THE FORGOTTEN CHILDREN

DON'T TELL MEG TRILOGY BOOK 3

PAUL J. TEAGUE

clixeo

ALSO BY PAUL J. TEAGUE

CHAPTER ONE

1992 David had known that he was going to hang himself since the previous Thursday. That was the day Gary Maxwell had told him that he would be chosen again. He couldn't take it anymore. It was time to end it.

There were people at the home that he'd miss. It was as if he had two lives there. The other kids were great – when you're thrown into a predicament like that, you tend to stick together, you make the best of it. They tried as hard as they could to protect the young ones. They kept them naive as long as they could, but there was only so long that you could shield them from the horror.

It should have been an incredible place to grow up. Sure, they'd all experienced horrible things. They all had sad stories to tell: mothers who'd turned to drink or had nervous breakdowns because of errant or violent fathers; absent fathers who wanted no part in their children's lives; parental deaths from car crashes, cancer, suicide and even one murder. David's parents had died in a plane crash as they jetted off for a holiday of a lifetime, while he was left at home with his gran.

All known tragedy was in that place. They were a bunch of forgotten children, cast out into the world because of misfortune or the inadequacy of the adults in their lives, and transferred into the care of Gary Maxwell, the man in charge of Woodlands Edge Children's Home.

Gary ruled by fear. If there was an inspection or official visit, they all got neatly in line. There was no dissent, no attempt to rock the boat. If there was as much as a hair spotted out of place, if they brought any kind of shame or unwanted attention onto the home, a horrific punishment would be waiting. You'd see it in Gary's eyes. He'd take whatever feedback he was given graciously and humbly. Maybe it was a remark about one of the children being spotted out late at night in town, or perhaps a love bite on a teenager's neck. But if it was commented on by anybody who could make life difficult for Gary Maxwell, there would be hell to pay.

You could feel the tension among the kids. Gary would say something like: 'That's really useful feedback, I appreciate that. Don't worry, I'll rectify that problem straightaway.'

They'd know what he meant. It would fall at their feet. If it was one of the girls, and she had a friend, her friend would get pulled into the punishment too. He was a bully, and there was nothing they could do to stand up to him. He was responsible for housing them, feeding them and looking after their welfare. And he was a monster. David had tried telling on him. Many times. His most recent attempt was the reason that he was now sneaking out to the tree with his dressing-gown cord wrapped around his hand.

They had teachers and counsellors, of course they did. They'd ask how things were going, how the youngsters liked it at the home, whether they had friends, how safe they felt.

But Gary never left any signs. There were never any bruises. They'd give all the right answers, anything to keep him away from them. Whenever David answered their questions, it was as if Gary was in there with him, sneering at him, poring over everything he said, making sure that there were no clues in there that might reveal his true nature.

David had tried to speak up soon after it had started. He was only thirteen, and was shocked and numbed. An older boy, Jacob, had been with him in that place. Jacob had tried to protect David. He'd attempted to draw the man's attention away from him. He'd failed, of course. That kind of person was used to getting what he wanted. He didn't understand the word no, and didn't care a jot about the youngsters.

Jacob hanged himself a fortnight after that night. He'd seen what had happened to David. He'd done his best to protect him, then comfort him, but there was nothing either of them could do. They had no voice. They were in the care system but no one individual cared for them. The people who should have looked out for them were gone. The children were on their own.

It was Bob, the only support worker in that place who genuinely cared about the youngsters, who found him. He hadn't seen Jacob at first as he cycled into work on that summer morning, but as he looked towards the trees, his attention was drawn by a thrush singing loudly among the greenery. It was perched on Jacob's shoulder.

The nylon cord from Jacob's dressing gown had supported him well enough to stifle the last breath from his miserable life. David never saw the body – they kept the children well away from the area. But they all knew what a relief Jacob had found in his death. He was safe. It couldn't happen to him again.

David sobbed for several nights over Jacob, but then his thoughts turned to what his friend had done. He looked at the long, sturdy branch of the tree which overhung the fence. It was strong enough to take a man's weight. Jacob must have stood on the fence to fasten the cord, placed the noosed end around his neck, and then jumped off. David worked through his death, moment by moment. The noose would have had to be pulled tight, really tight, as it took his weight. It would also have to have been knotted properly, or it would have slipped out. He'd have to research that in the library at school. Is that what Jacob had done?

The noose would have cut deep into the skin. His eyes would have bulged, and his head must have felt as if it was exploding. Hanging there, he could have got out of it if he'd changed his mind. It would have been possible to move his legs back onto the fence, to take his own weight again. David knew why he hadn't. Jacob wasn't making a half-hearted cry for help. He wanted out. He meant for his life to end.

David thought about how his body would jerk and convulse when he jumped from the fence. And he would jump. It would instantly tighten the noose, finishing him off faster. If they found him too soon, they might revive him. David didn't want that; it had to be final. A few moments of fear and pain, and then it would be over. At last.

He'd tried to tell Bob what had happened to him, several times, but the words just wouldn't come out right. He could barely explain it to himself, so how could he begin to tell Bob? He was so ashamed. David was sure that Bob knew that something was going on, but he too was scared of Gary. He had a wife and kids. He needed his work. Nevertheless, David was certain that he would have helped if they'd told him. It would have been difficult for him, but he would have stepped up. He'd have had to.

David came the closest to it that day. He almost blurted it out. He saw tears in Bob's eyes – he sensed what he was going to say. He wasn't stupid. The inquest had put Jacob's death down to depression. That was only half of it. He'd been on fluoxetine, several of them were on it; David was too. So yes, he was depressed. But his only release would be when he was eighteen years of age and could walk away from Woodlands Edge Children's Home, and Jacob couldn't wait that long.

David had seen Bob in Gary's office later on. He'd never seen Bob like that – he was really angry. He was shouting through tears, his face red, partly through anger, partly through frustration. Gary just sat there, giving him that cold, calm stare. Someone else would pay for it later.

The children were aware that Bob had stormed out of the home. The rumour was that he'd quit his job, there and then, on the spot. There was a hush among the children that night. They knew what was coming. In trying to help David, Bob had made it worse. He'd tried to hide the identity of his informant from Gary, but Gary wasn't stupid. He knew that David liked talking to Bob.

Sure as anything, David was chosen again that night, along with his friend James. He was just thirteen. Gary would punish David through James, but he'd make sure it was bad for him too. That's how Gary Maxwell maintained his control.

Suicide is often talked about as if it's done on the spur of the moment. But people who think about killing themselves know better. They've had it worked out for ages. They know where it will happen. They've thought through every detail. They've considered everything that could go wrong. They know the time, the method and the place. They will have toyed with it a thousand times before it happens. They will have stepped back, waiting another day, hoping that things would get better.

They might have considered the people they were leaving behind, wondering what difficult times awaited them after their death. But ultimately when you're in that dark, impenetrable place no light can get in. It's all you think about. David knew that he was going to kill himself that night. He knew that there would be no turning back.

As he perched on the fourth bar of the fence, the carefully tied knot pulled tight against his neck and he watched his frosty breath in the cold night air. There would be no breath left soon. He'd be half frozen by the time they found him; it wasn't getting light until after eight o'clock, it was right in depths of winter.

He jumped, with complete certainty that this was what he wanted. He felt the noose jerk tight, squeezing his neck. He was gasping for breath. His legs began to thrash, he wanted this more than anything, but his body was resisting, it was fighting to stay alive. David's eyes felt as if they were going to explode from his skull, and the cord dug more tightly into his neck as his body began to convulse. The last thing he was aware of as he slipped out of consciousness was the blood on his hand from where the nylon cord had cut so deeply into his neck.

None of it bothered him. He craved it. David wanted to die. He was pleased to see the back of his miserable, wretched life.

I looked out of the window of my second-floor flat and watched the youth screaming at his girlfriend – one-night stand – wife – whatever she was. He had tattoos all over his neck, wore a V-neck T-shirt and a cap put on back-to-front. The poor girl looked scared out of her life. I'd counted all of the expletives that I knew at least once and had clocked a few in there that I'd never heard of.

Apparently she was a slag because she'd done something that wounded his sensibilities. I wanted to warn her to run for her life. Get away from the oaf. Find a nice man. The look on her face told me that she'd be back. Whatever had happened in her life, she didn't think that she could do better.

What had I been thinking of when I moved onto this estate? It was a complete shit-hole, full of the terminally unemployed and unemployable. I suppose the flat itself was fine – modern, clean, and I had enough space, but I'd thought the landlady was a bit keen. She'd got me signed on the dotted line within five minutes of walking through the door.

I didn't have many choices. My house was worth less than I'd paid for it. Less than *we'd* paid for it – I hadn't seen the person who was supposed to be paying half of the mortgage costs for the best part of a year. That's why I was in a fix. I didn't earn that much as a radio journalist; it wasn't a bad salary, but I certainly wasn't rolling in it.

But it wasn't the mortgage that was the problem. It was the small matter of the murders that had taken place there. That tends to put buyers off. The asking price had gone down and down, eventually arriving at the breakeven point. When I thought it couldn't go any lower, I began factoring in a loss. I'd have a couple of thousand pounds to make up. Well, I didn't have it. My financial resources were depleted.

Our life had been set up around two professional salaries, and I'd had to pick up everything when Meg walked out of my life.

I knew things were getting desperate when I started to read one of those leaflets that gets pushed through your letterbox as if it were a literary classic. *Debt? Divorce? Death? Don't worry! We'll help you fix it. We'll buy ANY house, ANYwhere and in ANY condition.* It was the capital letters that did it. What did I say? A literary classic. I was at the end of my tether. I had no home of my own that I could live in and very little money.

I'd got my previous landlady killed. I'd been living in a static caravan at the Golden Beaches holiday park. Only that had now closed – because of me and the fact that my presence there had resulted in two deaths on the site, including its poor owner, a lovely lady called Vicky, whose death haunted me at night. I was a shit magnet.

In Meg's absence, I'd begun the process of selling the house to the company which had so thoughtfully thrust their leaflet through the letterbox of the flats. It was a miracle that I'd even seen it. The post arrived through a single letterbox at the front of the building. If you were lucky, you found your letters stacked on the bottom step of the staircase. If your envelope looked like it might contain money, you'd never see it again, unless the person opening it had been disappointed. In that case, you'd have to retrieve it from the back of the radiator in the shared hallway, avoiding the dog turds on the well-worn carpet, courtesy of the guy who lived in the ground-floor flat and was always too pissed to walk his dog.

I had to keep telling myself that I wouldn't be there for much longer. The house would be sold, and I'd be able to pay off the personal loan I'd taken out to cover the gap between what I'd paid for it and what it was now worth. Then I'd start to put my life back together. Probably without Meg. I had to accept that now.

My friend Ellie had lined up a great job for me in London, but I'd ducked out at the last minute when a three-month attachment had come up in Blackpool. After what Alex had told me about Meg living there, I had to take it. And I needed to get away from home; there were too many terrible memories. I had to find Meg and work out what was going on: if there was still a marriage to fight for, if I had a kid.

I was what is known as a district reporter. I worked from a tiny office, which was located on an industrial estate on the edge of the town. All I had to do was find a couple of news stories every day, turn them into three-minute radio reports, file them to the main office, and then I was done. No staff to manage, no rotas to maintain, just a straightforward reporting job in the seaside town where my wife was living. Or hiding, more like.

I didn't know where she was, but Alex had managed to track her down to Blackpool. That was her home before we met. It was the closest I'd been to finding her for months. We had to talk, I needed to get things sorted. She'd been running away from me long enough. There was only so long she could hide in a town the size of Blackpool in the middle of winter. The tourists were all gone; it was like a ghost town most days.

I had the three months of my attachment to find her. After that it was back to my regular job. I'd been in Blackpool for one month already, so I had just over eight weeks to sort everything out. There was a small chance my attachment might be extended, but it was unlikely. Whatever happened with Meg, I'd seek work in London then. The house would be sold, I'd be paying back the personal loan, the time would be right.

To think I'd had the offer of a room in Spain too. I couldn't take Alex up on her suggestion, not when I saw the Blackpool job advertised on the intranet site at work. I was straight in there. I knew the manager of the Lancashire radio station from my student days; we'd risen through the radio journalism ranks together. It was a bit of a demotion for me – same pay grade, less responsibility. He knew that I'd breeze the job. I'd be a safe pair of hands for three months. Everybody knew about the shit I'd been through, and the company was happy to cut me some slack.

When I returned from visiting Alex in Spain, I spent a few weeks in a grubby hotel and then managed to get the Blackpool job sorted out. I had a weekend to find a flat and I'd ended up in the only one that I could afford. At the holiday park I'd been able to supplement my income working in the bars, but I had no appetite for that now.

I knew I'd made a terrible mistake the minute I arrived to move my stuff into the flat. There was a syringe discarded to the side of the front step. I assumed it belonged to one of my new neighbours. Maybe it was a house-warming gift?

I was travelling light; my stuff was still in storage. That was another thing about this flat. It was furnished. All I had to do was load my clothes and laptop into the car and I was away. Forty years old and travelling lighter than I was when I was twenty.

I watched the idiot on the pavement outside slap the young girl across the face. She stopped dead and looked at him. He put his arm around her shoulders, guiding her towards the door to the flats. She didn't resist, but let him steer her back inside. And I watched it, too spineless to intervene. I didn't want to cause any friction with the other residents. I had to see them on the landing from time to time, although they tended not to keep the same hours as me. I let her go back into that flat where it would start all over again the minute the door closed behind them.

'You've lost your colour already! I'll swear that Blackpool actually reverses the tanning process it's so bloody cold.'

It was good to be laughing with Alex on Skype again. It was pissing with rain in Blackpool. My huge living-room window was steamed up as the internal and external temperatures fought it out for supremacy.

Her camera looked out onto a glorious, sunny Spanish scene. The garden was mainly covered with terracotta tiles; there was a swimming pool, and I could see that the sky was a beautiful blue colour. To think I'd been sitting out in that very garden only five weeks previously.

'It's not so bad. What else can you expect from the north of England in November? It's a bit shit up north! Hey, maybe Blackpool could use that as their advertising slogan?'

'Yeah, probably not!' Alex chuckled. 'Anyway, enough of the chitchat. Have you made any progress yet? How's your leg?'

'Nothing,' I replied. 'I've drawn a complete blank. And the leg is okay. It gives me occasional aggro, but nothing too serious. I'm going to go and talk to the old ladies at the Methodist church again to see if they can give me any more clues.'

'Oh God, they were funny!' Alex burst out laughing, recalling our first visit there. She'd behaved terribly, laughing at their occasional misuse of words and thinking that they didn't recognise her from the TV. Only they did.

Still, they were very nice about it. Alex had been horrified when she realised they knew who she was.

'I keep hanging around that cashpoint by the corner shop. The owner must think I'm some sort of pervert. You're sure that's where the money was drawn out?'

'I told you. It was the last time she drew money from a joint account. My digital forensics guy spotted it. It was that top-up card you used for holidays. No wonder you didn't see it on your statements. I bet you never even look at it, do you?'

'It's all online. We top it up when we need it. It had just over a hundred quid on it – well, you know that already – but she can't have got far on it. She might only have been passing by. It doesn't mean she's living in that part of town, does it?'

'No, I know, but it's a lead at least. And you know she's in Blackpool. It makes sense that she went back home. She knows the area.'

'How about you, Alex? Any plans to return to the UK yet?'

She'd given up her prime-time TV job presenting Crime Beaters and all of the celebrity appearances elsewhere that had entailed. As far as I knew, she still didn't have any plans to return to TV.

'I've had some offers, Pete, but I don't feel ready. After what happened, everything seems so petty now. I thought we were going to die that night. It's made me think about things more. I've had a lot of time to reconsider my direction in life.'

'You'll be lighting incense sticks and doing Tai Chi next. Please tell me you haven't started Tai Chi?'

'No way! But come on, Pete. You must know what I mean? You nearly had your head torn off in that bell tower.

You can't tell me you haven't been thinking things through?'

She was right, of course, but I couldn't get beyond my immediate problems. It was becoming a mantra: Meg – baby – house – job. Repeat ad infinitum. It was a drumbeat pounding in my head all day long. I couldn't move beyond it.

In the stillness of the night-time I thought about the deaths. I couldn't remember the last time I'd slept right through until morning. There'd been so much violence, so many deaths. And there was Becky too, stuck in a wheel-chair and going through endless rounds of therapy. She had tried to blackmail – and kill – me, but I wouldn't wish a life stuck in a wheelchair on anyone. I heard her whimpers of pain in my sleep. I'd never heard a noise like it – desperate, agonising human pain. It was horrible. I never wanted to hear that sound again.

I kept in touch with DCI Kate Summers. I'd seen a lot of her in the aftermath of the deaths. Endless questions. Who did what to whom, the usual inquisition from the police. Alex and I had agreed to go light on Becky. She'd been punished enough. We made it sound as if she'd been coerced by her crazy bloke, Lee. And we helped Ian Davies' case too. He'd saved our lives, even though he was pissed with us. He'd gone free; they decided there was no case for him to answer. He'd been following us and he'd rattled us at the time, but we didn't make a complaint.

'I do think about things, Alex. It bothers me a lot, but it's over now. Statistically we've had our quota of crap in our lives. That must mean that I have one hell of a great future ahead.'

'Did you think anymore about what I said? Do you think you'll change your mind?'

'I'm a journalist, Alex. I'd be bored working in a Spanish bar. I'd need something more to keep my mind engaged. You'd go mad too, wouldn't you? You wouldn't leave your celebrity life forever ... would you?'

I could see by the look on her face that she'd been thinking about it. I'd spent enough time with Alex to know what a hassle being in the spotlight could be. I didn't envy her that life. She'd be unable to escape it in the UK, but a life abroad would offer some anonymity.

'It wouldn't have to be a bar, Pete. It could be a restaurant or snack place. We could open a bookshop. I just don't think I want to go back to all that ...'

'The constant social media scrutiny and the selfies? I know how you feel. That week you spent with me gave me a taste of what you have to put up with. It's not for me!'

'I've had a few offers come in. I need to meet with my agent next week. I've got to fly over. I'm in London on Wednesday, and then I can come over ... if you want?'

Alex seemed unsure. I wasn't used to hearing her like that. She'd reached out to me last time I'd seen her and I'd pushed her back. I wasn't ready to discuss the future. Sure, Alex and I had been living together all those years ago, but I'd been married to Meg for a long time. I doubted if we could salvage the marriage, but we had to get things sorted out, legally if nothing else. My life was on hold. I was stuck until I could see Meg.

'You know who's appearing in Blackpool when I'm over, don't you?'

'No, who?' I replied, wondering why Alex had suddenly changed the subject.

'It's your clairvoyant mate, Steven Terry – the one you told me about, who warned you what was going to happen with Meg. That's him, isn't it?'

'"Steven Terry, clairvoyant to the stars" is how he bills himself. Where's he playing? I'd like to speak to him. He was spot on when he warned me about Becky. He was right the first time too. I bought his book, you know. I laughed at the title the first time I heard it: *Past & Present: My Life Seeing The Future.* I'm not laughing now, not after those warnings he gave me. He was dead right.'

'He's playing for three nights at the Winter Gardens – the Thursday, Friday and Saturday after I'm in London. How about I train it up to Blackpool and we look for Meg together?'

It sounded like a great plan. I'd been lonely since moving to Blackpool. Being a district reporter and working on your own in a small office isn't the fastest way to make new friends. Alex and I had had a great time last time we were in Blackpool together. It would be good to have her help.

'You know that my flat is really shitty, don't you? I mean, the flat isn't shitty, but the people who live here are. Not all of them. Some of them. But it's not as nice as your digs in Spain; that's what I'm saying.'

'It's fine, Pete. You know me. I'm not snobby about these things. I should have been off the TV long enough not to be too interesting to anybody. Has that episode of Celebrity Cake Makers aired yet? We filmed it ages ago.'

'Yes, I think so. I seem to have registered the series ending. You'll forgive me for not watching, I hope? If you want to make a cake while you're here, I promise to get really excited, if that helps!'

Alex laughed.

'See what I mean? My life is shite! I appear on TV programmes about baking cakes. Take me out and shoot me now. If my agent doesn't have anything interesting lined up for me, I'm telling you, Pete, I'm jacking it in. I've had enough—'

The doorbell rang. Sometimes it was kids, pressing all eight buttons connected to the units in my building.

'One moment, Alex. I'll see if it's kids messing around.'

I moved away from my laptop, wiped the mist from the window and looked down towards the front doorstep below. No sign of kids. The bell rang again. I could just about make out somebody down there. He stepped back and I rubbed the window again; it was misting up already.

He was in clear view now, but it took a moment to work out who it was. Damn it, it was the car finance guy. I knew I was sailing close to the wind. I was a few direct debit payments behind and they were coming to collect a cheque from me.

'Who is it?' Alex asked, hoping it might be someone interesting.

'Oh, it's only bloody kids,' I answered, pulling back from the window so that I wouldn't be spotted.

CHAPTER TWO

1991 There was a new child arriving. A new child always created a buzz of excitement in the home. It was instinctive. Kids love meeting new kids; it might be a new pal, a new playmate. But that natural desire to meet the new arrival was always tinged with fear and trepidation. If they were mature already, they'd be chosen by Gary. They wouldn't even have that short period of time where they were left out of it. The older kids would move in, try to make it better for them when the time came. If they were much younger, they'd be safe for a while. Not from Gary and his anger, but at least from them. The men in the suits. The ones that they despised even more than Gary.

The new child looked terrified. She was crying. That's often how kids arrived at the Woodlands Edge children's home. The tears would be the result of being parted from foster parents or perhaps an adoption process that didn't work out. Some of the children arrived barely weeks after the death of their parents. Hannah knew one boy who'd arrived at the home three hours after he'd seen both of his parents buried.

If only Gary could be the way he was when he was being watched by his superiors. He was exemplary then – eager to please, doing everything by the book. When he was back in charge, when all eyes were averted, Gary became the bully that he truly was. Hateful. Why did he work in that place since he seemed to despise the children?

Straightaway Hannah clocked the new kid as someone she wanted to know. She was fourteen years old and becoming aware that things weren't right for some of the older girls. They'd often not come to bed at night, and then sneak back into their rooms early in the morning. She could hear their sobs, but they'd be accompanied by the warning threats of Gary.

Nobody ever talked openly about what was going on, but there was a knowledge that permeated the home. It started with the younger children, an unsettling feeling that things were not quite right among the teenagers. They would become aware of hushed conversations among the older children, conversations which often ended with an arm around the shoulder, tears, a hug from one youngster trying to reassure another.

They would see the changes on the faces of the older ones. They would carry on as normal, get up in the morning, go to school, do their chores around the home, but something was extinguished, their eyes became dead and lifeless. Any joy seemed to disappear. The young ones saw it. They just didn't know what it was yet.

When the new girl arrived, it was a thrill for Hannah. She saw the tears, and she wanted to reach out and help. She knew that they'd be friends the minute she saw her.

It always took some time for the new arrivals to be free to meet the other children. They'd come with at least one adult, who'd be dressed in a suit and carrying a briefcase or a folder crammed with paperwork. They'd head for Gary's office, and Gary would seem like the best person in the world to be running a children's home. He'd joke around and be playful with the new child, sounding professional and efficient to the social worker who'd come with them. After the paperwork was completed, the child would be given a formal tour of the building and introduced to any of the other kids they encountered on the way. Finally, after what seemed to the other kids like hours, they'd be released into the wild, to their first night in Woodlands Edge.

'My name's Hannah,' she said at teatime. 'Where have you come from?'

The child shrugged.

'What's your name?'

Another shrug.

The girl was a little younger than Hannah. She wouldn't stop crying, so it was difficult for Hannah to speak to her. They'd all seen it before. Some kids came into the home cocksure and arrogant, but of course it was only a front. Others knew the care system well, and understood that you had to watch and learn first, work out the hierarchies, see who was dangerous and who was vulnerable.

This new kid was the scared type. Something had happened fairly recently. Usually it was dead parents or something horrible. Often there was no other family, and the authorities had no option but to place them in care. This girl had been passed from foster parent to foster parent, her addict mother unable to care for her on her own. Finally she had taken one pill too many and never woke up. With no father recorded on the birth certificate, the fostering was over and the care system beckoned.

Care for a child should be having a person to go to who loves them unconditionally. For the kids in that home, there was no such option. Care to them was an adult working through a checklist. There was no cuddle when they fell over, just a plaster, a kind word and a note in the accident book.

This girl needed a parent's love, but she wasn't going to get it. She'd have to toughen up and learn to live without it. Gary Maxwell was the man who made the rules now, and she'd have to adapt. Hannah wanted to make that process as gentle as possible. She knew to leave the girl alone with her thoughts and sat next to her as they finished their dinner in silence. Afterwards they watched TV. It was nothing that Hannah was interested in, but she sensed that this new girl would be happy to stay away from the rough and tumble of the other children while she adjusted to her new surroundings.

They sat in the TV room until bedtime, which for them was nine o'clock. Hannah sensed him before she saw him. Gary was approaching. She knew what was coming. He did it every time. He got in early, before they'd even slept through their first night. The fear needed to begin straightaway. It's how he held onto his power. He switched the TV off and came up to the girls. A couple of the other kids got up and moved away. They knew what this was.

'How's it going?' he asked, charming and friendly.

The new girl looked up at him, her eyes red where she'd been trying to hold back her tears. Gary's arm moved out suddenly and violently. He pushed Hannah's glass of juice from where it had been resting safely on the arm of her chair. The glass shattered on the ground and the juice splashed onto Gary's trousers. His transition to fury was immediate and complete. The new child tensed in her chair, not knowing what to do. This is why Hannah had come to her in friendship. She was there to guide the new girl, to navigate her through this.

'You stupid girl!' he shrieked at her. 'I've told you to be careful with drinks in here. Now look what you've done! Clear it up! Clear it up!'

The new girl had never seen an adult so immediately out of control. Her tears stopped as her survival instinct kicked in. Hannah leapt out of her chair and began to pick up the broken glass. Gary was shouting at her, telling her how stupid she'd been, what a fool she was, how it was her own idiocy that had resulted in the accident.

'Get some kitchen roll and wipe my trousers.'

Hannah looked up at him, wondering what this meant. Something had just changed for her. This wasn't good. She ran into the small kitchen, tore off a wad of paper and ran back to the TV room. All the other kids had made themselves scarce. Gary had been ranting at the new girl throughout, telling her what an idiot Hannah was, warning her not to do the same, or else.

He made Hannah wipe down his trousers. Then he pushed her to the floor and forced her to wipe up the remains of the juice on all fours.

'Like a dog!' he laughed at her.

She worked through it, step-by-step, knowing this process well. He wouldn't hurt her, not physically, at least. But a little piece of her would die inside. Her dignity, her hope would deaden slightly and Gary would exert a little more control. Ready for later. When she was older. That's how he did it.

Hannah saw Bob pass by the door as she'd been mopping up the juice. He'd hesitated, looking in, assessing what was going on.

'On your way, Bob!' Gary had ordered him. 'These girls

are just learning the importance of clearing up their own mess.'

Bob had waited a moment, trying to meet Hannah's eyes to work out if she was really okay. Hannah knew better than to look up. Bob looked as if he was about to say something, but moved on. It would be another year at least until he would confront Gary and lose his job in the process.

Gary strung it out for over ten minutes. He made sure that every drop of discomfort was wrung out before he released Hannah from her ordeal. He found every opportunity for humiliation that he could, but he didn't do a thing to the new girl. He didn't have to. This was all the induction that she'd need.

Eventually he was gone. He dismissed them both with a 'Go to bed!' and waited while they walked out of the room.

'It's alright,' Hannah began, as they walked slowly up the winding staircase together. 'It's over now. He just does that. I'm okay.'

The staircase was wide and long. It had been a huge Victorian house once upon a time. The new girl's hand found Hannah's and squeezed it gently.

They stopped on the staircase and looked at each other. It was Hannah's eyes that were red now; she'd done her best to check her tears, but she couldn't hold them in, however brave she was trying to be for the new girl.

'It's okay,' the new girl said. 'I'm sorry he did that to you.'

Hannah smiled. She'd known that this girl would be her friend.

'My name's Meg. I'm sorry I didn't speak much earlier.'

Hannah looked at her, still holding her hand. Then she saw Meg's face change, to a determination that she would observe many times in later years. Meg spoke again, different now, much stronger.

'Don't worry, Hannah. I'll look after you. I'll make sure that man doesn't hurt you.'

It was wild along the esplanade at Fleetwood. I had heard that sometimes the sea got so choppy it threw up stones capable of breaking a windscreen. I was a bit nervous but equally anxious to record the interview for that day's news report, get it edited and meet with Deirdre and Janet at the Methodist church at five o'clock. I'd spoken to the ladies before, but I wanted to know more. Their friend Cathy was unwell and not able to join us. It was a shame – those ladies had been a breath of fresh air when I'd met them with Alex.

I wanted to pick up my tickets for Steven Terry's first night too. I'd booked them over the phone from the office earlier that day, but I wanted them in my hands, just to be sure.

I was looking forward to Alex's arrival. She'd be a welcome distraction from the flat, an excuse to get out and have some fun. Although we hadn't lived together for years, we'd managed to hang onto our easy relationship, even while I'd been married to Meg. I was pleased about that – Alex had always been good for me.

I hadn't enjoyed any female company since the deaths – the most recent deaths, I should say. I never thought I'd end up having to differentiate between the murders that I'd been involved with. Two sets of murders. Who has that happen to them?

Steven Terry had warned me at our last meeting: 'The women you choose to stay in your life are what determines your path, Peter.' Well, he'd been right about that. It was sleeping with first Ellie and then Becky that had caused all of my troubles. Steven had warned me about it and I hadn't listened. I was ready to listen now. I was feeling shut down as far as women were concerned. I was ready to experience the life of a monk, for a short time at least – maybe until Steven Terry had given me the all clear.

I'd had the legal documents for the house sale in the post that day. The envelope had been opened before I got to it. The idiot on the third floor couldn't get out of bed to get himself to a job in the morning, but he always seemed to be awake enough to rifle through everybody's post in the hallway as soon as it arrived.

'Sorry pal,' he'd say, chirpy as anything. 'I misread the address, thought it was my mail.'

All I could think was: don't call me pal. I'm not your pal.

If he hadn't looked so tough, I might have given him a piece of my mind. Instead, I reassured him that misreading addresses on envelopes can happen to anybody, and I slunk away like a dog that understood his place in the pack. If you could gain superiority through verbal sparring, I'd have been king of the world, but the fact was that I had to take shit from guys who were stronger and more violent than I could ever be.

The house was ready to go. I'd lose ten thousand pounds on it in all. That was the difference between what I owed on it and what it was being bought for. It had been vandalised several times since the last murders. I'd had to get the doors and the windows boarded up. I was pleased to be rid of it.

I'd long since given up hope of Meg picking up her share of the debt, although I'd need her signature to let the sale go through. I'd even considered forging it at one point. Would anybody even notice or care? I doubted it.

I had the personal loan in place, and the money was all ready to move. The last time I had taken out a ten thousand pound loan was for a car. At least I'd been paying for something tangible, something that I could use. This was just debt, and I'd be paying it down for the next five years. What a depressing prospect.

I felt as if I was on the starting line of the next stage of my life. I needed Meg to blow the whistle. I wanted to begin the race, to start afresh. However it turned out with Meg, I was ready for change. I could feel it coming, it had to be close. Steven Terry would help me – he'd always been right before. Surely things had to start getting better soon?

I finished off my radio report and then locked up the office. It was some story about a guy who'd placed over thirty plastic windmills in his front garden and the neighbours were complaining. Real cutting-edge journalism, that's what my life had come to.

I was hungry after being out in the wind and rain all day, so pulled over at a chippy and bought a large tray of chips and gravy. Not great for my waistline, or my heart come to that, but I wanted to speak to the Methodist ladies on a full stomach.

They'd been very useful last time we spoke. They'd helped me to locate Meg's old family home, and given us some valuable information about the fire there, the one that had killed her parents. I'd thought of a hundred more questions that I wanted to ask them since.

'Hello ladies!' I smiled, walking up the aisle towards Deirdre and Janet. I couldn't remember which was which, they seemed interchangeable to me.

They recognised me immediately and stopped working

on a flower display to greet me. They were removing flowers that were looking worse for wear. The church looked lovely because of their work. I wondered what else they did other than coordinate the church's floral operations.

Scott Road Methodist Church appeared to be the best source of information about the Yates family. Hannah and Meg's mum and dad – their adoptive parents, Thomas and Mavis Yates – had attended the church, and Mavis had been particularly well known there.

After exchanging far too many pleasantries, and dealing with the ladies' disappointment over that 'lovely young lady' not being with me, we finally got down to the interesting stuff.

'After we'd spoken last time I realised that I never asked you, not properly. I just assumed that I knew the answer. What happened to Mavis Yates? Did she die in the fire? I assume she died with Thomas?'

'It's funny you should ask that,' Janet replied. Or was it Deirdre?

'She was alive when they finally broke into the house. Very badly burned though – we never saw her again. They took her to some burns unit down south. It was miles away. We lost contact when the girls went.'

'Do you know if she survived?' I asked. 'Did anybody ever hear?'

The two ladies looked ashamed for a moment. I'd hit a nerve.

'You have to remember, things were more difficult then. We didn't have the internet; we used to have to make phone calls from a phone box at the end of the road. We couldn't afford a phone in the house. We had to use launderettes too, in those days. It's easier now. We tried to stay in touch, but with no family living locally, what could we do? We never found out about Mavis. Poor woman, it was such a terrible affair.'

'What about the funeral?' I asked. 'Did any of you attend Thomas's funeral?'

'Yes, of course we did. It was a very sad affair,' said Deirdre, 'the girls were there, and lots of people from the home and along our street – and some very important people too. The head of the police was there.'

'You mean the chief constable? What was he doing at Thomas Yates' funeral? Was Thomas in the police?'

'No, no dear,' said Janet. 'Thomas worked at the home where the girls were looked after before they adopted them. He was a caretaker. That's how they got the girls. Friends in high places, I think. It was the old place on Burridge Road. What did they call it, Deirdre?'

Deirdre gave it some serious consideration, and then came up with her answer.

'Woodlands Edge, wasn't it? Woodlands Edge Children's Home on Burridge Road. It closed down years ago. Some scandal or something ...'

'It's derelict now,' Janet continued. 'I never go out there these days, but it was in a sad state last time I saw it. It used to be a beautiful old building.'

'So that's where Meg was based as a child? Before Thomas and Mavis adopted her and Hannah?'

'That's right, dear,' Deirdre confirmed.

These ladies were a goldmine of useful information. I made a note of the road name in the notes app on my mobile phone. I also took care to make sure that I had the name of the children's home written down correctly. As I was tapping away on my phone, another woman walked up to Janet and Deirdre. Her name appeared to be Phyllis. They exchanged a few bits of information about the flower-arranging rota and a bingo event taking place in the community centre later that week.

'And who's this young man?' Phyllis asked, turning towards me.

'Pete Bailey,' I answered, shaking her hand. 'I'm chatting to Janet and Deirdre about the Yates family. I don't suppose you knew them, did you?'

Her eyes widened immediately.

'You could say that!' she laughed. 'How funny you should ask about the Yates family after all these years. What a coincidence! I haven't thought about them for ages, and then all of a sudden ...'

'Do you know what happened to Mavis?' Janet asked. 'We lost contact after the ... after the fire.'

'Yes,' replied Phyllis. 'I occasionally get a Christmas card from her, although I haven't had one for some time. Don't you?'

Janet and Deirdre looked as if they'd been caught stealing a biscuit.

'We didn't think she'd survived the fire,' Janet said. 'So she's still alive?'

'Yes, she is,' said Phyllis, 'but she's been very poorly ever since. She's in care now, somewhere near Aylesbury. She had terrible problems with her skin after the accident – they never got it right. But yes, she's still alive. I haven't seen her since the fire, but I started getting Christmas cards from her about two years afterwards. I used to see the girls in the street. Lovely young ladies they were. That's why it's funny you should be here.'

'Oh yes?' I asked, keen to hear what she had to tell me. It was excellent news to hear that Meg still had family alive. It was also surprising. I'd thought all of her family were dead. That's what she'd led me to believe.

But there was better to come as Phyllis finally got to the point.

'It's funny how these things happen. Here we are talking about Mavis Yates after all these years – and those girls. Yes, I used to know them well, that's why Mavis sent me the cards. Now here you are asking about the Yates family, and who should I see only last Tuesday, walking through the town centre?'

She waited a while, knowing that she had dramatic news to share with the small group of people, all hanging onto her every word.

'It was only Meg Yates! You can't mistake her, even after all these years. I was sitting in the window of the tearoom near Wilko's, and who should walk right by? I recognised her immediately. It was Meg Yates. She had a baby with her. And the pram was being pushed by some young man. Very handsome he was too. Very handsome.'

Alex and I were sitting at the end of a row of seats on the balcony overlooking the large stage in the Winter Gardens. I was impressed with Steven Terry. He'd started life as a pub-and-club clairvoyant and had moved up to three nights in this place. Not bad. Most of it was the result of his best-selling book. That's how we'd first met – I'd been sorting out the studio for him at the radio station. It was a national tour too. The TV programme had helped to sell the seats, but I had to admire a man who'd spun so much gold out of a handful of straw.

'Ladies and gentlemen, please take your seats and get ready to watch clairvoyant to the stars, Steven Terry! The show will be starting in ten minutes.'

'I'm looking forward to this,' I said as I turned to Alex. 'I thought it was a load of nonsense when I met him for the first time, but I'm becoming intrigued. I know he's all showbiz and sparkle, but I do think he's onto something.'

Alex had grown her hair longer. It had also faded a little in the Spanish sun. And she was wearing glasses now – I think she'd decided to ditch the contacts. She looked good. Different. And more importantly, it was sufficient disguise for nobody to notice her. We were as anonymous as any other couple in the audience.

Alex's phone buzzed and she hurriedly took it out of her pocket.

'Shit, I'd better mute that before the show. That's all I need: Steven Terry asking, "Is there anybody there?" and my Homer Simpson ringtone going Doh!'

She dwelt a moment on the phone screen, and then handed it over to me.

'That's my police contact in Buckinghamshire. Mavis Yates is in Nightingale House Care Home on the outskirts of Milton Keynes. Are we going to see her?'

'You bet we are!' I replied. My hunt for Meg had taken on a new impetus since speaking to the ladies at Scott Road Methodist Church. It was astonishing to learn that Meg had a mother who was still alive. Why hadn't she told me? Why did she never share any of this?

Surely she'd have visited her mum? I thought back. It's easy to hide things when you're embroiled in corporate life. Both Meg and I were always being summoned to training courses. If it wasn't Health and Safety, it was Negotiating in the Workplace, Handling Staff Better or Being a Better Team Member. Usually it was London, and sometimes it was a slightly more glamorous location. Like Newcastle. It was my weekend work trip to Newcastle that had started this chain of unhappy events.

Where had Meg been for training? Sheffield, Portsmouth and Leicester were the main locations that I could think of. But I never checked. When I thought about it, she could have been having an affair for all I knew. It was possible that she might have visited her mother without me knowing.

'How about we travel down on Saturday? It'll have to be the train again, I'm afraid. Milton Keynes is a bit of a stretch in my current vehicle.'

'It's no problem. I don't mind the train. I used to hate it before tablets, but nowadays I usually get so engrossed in a film that I have to be careful not to miss my stop. It's much better than when we were students. Trains were really crappy back then.'

'Ladies and gentlemen, please take your seats and get ready to watch clairvoyant to the stars, Steven Terry! The show will be starting in five minutes.'

People were beginning to make their way to their seats. I began to regret booking seats at the end of a row. It was easier to sneak out for a pee if you needed one, but it was a pain getting up and down so that the late arrivals could get seated.

'We can get a taxi from Milton Keynes station, or maybe they've got Uber.' I looked at Alex. 'I like your hair like that. It suits you.'

I didn't usually notice things like that, but she looked great. The Spanish sun had done her the world of good. She seemed relaxed and more at ease than when I'd seen her last. That was understandable – we'd both almost lost our lives. It tends to put you on edge that.

'What about Meg?' Alex asked. 'Any progress?'

'No. I popped into the tearooms near the seafront before you arrived, and took a snoop around. There's a post office nearby and some banks, also a baby shop – plenty of reasons for her to be in that area.'

'You know Mavis is likely to be in a bit of a state, don't you? She was badly burned in the fire. It's not going to be an easy meeting. Do you think we should ring ahead to let them know we're coming?'

'Who knows?' I replied. 'We're damned if we do, damned if we don't. They might ask us not to travel down if we ask for permission. I daren't risk that. But they could turn us away if we arrive unannounced. I don't know. I say we travel down, turn up and tell some white lies. I need to speak to her, that's for sure.'

Alex nodded. It was a tricky one. Out of nowhere we'd discovered that a person we'd thought to be dead was still alive. Mavis should be able to fill in some of the gaps about Meg's life, and if we got lucky she'd lead us to her. I was desperate to know about the child too. Was it mine? And who was this man she was with? Maybe she'd created a new life for herself in Blackpool. I was now closer to getting the answers than I'd ever been. And the next day, first thing, Alex and I were going to that children's home. I wanted to take a look at it for myself, get a feel for the place my wife had lived as a child.

A family of five shuffled in front of us as the lights went down. Dramatic music began to blare from the speaker system. Steven Terry entered the stage to thunderous applause.

'Ladies and gentlemen, welcome to the Winter Gardens in Blackpool. It's wonderful to see you here tonight!'

There was a massive cheer when he mentioned Blackpool. I wondered if there was a place where the audience didn't cheer. Cleethorpes perhaps. He was good, I'd give him that. The minute he walked onto that stage, he commanded the audience. His voice quietened, almost to a whisper. It was as if he were turning the volume down. They listened attentively.

'Ladies and gentlemen, we're here for a very special reason tonight. As you know, I have second sight. I have the gift of precognition. I see things others cannot. This can be both a gift and a curse. This is more than mere clairvoyance, ladies and gentlemen, because not only can I receive messages from loved ones who are longer among us, I also see glimpses of the future. Sometimes they are weak, but many times they are strong.'

I had to resist my natural urge to cynicism. I'd seen it for myself. My instinct told me it was a load of old bollocks, but my personal experience of speaking to Steven indicated that he did, indeed, possess some unique gift.

The audience was spellbound. He was speaking quietly in a room packed with a couple of thousand people, yet you could hear nothing else but his voice. No coughs, no snuffles, no rustling papers and no fidgeting. He had us exactly where he wanted.

'Ladies and gentlemen, some of you will go on an amazing journey tonight. You may leave in tears after speaking once again with a loved one now departed and sharing the thoughts that you wish you'd passed on when they were alive. You may be fortunate enough to glimpse your future ... but let me warn you, it's possible that you might not like what you hear. And somebody in this audience tonight is going to hear a message which will rock their life to its very core. I can feel it, ladies and gentleman. There is somebody in this audience tonight who is surrounded by demons. This ability of mine is as much a curse as it is a gift, ladies and gentlemen. Tonight I must pass on difficult news to one member of this audience. I don't know who it is yet, but by the end of this evening the truth must out!'

The audience applauded, the dramatic music returned and Steven Terry sat on a single stool, floodlit in the middle of the stage. At the time I thought that he was just building dramatic tension. How could he single out an individual in an audience that size? But later I would understand the truth of the matter. That person in the audience was me.

CHAPTER THREE

1991 It didn't take Meg and Hannah long to form a friend-ship. There was a shorthand that Meg learned fast, the sort of code which helped the new children to survive at the Woodlands Edge children's home. It involved steering clear of Gary Maxwell. The other support workers in the home were generally okay; it was Gary you had to watch. The culture he'd created was one of fear and control. You seldom heard any shouting in the corridors. Gary was more dangerous when he was speaking quietly to you. It's when you couldn't hear his voice that there was usually some trouble going on.

Meg saw several things that concerned her. But when a place is your home, when you're a youngster without a say in things, you have to put up with it. So it was with Meg. She watched and learned, as her hatred for Gary grew.

Meg once looked on with horror as he spilled his hot drink on Hazel Lomax, a plain, overweight girl whom Gary seemed to actively dislike. Hazel was always running away. The police would be involved, tracking her down, but she'd always be found in the same place: at her mother's bedside in the Sunny View psychiatric hospital in Bristol. It wasn't the best escape plan on earth, but Hazel always returned to where she felt loved. To her mother.

Meg didn't know if Hazel even had a father. She'd only ever heard her talk about her mother. She'd had some sort of breakdown and never recovered. She needed a lot of supervision and Hazel had become a young carer. When she'd finally been discovered by social services, prompted only by her absence from school rather than the fact that she'd been left caring for her mum, the household had reached breaking point. Hazel's mother was covered in bedsores and was so dirty that she'd developed a form of dermatitis. Her hair was a mat of grease and dirt. Hazel had done the best that she could, but was simply too ill equipped to cope after her mother's recent problems.

Her reward for doing the best that she could with her mother was to be placed in the Woodlands Edge children's home. She was not sufficiently pleasing on the eye to be taken at night, so Gary just made her life hell in the home. Every time she ran away, he'd be seen to go through the routines of paperwork, care plans and sessions with the counsellor, but Hazel's unauthorised trips to see her mother would always be followed up by a mysterious accident.

It shocked Meg the first time that she saw this happen. She watched as Gary placed his foot in front of Hazel so that she fell hard on the floor while carrying a tray laden with her dinner and pudding. He then forced her to clean up the mess on her hands and knees until the floor was spotless, all in front of a crowded dining room of youngsters. He told her how clumsy she was, how careless and unaware of her surroundings she'd been. Hazel silently took her punishment. She must have been desperate to see her mother, knowing that such a humiliation would be the result.

It was only Bob who came to her aid, helping her clean the pile of food off the floor.

'Leave her, Mr Taylor!' Gary had warned. 'Hazel is clumsy and needs to learn the consequences of her actions.'

Gary was never one to miss out on an educational opportunity.

'Surely we can help the poor girl to clean up the mess? It won't take a few minutes. I'm happy to do it—'

'Thank you, Mr Taylor. Your concern is appreciated. We wouldn't want to deny Hazel a chance to take *responsibility*, would we? It's so important to own up to our mistakes in life, wouldn't you say?'

Bob looked at him. Meg could see that there was something else going on here: a warning to Bob. He backed off, waiting at a nearby table until Hazel had been released from her punishment. He rushed straight over to the sobbing girl, offering what comfort he could. Gary seemed to have some power over him – he seemed to have a hold over all of the adults working in the home, either that or they were in collusion, part of 'Gary's team', as the children described it. But Bob was undoubtedly one of the good guys.

Two of the boys also came in for particular attention from Gary. They were good kids, a couple of mates, David and Jacob. They were well grown and looked like men already even though they were in their early teens. Gary viewed boys as a potential threat. He made every effort to subdue them before they became too strong. If they became powerful men, they might challenge his authority.

Gary was not a big man, but when he entered a room he exuded power and dominance. He soon broke the boys; he ensured they were taken at night. Meg had known that something was going on soon after she entered the home.

There would be hushed conversations, quiet taps on doors, and then reluctant shuffling. Meg would wake to hear them returning in the early hours. Sometimes she'd hear sobbing, but always it was there, Gary's quiet and controlling voice.

Meg liked David. She took an immediate shine to him. He was funny, bright and gentle. There was a spark between Hannah and Jacob too, and the youngsters would often sit at the same table in the dining room, chatting and laughing. Sometimes the boys' faces would light up as if they'd forgotten everything else that was going on in their lives. Meg loved it when they could forget, when they could pretend that theirs was just a regular life.

David was a little older than Meg, Jacob one year older than Hannah. As they grew up, the group became closer. In the room that they shared, Hannah and Meg would often talk to each other about the boys. They treated them as brothers: living at Woodlands Edge, all of the kids felt like your brother or sister in some way, but with David and Jacob there was something special. They made a great little gang.

Gary would often pull a chair up to their table if they were laughing and eating. The conversation would stop. He'd eat with them in silence, clean his plate and say something like, 'Hannah and Meg are going to enjoy meeting Mr Black, don't you think?'

Jacob was sick at the table the first time he said this. Gary was always mentioning Mr Black, and it would bring the same response from the boys. Their eyes would deaden, and they'd go to their rooms, unwilling to chat anymore.

Meg knew that the boys were troubled by something, but they wouldn't say what it was. They compartmentalised their lives. They were happy to talk and laugh about teenage things – pop music, TV, school, their favourite books – but they would clam up if Meg or Hannah tried to draw them on what was happening at night.

And then it happened to Hannah. They'd been asleep. Earlier they'd been in the TV room having a good laugh at one of the groups on Top of the Pops. It had been a good evening – on nights like that living in a home with a group of kids your own age was almost better than regular life. Meg had been sleeping soundly when she was woken by movement in the room. At first she thought that Hannah was visiting the toilet, but there was somebody else in there with them. It was Gary Maxwell. He was telling Hannah to get dressed. They were going on a late-night journey.

Meg lay still, pretending to be asleep. She could hear other youngsters getting ready along the corridor. She saw Jacob walk past their bedroom door fully dressed. He looked empty, not the Jacob she knew. Hannah was protesting, asking questions, wondering what was happening. Gary instructed her to be quiet.

'If you wake up Meg, it'll be worse for you. Do as you're told. Get dressed and wait outside with the others.'

Meg could sense the tension. She wanted to get up and intervene, but she knew what Gary was like. She daren't.

Hannah and Gary left the room. The door was quietly closed and she heard the small group making their way down the stairs. There was the distinctive sound of the diesel engine as the minibus used by the staff at the home was started up. Doors slammed and the vehicle drove off. Meg rushed to her window to look. She caught sight of Hannah, Jacob and three other older children from the home. They were sitting in silence in the minibus, and she could see even from that distance that there was no teenage chatter in there. She didn't recognise the man who was driving, and there was no other adult in the vehicle.

Meg wondered where Hannah was being taken. She knew that it wasn't good. To Mr Black probably, whoever he was. She lay in bed, fearful for her friend. She fell asleep, but was disturbed a few hours later by the sound of Hannah coming back into the room. She didn't get undressed, but took off her shoes and climbed into bed. Then she began to sob, quietly. Even from across the room, Meg could sense her body tensing and shaking.

Hannah had promised to protect Meg when she'd first entered the home, but Meg now realised that this was not going to be possible. There was nothing that Hannah could do to save her. It wouldn't be long until Meg was being taken at night too. Meg slipped out of her bed, walked silently across the room and slipped into bed alongside Hannah. There was no conversation. Meg moved in close and held her friend tight, saying nothing.

Steven Terry's show was a complete eye-opener for me. I'd seen advertisements for clairvoyants in the newspapers, assuming them to be aimed at old ladies and the gullible, but it was a great show. Steven was a fabulous entertainer, a real force on stage, and he had me completely captivated for the two hours that he was performing.

There was something about him – I couldn't put my finger on it. The journalist in me wanted to question everything that was going on. I scrutinised every sentence, wondering if what he was saying could apply to anybody. Whatever was happening on that stage, he was reaching people and connecting with them in way that I'd never experienced before.

There were tears, there was joy, there were moments of

tension and revelation. He moved among the crowd, a camera following him so that he could be seen on the large screens at all times. His face looked huge – you could see everything. I saw a scar on his cheek. I'd never noticed that before. It was concealed by the light growth of stubble that he sustained at all times. I'd assumed that to be a small vanity, part of the image. I wondered now if it was there to conceal the scar.

I searched for signs of dishonesty and deception, but Steven Terry seemed completely genuine. He was either an excellent actor or, as I was beginning to realise, he believed passionately in his gift. Whatever was happening at Blackpool's Winter Gardens that night, it was a force for good, not evil. People left that place feeling inspired and elated; there was nothing destructive in what he was doing.

'What do you think?' I asked Alex in the bar during the interval.

'He's good, I'll give him that!' she answered, taking a sip of her red wine.

'I always wrote him off in the past. He was in and out of the radio station doing interviews for this, that and the other. In fact, I'd even go as far as to say that I despised him. But I think he's onto something. I don't believe that it's paranormal or anything like that, but he has a gift, that's for sure.'

'I've said no to the offer,' Alex said out of the blue. 'While you were peeing, I got back to my agent. I'm not doing that new show.'

Alex had come away with a couple of new offers while she'd been visiting her agent in London. She'd rejected one immediately. The money involved made my eyes water. She'd earn as much as I did in one year for two months' work. They'd wanted her to co-present a show called

Britain's Talented Babies. Her co-presenter was going to be some guy who was twenty-four and had been in the papers for having fathered nine children with six women. I couldn't blame her for turning that one down, but the money was amazing. We'd never discussed how much she earned before, but I knew that it would make me want to cry. When you're earning six figures per contract, and all your clothing and day-to-day expenses are being taken care of, you can accrue a lot of money very quickly.

The show that she'd just knocked back was a new version of Crime Beaters, which one of the satellite-only channels wanted to create. They knew that if Alex was at the helm it would get the programme established immediately. They'd offered her twice her regular payment per episode to join the show for season one. The money was ridiculous. I was in the wrong game working in radio. She'd thought hard about that one. I'd sensed the gears in her mind grinding while Steven Terry was doing his thing on stage.

'I'm taking a break,' she continued. 'I'm going to stay away from TV for a while. I can take the house in Spain for another six months, and I might even think about buying out there. But I want to do something different. I'm going to make it a sabbatical.'

The announcements started, letting us know that we needed to make our way back to our seats. We hung back, knowing that if we returned to our places too soon, we'd be up and down making way for everybody else in the row to get to their seats.

The second part of the show was just as entertaining. I was astonished when he called out a woman for having an affair. She was sitting with her husband, and it all got a bit tense for a while as the audience – myself included –

wondered where he was going with it. It turned out the bloke was gay and had been hiding it all of his life. On some level his wife had known – hence the affair. It was remarkable how skilfully Steven turned the situation around. The guy got a standing ovation for admitting that he was gay. He loved his wife dearly but had been attracted to men for as long as he could remember. She loved him but had sensed there was something wrong. They were about to be whisked away, crying but hugging each other, to a five-star hotel in the resort.

'Let's give this lovely couple some time to talk and make peace with their new lives. Ladies and gentlemen, what happened here might seem dangerous to you, it might feel like we've shaken this couple's life to the core, but, believe me, although their love for each other will live on, their lives will be happy now. They will both find the peace that they've been craving.'

There were cheers, a massive round of applause. The couple were a few rows down from us. Steven had them standing in the aisle while they were talking. As applause thundered through the auditorium, Steven turned and caught my eye. He looked as if he'd been hit by a bus. He walked up to me, the applause beginning to fade. He switched off his radio microphone and moved in close.

'Peter. Peter Bailey. I sensed that you were here tonight. Come and see me after the show in my dressing room. Ask for Carlos backstage. I have to speak to you.'

He stood up, switched his microphone back on and said, 'Ladies and gentlemen, let's have another round of applause for our lovely couple, Edward and Louise!'

He milked the applause until he was back on the stage, and then moved the show into the finale.

'What was that about?' Alex whispered.

'He wants us to see him after show. Remember Carlos. We need to speak to Carlos backstage.'

'Ooh, look who's a friend to the stars now, Pete Bailey!'

She pushed me playfully, but I wasn't feeling particularly humorous about it. Steven hadn't yet revealed the audience member who was surrounded by demons, unless he'd meant Edward and Louise, but I thought not. That's not the way he'd played their story. I had a nasty feeling that he'd just found his guy, only whatever he wanted to say to me needed to be private, it was not for the audience.

I was anxious for the show to end after that, desperate to know what he wanted to tell me. He'd been right twice before about all the shit in my life. There couldn't be any more left, surely?

After the show, as the buzzing audience slowly made its way out of the Winter Gardens, Alex and I sought out Carlos. As a radio journalist, I was used to doing this. People think that celebrities are inaccessible, but you can usually get to them via the network of support staff that are always around, should you care to look for them.

Carlos had clearly been briefed to expect us. He showed us into Steven's dressing room.

'Peter – I beg your pardon, you prefer Pete – and Alex too, what a lovely surprise! Your scar is healing well now, Pete. I hear that you had quite a time at the hands of that couple. I'm so pleased that it all turned out as well as it could for you.'

How did he know about the Peter thing? Had I told him that? I couldn't remember. And things hadn't turned out that well, the way I saw it.

'Good show tonight, Steven,' I said, shaking his hand as if he were an old pal. There's something about seeing familiar people in unfamiliar places that makes you more friendly towards them. That's how I felt with Steven Terry that night.

With the pleasantries out of the way, Steven got straight to business.

'I'm so sorry about what happened, Pete. I read about it in the newspapers, of course, but I had a premonition that it was going happen when we met the last time.'

'You were right again, Steven. I don't know how you do it, but you were bang on.'

'I had a strong sense from the minute I walked out on that stage tonight that you were here. There's something about you, Pete, something in your life that's very strong. I called it a demon on the stage, but of course there are no such things as demons. They come to us in human form.'

Silence, for a moment. He did this on stage. It worked well. He left his words hanging. Was this just more showbiz?

'I said it before, Pete, and I'll say it again. You have to make very careful choices about the women in your life. There is a demon among them. She is still around, Pete, I'm sorry to tell you. In spite of all that has happened to you in your past, the real demon is still in your life.'

'What do you mean by *demon*, Steven? You keep using that word, but what does it mean in human terms?' Alex asked. She was as riveted by this as I was.

'You're quite right, Alex. I need to explain. I call them demons, but they are just people who walk among us. They are dangerous. They seduce us, mislead us, make us stray from our path and undermine us. At worst, they can be pure evil. You have known plenty of that already, Pete, but I'm sorry, there is more to come.'

If Steven Terry had looked as if he'd been hit by a bus earlier, it was my turn now. All my previous troubles had been predicted by this man, and here he was again telling me it still wasn't over.

'There can't be more to come, Steven? It must be over now. I can't take any more.'

I wanted to cry. I honestly thought I was going to start crying. I felt so worn out by it all. I hadn't realised how exhausted it had made me.

'I'm sorry, Pete. I have told you before: this ability of mine ... it can be as much a curse as it is a gift. But I felt it the minute I walked out on that stage tonight. I'm sorry, Pete. There is a demon in your life who has yet to be banished. It is this demon that you must fight if you are going to have lasting peace in your life. I'm so sorry, Pete, but it's not over yet.'

***

The Woodlands Edge children's home was boarded up and surrounded by security fencing. The site was up for sale. The grounds were overgrown and it didn't look as if it had been occupied for several years. It reminded me of my own house: vandalised, rotting, uninhabited, slowly falling to bits. I shuddered at the thought of all the money I was about to lose and how long it would take to pay it all back.

'How long do you reckon this place has been closed?' Alex asked, reading my thoughts.

'Must be at least five years. I'm trying to work through the ages. Meg must have been here in the early nineties, and it looks like it stayed open a while after that. It's a nice enough location for a home, mind you.'

The house had extensive grounds. Overgrown, as they were now, they were a bit of a headache. If they were well kept, with the home occupied, it would have been a wonderful environment in which to grow up. The gardens were bordered by woodland. A large oak stood tall and proud by the side of a dilapidated fence, which was covered in lichen, many of its bars fallen from the rusted nails. I noticed that one of the lower branches of the old oak had been removed. It seemed strange that it should have rotted – the tree looked strong and safe.

'Are we going in?' Alex asked, smiling. 'It would seem rude not to.'

There was no way we were visiting this place without a snoop around. The fencing was only the temporary type, the sort that builders use to contain hazardous areas. It didn't take much to manoeuvre one of the posts out of its concrete stand and create a gap that was big enough to squeeze through.

'Why didn't Meg tell me that she'd lived in this place? Why did she keep it to herself? She can't have been ashamed of it, surely?'

'Who knows what happened here, or why she ended up here in the first place. You know what these bloody homes were like. In some of these places the kids would have been safer fending for themselves on the streets than being at the mercy of the bastards who were running them.'

I knew what she meant. The number of cases that I'd dealt with in my journalistic career was unbelievable. It never ceased to amaze me how these things had gone on. I wanted to find out why this home had closed, that was for sure. An earlier online search had yielded nothing interesting; it was going to be a job for the microfiche in the local library. They'd have all the old newspapers in there, and that's where I'd find my answers, if any were to be found.

We'd reached the front door. It looked as if it had been protected by chipboard once upon a time, but that had dropped off – or been ripped away – and was now moul-dering among the undergrowth in the garden. I tried the door, but it appeared to be locked. The downstairs windows were boarded and covered with different coloured spray paints. Most of them were nicknames and dates, but one caught my attention. It was in red paint. *Cover-up!* was all it said, scrawled all around the sides of the building. That microfiche machine was getting a visit – my journalistic antennae were tingling. Alex had clocked it too.

'Pete! Pete! I've got the door open.'

Alex had gone off alone while I was studying the sides of the building.

'How did you manage that? It was locked.'

'It was jammed. It's badly warped, but a good shove budged it. It was blocked off at one time; you can see the nail holes around the doorframe. Shall we go in? Although I know that you won't want to ignore the useful health and safety warnings that have been put up.'

She smiled again. We'd been in some right shit together, but playing detectives with Alex was fun. She made it fun. She had the same instincts as me. We'd met while studying to be cub reporters, so that made sense. We were both nosey. We were paid to be that way for a living.

'Fuck health and safety, I'm going in!' I said, giving the door a final push so I could squeeze through.

There was a wide stone staircase winding up the three levels of the building from a massive hallway. The ceilings were high, as you'd expect in a house of that age. It must have been a wonderful building once, but now it was falling to bits. Old plaster was flaking off the walls and it smelled damp and abandoned. The ground-floor windows were boarded up. There was some light coming down the landing from the upper windows, but it felt a bit dark to be going in without a torch.

'Have you got a light on your phone?' I asked Alex. 'Mine has one, but it looks a bit dark in there.'

'Sure, yes, hang on. I'll find it. Yes, there you are. We look like a couple of American TV cops.'

She was right about that. We entered the hallway cautiously, using the beams from our phones to check the way ahead, and then to get a closer look at the walls and decor.

'Can you believe it. The place has been empty for ages and they've still got a pile of bloody junk mail!' I laughed as I rummaged through the free newspapers, takeaway leaflets and charity bags that had been piled up to one side of the door.

'February 2002,' I read from the paper. 'That's the latest date on these papers.'

'Hell, it's been empty for over a decade,' Alex replied. 'You'd think somebody would have developed the site for housing.'

'It's probably council owned or something like that. If it's tied up in any legacy, it might get even more compli- cated. I did a radio story once about some old people's home that had been left in trust. It was easier to let it rot than to try and sort the trust out.'

'Maybe,' said Alex. 'This place must have an amazing history.'

She moved towards the first door, which still had the word *office* hand-painted on it.

'Watch out,' I warned, uneasy about the bare, creaking floorboards. 'Take care. If this place has been empty that long, those health and safety warnings might be making a fair point.'

Alex entered the office, stepping carefully and making sure that she scanned the path ahead.

'Anything in there?' I called across the hallway. I was taking a look at the lounge area. There were still some old chairs – it looked like it had been a TV room at one time.

There was no reply from Alex.

'Anything there?' I called again.

'Only some papers, nothing private, but interesting. Social services handbooks, crap like that. How about you?'

'Just a lounge area. It opens onto what looks like a dining room; it's got some of those old school trestle tables in there still. Looks very Oliver Twist to me. Must have been horrible for those poor kids.'

There was a sudden rustle from one of the old hessian chairs, and then a scratching sound on the floorboards. I shone my torch to see a large rat scuttling across the room.

'Oh shit, rats!' I called to Alex. 'It's coming your way, look out!'

I heard a short cry of alarm from across the hallway, and then a loud crack from inside the office.

I ran in the direction of the rat, but I couldn't hear it anymore, it had taken shelter.

'Alex? Alex? Are you okay? It's gone now.'

I walked into the office area, shining my torch. There was no Alex.

'Alex? Where are you?'

I looked around for another door, but there was only one entrance. I shone the light from my phone across the floor and around the room. I found the papers that Alex had been talking about. I moved towards the table, and then I saw what had happened. She'd fallen through the floorboards. There was a dark hole in the area where she must

have been standing. I couldn't see a light from her torch –
neither could I hear her making any sound.

'Alex? Are you alright?' I called, shining my torch down
into the hole created by the shattered floorboards and terrified of what I was going to find on the floor below.

CHAPTER FOUR

1992 There were not many members of staff that the youngsters bonded with at Woodlands Edge Children's Home. Bob Taylor was one of them. He was a favourite of most of the children whose misfortune it was to end up there.

Most of the staff were indifferent. They were professional, kind enough, but always businesslike. The children in the home craved a close connection with an adult, and Bob Taylor was someone they could trust. His eyes were kind and he was always happy to listen. He'd frequently stay after his shift was over to work through some problem related to school or members of the opposite sex. He was like a real dad, and he genuinely enjoyed the company of the young people in his care.

Then there was Tom, one of the caretakers at the home. He worked alternate early and late shifts. The second caretaker was grumpy and impatient; he had no interest in the kids, but Tom made time for them, he'd be happy to chat as he was going about his work. There was a reason for that. Tom was unable to have children with his wife, Mavis.

They'd met and married in Blackpool and always hoped to start a family there, but after several years of trying, they had not been given the child that they craved.

Tom knew how sad it made Mavis, and it goaded him constantly that he couldn't give her that one thing. They had fostered, to bring the presence of children into their lives, but it broke their hearts when their young visitors had to move on. They wanted their own children. They were trying to adopt. It was a long and tortuous process, but they lived in hope that they would be able to have a child in their lives before they were too old.

There was no way a baby or toddler would be placed with them now, but a teenager was possible. It was a daily torture to Tom to work in that place. All those kids desperately craving the love of a stable home and he and Mavis who would adopt any one of them at the drop of a hat.

Tom was always happy to pass the time of day talking the boys through practical tasks like bleeding radiators and fixing door handles. He figured that they'd need skills like that when they were older, and without a parent to teach them, who else would?

Tom was popular with the girls too; he was unusual in that he didn't differentiate between them and the boys. He was equally at ease teaching Hannah and Meg how to use a hammer as he was showing Jacob or David the best way to replace a washer.

He was a quiet man, intimidated by the social workers and professional staff, and much more at ease with the children. Although he felt the sadness in many of the children, he'd always assumed that was because they were so desperate to find families to live with. He'd never got a sense that anything else was going on. The older youngsters were able to separate the horrors of the night-time from the safety of daytime – they suppressed it and never discussed it among themselves or the adults.

He got on well with Meg and Hannah. They were a right couple of characters. They'd chat and laugh and loved helping him as he went about his chores. They were a double act, joined at the hip, and always enjoying each other's company.

He sensed trouble coming with David and Jacob. They were nice lads, but all those hormones were exploding in one building. He would never dare to mention it to any of the staff, it wasn't his place, but he could see that David had eyes for Meg. And she was certainly no reluctant party. He hoped that the social workers were keeping an eye on them all. It wasn't his business, they must be used to dealing with teenagers who were becoming sexually aware.

Life went on at Woodlands Edge. Tom grew closer to Meg and Hannah. He'd discuss the girls with Mavis and they dreamt about how, one day, they might be able to care for them in their own home – if there was ever any movement on their adoption paperwork.

It all changed the day that Jacob died. It shook Tom to the core. He'd liked Jacob. He was cheeky – what young lad isn't? But Tom hadn't put him down as being that unhappy. It was one of the lowest points of his life. It wouldn't be the last.

He was on the early shift that day and he'd stopped to brew up. At first he thought it was the radio, but the shouting was persistent and urgent. It was coming from outside. Tom rushed to the front entrance, from where he could see Bob struggling with something over by the big oak tree.

He knew before he even got there that it was a body. Bob was frantically trying to support it, hoping that he wasn't dead. It was too late, of course. Jacob had been dead for a couple of hours.

The boy's face haunted Tom for several months afterwards – you should never have to see a child like that. The police came and the body was removed; the news was broken to the youngsters inside the home and a terrible darkness descended over them.

Several young people knew why Jacob had done what he'd done, so why did none of them speak? Gary had gathered them in the lounge to break the news. He'd actually managed to shed a tear for the benefit of the other staff. David wanted to kill him.

There were questions, a full investigation, caring social workers, counsellors, the lot, but not one of them walked away with the information that could have explained and rectified it all: Gary Maxwell was a bullying and manipulative monster and he was making their lives a living hell. The younger children liked Gary, but he was grooming them for later, making sure they were ready. He only began to intimidate them when they moved on to secondary school. That's when things changed. They didn't know. How could they? Every word that came out of his mouth helped to weave a web of control around them.

Tom saw snatches of this. He was not party to confidential chats, but he could observe from afar. He knew that David was taking antidepressants. A kid of his age, on antidepressants. He'd lost his best friend, of course he was bereft, but drugs? Who was looking out for these kids?

Tom had watched as Meg and David grew closer. It didn't exclude Hannah, but there was something else there. A craving in David for love, that's what he put it down to. What must it be like for those kids to have nobody to hug them? He tried to guide David to talk to Bob, but he couldn't intervene, he was only a caretaker. He knew the staff, but he was deferential to them; he would never dare to speak his mind. He was there to change light bulbs and fix plugs. It was not his place to advise on the children.

The first thing Tom knew about Bob's departure was movement in the entrance hall. People were looking out of windows, checking to confirm that Bob had actually done what they'd thought – he had left after a blazing row with Gary. There were hushed conversations among staff and children; nobody knew exactly what had happened. Everybody kept out of Gary's way. He was furious. Tom averted his eyes and didn't get involved. It was not his place to speculate about what had gone on.

Then it happened again. It was Tom who found the body this time. It was hanging from the same branch that Jacob had chosen. David had taken the same terrible way out as his young friend, copying his method exactly. Tom wept as he took the body down and checked for signs of life. Like Jacob, David was cold and dead and had been for hours. He'd planned it that way, using the cover of darkness to conceal his actions.

What could be making these wonderful young men so desperately unhappy? Why had these two boys taken their lives so violently? Tom wanted to scream these questions at Gary, but the adoption paperwork was progressing well, and he had high hopes that he and Mavis would be able to care for their own child before the year was out. Now was not the time to rock the boat.

Meg and Hannah were distraught at the loss of their friend. Tom didn't see them for some time after David's death, and it was only after everybody returned from his funeral that they came up to chat to him again.

'Did David look at peace when you cut him down?'

Hannah asked. 'Please tell me he looked like he'd found some peace.'

Tom lied. There was no way he was going to tell them what David's body had looked like. Not their friend. They didn't need to hear that.

'He looked like he'd found the escape he was looking for,' Tom replied quietly. He didn't mention the bulging eyes and blue face.

Meg couldn't speak to him, she was so upset. She'd always seemed a tough cookie to him, and he'd never seen her so distressed and vulnerable before. It was a few weeks later that he'd find out why, along with the rest of the staff, to their horror.

Before David killed himself he'd had enough time to make Meg pregnant. At the age of only fourteen, Meg Stewart was pregnant with a dead boy's child.

'Shit, it's time I lost some weight!' came a voice from the darkness below.

'Are you hurt?'

I was frantic. I could barely see a thing – it had to have been quite a fall if Alex had gone through the floorboards.

'Only my dignity,' she replied. 'And I thought it couldn't get any worse than when I appeared on CeleBritish Holidays. Turns out I was wrong!'

At least she was joking. I cautiously moved as close as I dared to the broken floorboards and peered down. I could see her lying on the floor, cushioned by boxes of old newspapers.

'These broke my fall,' Alex said, blinking in the glare of

my flashlight. 'It's a bloody good job. It's a stone floor down here.'

'You sure you're okay?' I asked again. I couldn't believe that she hadn't broken anything. She tried to move.

'Oh shit. I've hurt my ankle. Sprained I think, not broken. God, that hurts!'

'I'm going to work out how to get to you. Do you need an ambulance or anything? How bad is it?'

'Just a shoulder to lean on – please don't call an ambulance. If the local press get a whiff of TV presenter Alex Kennedy falling on her arse in an abandoned building, we'll never get them off our tail. Come down here to give me some support, if you can. I'll be okay.'

'Find your phone, I'm coming down.'

It was too dark in the cellar to leave Alex without any light, but once she'd found her phone I could use my own flashlight to illuminate my path.

I trod warily on the floorboards. Alex's accident had made me doubt the safety of the building. Perhaps we'd been a bit gung ho sneaking in – there were plenty of warnings, after all.

I moved along the corridor, looking into the rooms as I passed them, and eventually reached the door leading down to the cellar. It took some opening – all of the woodwork was swollen with damp. Behind the door was a steep wooden staircase. No wonder they'd closed the building down. No health and safety legislation would let kids anywhere near stairs like that. I gingerly placed my weight on the first step. The woodwork creaked, but seemed to be sturdy. I heard a rustle below.

'Alex?'

No answer. Shit, probably more rats. I wondered for a moment if the ambulance guys might be the better option.

Was I seriously thinking of abandoning my friend because of a vermin problem?

I made my way down the stairs, scanning the floor for rats with the limited light given out from my smart phone. It was an empty cellar with the exception of a punchbag hung up from one of the joists, some discarded linen piled up in the far corner, and a couple of old chipboard bookcases leaning against one of the walls.

'Alex?'

There was no sign of her. There had to be another entrance.

'Pete, where are you?'

I could hear her voice coming from a room beyond. I walked towards the bookcases and gave them a kick, giving any rats a chance to make a run for it before I shifted them. They were only lightweight and moved easily enough. It turned out they were concealing a second door. I opened it and there was Alex, painfully trying to stand up unaided.

'Sit down. I'll take a look,' I said as I rushed over to her. I scanned her via the light from my phone. She had some scratches on her arms and a bloody mark on her cheek. I dabbed that with a tissue first, and then turned to her leg.

'What movement do you have?' I asked, the most cack-handed doctor that you could possibly have the misfortune to be examining you.

'Honest, Pete, I think it's only a bad sprain. It'll take my weight – just – but I'm okay. I'm more interested in all these old newspapers.'

I looked down to see that she'd already been working her way through the ones on top.

'Take a look at this,' she said, handing me a copy of the Today newspaper from 1992. I hadn't seen a Today newspaper in years, and the distinctive blue logo immediately took me back to a time and place when I was much younger and living at home.

Second Death At Controversial Children's Home read the headline. The article related to Woodlands Edge. There were piles of them: national newspapers, local newspapers, professional journals, each one outlining the history of the place where my wife had lived.

This was irresistible to a couple of journalists like Alex and me. We rapidly made our way through the boxes of papers, trying to get a rough timeline of the problems they'd experienced there.

It looked as if there had been four deaths in all: three boys and one girl. Two suicides by hanging, one by pills, the other by cutting wrists. Then there was a big inquiry, and the hauling of staff over the coals: a man called Gary Maxwell, the guy in charge of the home, and a support worker called Bob Taylor, who'd been scapegoated in the investigation. The chief constable at the time, Tony Dodds, and Russell Black, the head of social services, were heavily implicated. It was remarkable reading. But at the end of it all in 1993 the home was given a clean bill of health. It was 1994 when it was resolved. Meg would have been sixteen at the time. Was she involved in this?

There would never be any pictures of the kids – even then press regulations would not have allowed it. But somebody had painstakingly kept newspaper records of everything that had gone on here. It was an entire, sorry history told through sensational headlines.

Head Of Children's Home Jailed In Abuse Inquiry

Police Chief Claims Personal Grudge To Blame For Costs Of Inquiry

Woodlands Edge Home Renamed After Abuse Inquiry

Even in the nineties they'd got the hang of rebranding it

seemed. But Meadow's End? Really? Which committee of fuckwits thought up that one? It told you all that you needed to know that the locals had completely ignored the new name and continued to call it by its original name for years afterwards. The story that we were reading had all the hallmarks of a seventies-style cover-up. As journalists we're supposed to be impartial about these things, but my cynical sixth sense was telling me that this had all the makings of a horrible story. And this is where Meg and her sister had been.

'Are you thinking what I'm thinking?' Alex asked.

'What? It looks like a load of shits walked away with unblemished careers after a whitewash?'

'Ooh, you've become so cynical. No, but I agree, it stinks. I thought we should get Steven Terry up here. If kids died and stuff like that, he might be able to sense something. What do you reckon?'

'I think it's a great idea!' I said. 'He's in Blackpool for two more nights. I wonder where he's staying?'

'He gave you his card, didn't he? He did say to call him anytime. He'd have a field day in this place. Let's call him. Seriously. It can't do any harm.'

'We need to get you out of here first, and take a better look at that—'

I stopped in mid-sentence. Alex had rested her phone against her thigh and it was shining on one of the newspapers. I recognised the face in the photo, but I couldn't place it at first. It was grainy and faded – the light was poor. I got it eventually. It was Thomas Yates.

I picked up the paper, and moved the beam from my phone closer so that I could read the tiny text in the darkness.

It was Meg's dad alright. It turned out that he'd been a

caretaker at the former Woodlands Edge children's home. He was in the paper because of his connection with the guy in charge of the home, Gary Maxwell, and all the other high-ups who were named in the various newspaper articles. The original case had collapsed when Thomas Yates withdrew the allegations that he'd made alongside Bob Taylor. Bob Taylor became immediately discredited and the suits walked away. My journalistic instincts were fully aroused.

———

Alex had been right about Steven Terry. He took no persuading to pay an impromptu visit to Woodlands Edge – or Meadow's End, as nobody called it, ever.

After discovering Thomas Yates' involvement in the whole affair, things were beginning to take a little more shape. It was making more sense to me that Meg might not want to rake over this entire story again. I think that I'd want to forget it all too.

Alex and I skimmed off a selection of the papers before we made our way out of the cellar and back to the car. It was a slow and painful journey for her, but we made it and she was soon on her way to A&E. She was reluctant, but I persuaded her to get it checked out. We got lucky; we'd avoided the weekend and evening rush hours so we only had to wait for a kid with Lego stuck up his nose and an old guy who'd had a bad fall before it was our turn. The doctor was far too professional to play fan girl, and just did her job, sorting out an X-ray for Alex, and then confirming that it wasn't broken. Her ankle had bruised though and looked like an over-ripe banana. One of the nurses was assigned to bandage it up and Alex was given some painkillers. All in all we were in and out in a little over an hour. Not bad.

I called Steven Terry from the waiting room. They seemed to have relaxed the rules in hospitals. There was a time that I'd been scared to switch my phone on in case someone's life-support machine exploded at the mere whiff of a 2G signal. It was the same with planes. Apparently, the onboard instrumentation is so sensitive that if you dared to call your mum to tell her you were on your way back from sunny Spain, you'd instantly start to plummet from the skies.

'How lovely to hear from you, Pete. Have you been mulling over what I said to you?'

'Actually, Steven, I want to know if you're up for an adventure.'

I explained what we'd been doing and warned him that he'd have to sneak through builder's fencing to access the building. He was immediately up for it.

'It may look glamorous doing a touring stage show, Pete, but I do find the days a little dull. All that applause and adulation, and then I'm left to my own devices until the next one. In short, I'd love to join you. It sounds like just my thing!'

I hadn't put Steven Terry down as an adventurer, but he couldn't get over to Woodlands Edge fast enough. I had to tell him to hang fire until Alex and I were finished at the hospital.

I looked up the Milton Keynes train times on my phone while Alex was having her X-ray. She'd assured me that she would be fit to travel the next day, but I thought it best to delay buying tickets until a bit later. I knew that I was sailing close to the wind with my credit card too, I was keen to put off spending the money until I knew that we could make the journey. There's only so much humiliation one man can take. I'd already screamed at the sight of a rat – I didn't want to make a big deal of how broke I was.

We'd have to catch a shitty shuttle train over from Blackpool, but then it was straight down from Preston on a decent InterCity train. I hoped Meg's mum would be able to explain everything that we'd discovered in those papers.

With Alex dispatched from the pharmacy with painkillers in hand, we bought a bottle of water from the hospital shop so that she could take her first pill, and then made our way back to the car.

'I'll text Steven now. He said he'd have to take a taxi, so we might have a short wait. You okay?'

'Yes, fine. I know it looks bad, but it's not as painful as it was when I first fell. What a daft cow I am. I can't believe I did that!'

'How about we pop into the catalogue store on the way over and get you a walking stick. Would that help?'

'I can't believe I'm saying this, but yes it would.'

'You can get the old-lady experience; it'll give you a taste of what you're in for in years to come!'

I was in and out of the store in no time. They had a cheap metal walking stick, which cost me less than a tenner. My credit card was still obliging. How far would I be able to go until I got blocked? I could see immediately that Alex was more comfortable with the stick taking the weight off her foot.

***

Steven Terry was there already. I saw him as soon as we drew up. He'd located the same gap in the fence that we'd used and made his way past the big oak tree to the house.

He'd been crying when we reached him. He made no attempt to hide it.

'Sorry we're late, Steven. Are you okay?'

'Yes, don't mind me. How about you, Alex? Is your ankle alright?'

Alex filled him in with the details.

'What have you picked up then, Steven? What's so special about the tree?'

I was testing him. I knew that two boys had hanged themselves from that tree, but I wanted to know how genuine he was.

'I don't think I've ever felt so much sadness in one spot,' he began, his eyes reddening again at the thought of it. 'Two young men ended their lives here. They were in great pain – terrible things had happened to them. They were friends too, good friends. The death of one was copied by the other, and they followed each other to the grave.'

He paused. Whatever signal or information he was receiving from this area had given him quite a jolt.

'These boys felt lost and trapped when they killed themselves. They had everything to live for, but they couldn't carry on with their lives. They felt as if they had no other option. You see where this branch has been cut down? That was done to prevent any more children from doing the same thing. It's terrible, this place is very dark.'

'Shall we try the house? Is there anything else that you need to look at outside?'

I was stunned by Steven's accuracy. There was no way I was telling him how correct he'd been. He can't have looked it up on the internet; the story was too old, nothing had come up when I did an online search in the hospital. This was an old story. Its details were confined to musty old newspapers and the library microfiche.

We headed towards the house.

'Mind if I sit on the step?' Alex asked. 'I'd rather give it a miss in there for now, bearing in mind what happened earlier.'

We left her tapping away on her phone and entered the building for the second time that day. Steven stopped sharp in front of me.

'What?' I asked.

'There was joy in this place,' he answered, 'but there has also been so much pain. I can hear the echoes of children laughing. They would play in this hallway; they loved to have games of hide-and-seek and chase. But I only see that happiness on the younger faces. The older children carry a burden – I can't tell what it is.'

'Do you actually see faces? Or is it more a feeling?'

The cynic in me had long gone as far as Steven Terry was concerned. I was hanging on his every word.

'It's more of a sensation, Pete. It's very strong in this building. I'd love to film my TV show here; I think we'd get a couple of episodes from it. What went on here?'

I hadn't revealed that yet. I wanted to see if Steven would sniff it out himself.

'Let's walk up the stairs,' I suggested. 'Alex and I never got that far.'

Using the lights from our smart phones, we made our way up the wide stone staircase. As we entered the landing, it got lighter. The upstairs windows weren't boarded up. I opened a few doors and we were able to switch off the flashlights.

These rooms had to be bedrooms. Each room had a washbasin in it, and one or two had the frames of collapsed wooden beds. There was no ensuite in those days, and the toilets were accessed via the second-floor landing, girls on one side, boys on the other. It looked like the boys had the bedrooms on the right-hand side of this floor and the girls the ones on the left.

Steven stopped dead again. I was getting accustomed to the drill now. All the good information would begin to flow soon after he stopped walking.

'There was a demon in this place. Remember I told you last night about demons? They're evil people. They can't help themselves. They're just pure evil. There was one here. The children lived in fear of him. So did the staff. I can still feel his presence here. He hasn't been here for many years, but his scent still lingers for me.'

He paused again. It was as if he had to sort it out in his own mind before he could communicate it to me.

'Let's walk into the rooms, Pete – see what's there.'

We walked in and out of the bedrooms. A shiver ran through me as we reached one on the boys' side.

'They're here, Pete. They're with us now.'

'Who? Who's with us?' I asked, looking to see if Alex had joined us.

'The boys. They used to share this room, the ones who hanged themselves. They're with us now. They want us to carry on.'

'I looked around. I couldn't see anything.

'Are they actually here with us now, at this moment?'

'Yes and no, Pete. I feel them strongly. I can sense everything that happened in this room. It has been a happy place. There has been joy in this room. But it's these boys whose mark has been left most strongly. They were wronged. I can sense only anger and despair. They felt helpless and trapped when they ended their lives.'

I was completely gripped by what Steven was saying. Baloney or not, there was no way he could have known any of this information. It had to be for real, but my instincts kept telling me that it was impossible that he could see these ghosts. It was just too incredible for me.

We walked across the landing. He was like a water diviner, sometimes he sensed something, most times he didn't.

We walked in and out of the girls' rooms. He said nothing. I was beginning to think that that was all he was going to come up with. Then, without warning, we entered the last of the rooms on that side of the landing. I thought he was having a heart attack. He looked as if he was about to drop down on the floor.

'What is it, Steven? Are you okay?'

'Oh my dear God, Pete. Just give me a moment. I need to consider how to tell you this.'

I looked at him. His face was white. I gave him time to recover, but I was desperate to hear what he had to say.

'Two girls shared this room, Pete, two good friends. They were in love with the boys who killed themselves, or at least they thought they were.'

This was of no particular interest to me, but I knew that I had to bide my time. There was more that he wanted to say. He started to speak again.

'These girls shared many secrets, Pete. They were forever bound by the ties of their lives. But someone very dangerous has been in this room, Pete. She's another demon. She's one of your demons, Pete. You need to take great care.'

CHAPTER FIVE

1992 The Woodlands Edge children's home was a quiet place for the next two weeks as the youngsters there adjusted to a second tragic death. Meg Stewart was inconsolable. It was only when she fainted one teatime that a medical examination revealed the truth about her health. Grieving turned to shock and gossip, and David's death was quickly placed on the back burner as far as the residents were concerned. One of the girls had become pregnant, and she was below the legal age of consent.

Gary was a man under siege. Not only had the home lost two children in a matter of weeks, it now had to face the ignominy of an underage pregnancy and the associated implication that the boys and girls in its care were perhaps less well supervised than they might be.

It was never good when Gary was under pressure. He was curt with staff and dismissive of the youngsters, unless someone wearing a suit was visiting his establishment. Everyone kept their heads down. Tom did his work and stayed out of it. The task of removing the branch from which the boys had hanged themselves fell to him. He supervised the tree surgeon who came to saw off the branch, and he was pleased to see the back of it when it crashed to the ground. It had been one of the worst experiences of his life as he'd tried to support that young lad to keep him breathing if he was still alive, desperately crying out for help to get him cut down.

Meg had suspected that something wasn't quite right. She and David had found comfort together, so she knew what the changes in her body might be, yet she was terrified to admit it to herself. She prayed that the situation would somehow pass of its own accord. She knew that she would have to deal with Gary when the news came out, and she wanted to postpone that as long as possible.

Gary had already taken his first swing at her after David's death by putting her and Hannah in different rooms. She was now roommates with Debbie Simmonds, whom she detested. Debbie was a needy, overweight girl it was difficult to warm to. She was close to Gary, one of his favourites, and this made Meg's situation even more unbearable. She missed her night-time chats with Hannah – she would have confided in her best friend, but there was no way that she could open up to Debbie.

Gary had sought to punish Hannah and Meg for the boys' deaths. They were close, they must have known that the boys were unhappy. They might also have heard them talk about ending their lives. Either way, their deaths had brought considerable heat for him. There were questions and investigations. The home was assessed and inspected, but Gary lived to fight another day.

There was speculation that the problem had been swept under the carpet. Gary was visited frequently by Russell Black, the head of social services, and Tony Dodds, the chief constable. They'd greet Gary warmly, but with concerned looks, and he'd usher them into his office. The door would be closed and there would be intense conversations and sometimes raised voices.

The older kids would make themselves scarce when these men were in the building. They'd retreat to their rooms like frightened animals. They knew these man, but not in their official roles. These were their monsters in the night.

It was on the evening that the home got the all clear that Meg fainted. Gary had been completely exonerated. Woodlands Edge was deemed to be a safe, secure and happy place under his leadership. The boys who had killed themselves were troubled youngsters from broken homes, navigating their way through difficult teenage years. Both had been taking medication for depression. Russell Black and Tony Dodds appeared in interviews, explaining the root-and-branch extent of their investigations. They declared that they were completely happy with the leadership of the home.

It would have been crass for the support workers to watch the TV reports in an environment that was shared with the children, but with jobs and careers in the firing line, they couldn't wait until they got home at night to catch up with the latest news. The home was in the clear. Gary had passed scrutiny, and things would go on as they always had.

Meg was already feeling weak when she entered the dining area; she'd heard the news and it made her feel nauseous. As she sat down on the bench with her tray in her hands, she became light-headed and fell to the ground. Her tray crashed to the floor, making the room fall into silence as everybody sought out the source of the noise.

Gary, who had been working his way around the dining

room, moved directly towards her, angry that he was being faced with a new situation so soon after being cleared of any wrongdoing after the death of the boys. He carried Meg to the sickroom himself and, along with another member of staff, ensured that she was made comfortable on the Z-bed that was in there. He noticed as he carried her that she had a womanly shape now.

He was startled to hear the doctor's diagnosis that she was pregnant. The first thing that he could think of was the attention that this would bring to the home. There would be more questions and closer scrutiny of the care regime which he operated there. As the doctor left the building, confirming that Meg would require ongoing medical attention and an urgent hospital visit for a full check-up and scan, Gary looked as concerned as a parent would be. With the doctor gone, he made straight for the sickroom where Meg had been left alone to rest.

It was dark in there, but he turned on the lights without warning, rousing her from her sleep and leaving her blinking at him, trying to orientate herself in the unfamiliar room. He sat on the bed, right next to her, and leant on her stomach as he moved his face right up to hers. She flinched instinctively, aware now that there really was a baby inside her.

'If you think you're in for special treatment now, you're very much mistaken, you silly little slut. How dare you do this to me! You will go to the hospital, you will speak to the doctors and you will say nothing. If you do, your friend Hannah will pay for it, you understand? And if you think you're keeping the baby, think again. It's getting adopted. Do you understand me?'

There was the sound of a mop handle falling to the floor in the storage cupboard next door to the sickroom. Gary pushed into Meg's stomach harder as he got up from the bed. He went to investigate the nearby sound. He'd thought he was alone while threatening the girl.

It was the caretaker Thomas Yates messing around in the storage area. Although he tried to disguise the fact by screwing a mop head onto a new handle, Gary sensed from his expression that Tom had overheard his conversation with Meg in the opposite room, or, at the very least, he must have been aware that their conversation was a tense one.

'Oh, hello, Mr Maxwell, I didn't hear you there. Is everything alright? Can I help with anything?'

Gary knew that the girls got on well with Yates – he'd seen them chatting and laughing around the home, and he knew that the caretaker would have some sympathy with the girl.

'How's the adoption process going?' he asked directly. 'Any progress yet? You know I was discussing your case only last week with Russell Black. I shouldn't tell you this, but it looks like things are getting close. Your wife must be excited.'

Thomas Yates received the message loud and clear.

'Yes, Mr Maxwell, we're very hopeful. It could be any day now. We're grateful to Mr Black, he seems to be moving things along nicely.'

'Let's hope things continue to progress well for you. I put in a good word for you to Russell – he's a good friend of mine. I'll do my best to get things sped along for you. We wouldn't want any complications slowing things down, would we?'

Thomas Yates knew exactly what he meant. He lowered his eyes and continued screwing the head on the mop handle.

'By the way, Mr Maxwell, I can't hear what's going on

down here. These walls are so thick. It's difficult to know what's going in the room right next to you sometimes.'

Gary smiled.

'I know what you mean,' he replied. 'It's so easy to mishear things in this place. Good to see you, Thomas. I hope things continue to go well with the adoption.'

He exited the storeroom and returned to Meg, where he said nothing. He looked at her and put his finger to his lips. She looked at him, terrified now, knowing that her life was about to become very difficult.

She detested this man and she would be happy to see him dead.

The problem with Steven Terry was that he was a bit of a cock tease. He'd take you almost all of the way then roll over and go to sleep. Alex and I had been whipped up into a frenzy by our visit to the boarded-up home, but what had he really told us? Sure, we'd got a hint of what might have gone on. I was shit scared about his warning, but there weren't any names or specific information. Just a vague sense of what might, or might not, have happened.

He said as much himself.

'I don't see details, Pete – it's more a sense that I get, echoes of ghosts and glimpses of the past. I don't know these people, I just feel their sadness or yearning, and sometimes it can be difficult to interpret. I know, though, that this was not a happy place.'

We'd got the message. There was nothing else that he was able to tell us. As well as continuing my hunt for Meg, we needed to take a closer look at this home and the people who'd been in it.

Steven Terry seemed chatty. He was probably lonely on his gruelling tour. I was anxious not to miss the library. They closed at five o'clock on a Friday, and I wanted to get my hands on the microfiche machines. I hurried Steven along once we'd squeezed out every bit of juice from him. Alex gave me a glare, letting me know how abrupt I was being, but I wanted to be on a train to Milton Keynes the next day.

We wished Steven well with the rest of his tour, thanked him very much for his help, and dropped him off back at his hotel. His last words were exactly what you'd expect: ominous and downright scary.

'This ends for you soon, Pete. But the choices you make and the people you decide to trust will determine the outcome. It all moves around you. I wish you luck, my friend.'

And off he went. I'd have settled for a 'Cheerio!'

'That man really knows how to spin a yarn,' Alex said when he was out of earshot.

'I'm not sure where it leaves us, but we've got to keep digging, I know that. I want to catch the library before it closes. We need to check out this story on the microfiche, and the fire too. I want to find out more about the fire before we drop in on Mavis. Are you up for it?'

Of course Alex was. We were journalists through and through. We'd caught the faint whiff of a story and we were like hunting dogs following a scent.

By the time we got to the central library, we were pushed for time. We were lucky that the local history buffs had buggered off for the weekend and left a couple of machines free. The librarian reminded us that they closed at five sharp on a Friday. Why? I wondered. What were they all going to do – rush home and read more books?

Alex took one machine, and I headed for the other.

'You take 1992, I'll take 1993, and if we get enough time, let's look at 1994 and 1991 too, just to be sure we mop everything up. I'm looking for the fire and the home. Anything. And those two guys too, Russell Black and Tony Dodds, they should be all over the papers, not only in connection with what we're looking for.'

Bloody microfiche. We both wasted precious minutes as we buggered around threading the roll of film and figuring out which way to turn it. It was like using a prehistoric version of the internet. I wished that some entrepreneur would come up with another way to do it and fast track it through Dragon's Den as soon as possible. What a nonsense.

Between us we scoured the local papers. It was a tornado of local galas, controversial planning applications and celebrity visits. Every now and then Tony Dodds or Russell Black would make an appearance, shaking hands with some councillor or politician. We found most of the stories that we'd already seen in the newspapers from the cellar; there was nothing new there.

Alex moved back to 1991 and I took a look at 1994. I was aware of a librarian beginning to make his 'we're ready to close soon, fuck off please' moves. He was throwing away discarded coffee cups and water bottles and collecting newspapers which hadn't been put away. I had a bit of luck, finding a larger picture of Thomas Yates and Bob Taylor, but no more information. I took a picture of the photos with my smart phone – I couldn't face trying to work out how to print them off. It probably involved diesel fuel, an elastic band and a cranking handle.

The librarian was moving in closer now. Bollocks. We'd have to finish soon and we were leaving empty-handed.

'Have you finished with this paper, sir? Do you mind if I take it? You know that we're closing in a couple of minutes?'

'Yes, yes, take the paper. We're not using it, it's fine. We'll get cleared up here. Sorry, we were hoping to find something.'

Normally a librarian wouldn't be able to help himself with such an unanswered research question, but he resisted. It must have been reading group that night. He wouldn't want to be late for that.

'Woah, hang on a minute!' Alex interrupted. 'Can I hold onto that paper? Are you throwing it away?'

'Here, fine, take it,' the librarian answered, doing that thing where he was trying to place where he'd seen Alex before. 'They go in the recycling bin at the end of the day – take it if it's useful.'

Alex took it from him and asked me to open up the pictures I'd just taken on my phone.

'Not Thomas Yates, the other guy. Bob whatshisname.'

I opened up the grainy photograph and handed my phone to Alex.

'How fucking excellent am I?' she smiled. 'Look who this is!'

I studied the photo of the retiring lollipop man on the front of that day's local paper.

'Well, bugger me, it's only Bob Taylor! He became a lollipop man after he left social services. Look at that – twenty-five years' service in the pot. Very impressive. And he still has a month before he officially finishes.'

'What's his school run?' Alex asked. 'We can drop in on him on Monday, ask him a few questions about the inquiry.'

The reporter had kindly added the name of the school in the article. I knew it well. I'd been there on a news story myself. If only I'd known the importance of Bob Taylor then. I'd probably driven straight past him.

Our time was up. The librarian was no longer dropping polite hints. The lights were being turned off, one by one. Our weekend was sorted. We were heading off to meet Meg's mum down in Milton Keynes, and then Bob Taylor was getting an early morning visit on Monday. There was no way Meg would be able to evade me after that.

A train journey to Milton Keynes isn't most people's idea of a great day out, but Alex and I were becoming consumed by Meg's previous history. In fact, discovering the truth about her past had become almost more important to me than locating her.

I was in two minds about it all. Part of me could understand why she might want to keep everything to herself. If it was a part of her life that she hated, why not reinvent herself and move on? However, if we were as in love as I'd felt we were when the relationship was good ... well, why not share that information? A trouble shared is a trouble halved and all that.

We were on our way to visit Mavis Yates at the Nightingale House care home. We had decided against warning anybody that we were coming. We'd agonised over this, but decided that the element of surprise might be best. Mavis was an adult, so she'd be more accessible than a child would be.

We were travelling first class, courtesy of Alex. I didn't like her paying for the tickets. I was supposed to be her host, after all, but she did a good job of selling it to me.

'You're paying for the food, accommodation and petrol, Pete. It seems only fair that I chip in.'

Put like that, it felt okay to take her money. I was secretly delighted. I hadn't told her yet about the visits I'd been getting from the car finance company. I'd started to juggle my payments, getting behind on a few key bills and then paying them off before I received too many warning letters. I didn't have enough cash to go around, it was as simple as that. Most people would just flog their house, reshuffle the finances and move on, but I was shafted on two fronts: I needed Meg for the paperwork, and the house was worth a fraction of the price it would normally have sold for. I'd even begun to receive letters from the neighbours cursing me for screwing up their retirement plans or being single-handedly responsible for lowering the house prices in the neighbourhood.

There had been an embarrassing ring of the doorbell before we caught the train. The finance guy, wise to the ways of people like me who were avoiding paying their bills, had caught me early. I was enjoying my first brew of the day and chatting to Alex about something trivial that I'd spotted on Facebook. Alex answered the intercom. She was too fast for me to beat her to it, and by that stage I was committed.

'Some guy from Ready Solutions Finance to see you,' Alex said. 'Are you expecting him? Shall I tell him to push off?'

I felt my face turning red. This is the guy who'd been on the doorstep when Alex and I were having our Skype call prior to her visit. He'd been a few times since, always leaving his business card and urging me to call. I tried to look nonchalant.

'Oh yes, damn. I forgot he was coming today. I'll nip down and see him at the front door.'

I was still in my boxers and T-shirt so I pulled on a pair of jeans and put some plimsolls on my feet. Good job I did – the ground-floor dog had been out for its morning crap in the hallway. I missed it by a couple of centimetres. I had to get out of that dump.

'Good morning, Mr Bailey. I'm sorry to trouble you so early, but you're a difficult chap to catch.'

He was only a young guy, beginning to make his way in the world, with a cheap suit and too much hair product. He was nice enough – bright and friendly.

'At six months in, we'll have to take steps to repossess the vehicle. If you're able to make some form of payment today, we'll be able to postpone that process. Are you able to make a payment?'

The chap with the charming attitude towards his girl-friend came into the hallway and smirked at me. He didn't say anything, but walked past me, grinning and finding it highly amusing that I was having to discuss my financial troubles on the doorstep.

I got my own back, though. He was so busy looking at me that he walked straight through the pile of dog crap on the floor. Revenge can be sweet, and in this case it wasn't too long coming.

If I wrote a cheque to this guy, it would probably bounce. I did the maths in my head. I had another mortgage payment due by the end of the next week, and my salary was due in the week after that. I daren't miss the mortgage payment. I wondered if declaring bankruptcy at some point might solve my problems. At least I'd be able to walk away from things.

Alex joined us. She'd been alerted by the cussing of my smirking pal in the hallway. He was banging on the door of Flat 1, shouting at the guy inside.

'Why can't you let your dog crap on the pavement like everybody else?'

I think he'd rather missed the point, but still, if he made a breakthrough it would at least make walking through the hallway more pleasant.

'How much will it take to clear the arrears?' Alex asked.

'No Alex, it's alright, I've got this—'

'Pete, I'm settling it. Pay me back later. You can't go on like this. You need to pay your bills.'

I felt small and humiliated. It was nothing to do with Alex. Part of me was grateful for her help. I certainly needed it. I'd been on a reasonable salary all of my working life, and I'd never been late with bills. I hated not being able to keep up with my expenses. It was grinding me down.

'It's £597 to bring it up to date, and another £199 would make it £796 to get next month's payment sorted as well,' said the young guy.

Alex did a quick mental calculation and wrote a cheque for £995.

'That's two months' grace,' she said as she handed it to him. 'Can you receipt it for me, please?'

He wrote out the receipt, and went to hand it to Alex, but gave it to me instead. He was on his way.

'Thanks, Alex. I'll pay you back, honestly.'

'Pete, forget it! I understand. It's not like you're some pisshead or anything. Once you get sorted out with Meg, it'll all be fine. I know that. It's yours if you want it, but I know you. You'll probably pay back every penny. Just understand that I like helping you. It's good for me. I earn too much money anyway.'

She'd already bought the first-class train tickets, so the amount that I owed her now, totted up in my head, was way more than a thousand pounds. Once the house was gone, I'd make my financial recovery within a couple of months. It wasn't getting out of hand just yet.

'Can we get food on a Saturday?' Alex asked as we made ourselves comfortable on the train, 'or are we condemned to a UK weekend service?'

'I think it's hot drinks only,' I replied. 'I can't see any evidence of food anywhere.'

We'd got a couple of facing seats. It was only me and Alex, and the train was quiet. No football fans either, I couldn't believe our luck.

'You know, Pete, I really don't mind helping out with the money side of things. We're in this together. I'm always your friend, however things turn out with Meg.'

I reached out and squeezed her hand. She made it so simple, and I never felt that she was judging me. Every ounce of my body wanted to reject her financial help, but paying off those loan arrears would help me tremendously.

'You've always been so generous with me, Pete. Like that time I had depression when we were together. Most guys would have dumped me and moved on. You were always there for me. I owe you.'

It was so long since we'd been through that. How many years? Too many to count. I'd never experienced depression before. Alex had been struck by a terrible bout of it, and this was even before we lost the baby.

'How are things now? I never asked. I'm sorry. You seem okay these days. Does it ever come back to plague you?'

Some new passengers struggled by with their suitcases, and Alex let them pass before answering.

'I still get it, but I'm getting better at living with it. I know that it's going to pass these days, but that first time it knocked me for six.'

I thought back to how things were and how low she'd

been. I never thought of Alex as being the depressive type; maybe it's because she always seemed so bright and upbeat. Perhaps that was the curse though – perhaps that was how she paid. I was a miserable old git all the time, but I was never troubled by dark thoughts like Alex.

'You never ... you didn't try to ...'

'No, that was the only time. It frightened me as much as it did you. I don't know what made me do it. I couldn't see any way out. It's ridiculous. I had you – you were lovely, but I just wanted it to stop.'

I squeezed her hand again. I hadn't thought about that event for some time, but we'd certainly clocked up some air miles in our short time together as a couple.

As we sat chatting on the train, speeding at over 120 mph towards our destination, neither of us realised that there were still much darker times ahead.

CHAPTER SIX

1992 Meg Stewart's baby arrived four months after her condition was identified. She had no power in the situation and no advocate who stood up for her choices. A whirlwind of adult decisions was swirling around her, and a mediated adoption was deemed the best course of action. The father was dead, and she was below the age of consent, with her whole life in front of her. It would be best if the baby were adopted.

For Meg it was one of the lowest points in her life. The birth was painful and traumatic; she barely got to see the baby before it was whisked away and the paperwork completed on her behalf – facilitated by the efficient social services offices, headed by Russell Black.

When Meg returned to Woodlands Edge her eyes were red from crying. She'd be monitored for postnatal depression. The tears were not wholly unexpected; her hormones had taken a pounding as a result of giving birth. She returned from the hospital late at night, with Debbie already fast asleep and snoring. She sobbed quietly in her bed, desperate to see her friend Hannah, craving somebody to talk to about what had happened.

With Bob Taylor now gone and David and Jacob dead, Hannah was the only person that she could confide in. Gary Maxwell had even screwed that up for her. She was alone and inconsolable and very soon moved onto a regime of antidepressants prescribed by a doctor who'd seen those symptoms many times before. She was young and resilient, and she'd soon recover and understand that it was best for everybody for the baby to be taken away.

Life at the children's home carried on as normal. The more considerate support workers fussed over Meg for a while, but she rejected them, feeling hostile and betrayed. The other kids reached out to her, but she brushed them aside. How could they understand what she'd been through? They were too young; she'd become an adult very quickly, yet here she was, still at the mercy of the care system. She longed for the day when she was eighteen and could walk out of that place. She was spoiled goods from an adoption point of view, difficult to place. Most adoptive parents wanted a ready-made, happy family. It took a partic-ular kind of person to adopt a teenager with Meg's history.

But then it came, out of the blue. At last it was a chance to leave that place. Many adoption opportunities came and went – either it would fall through for the adopting adults due to some lifestyle or domestic issue, or they would baulk at taking the children at the last minute. The kids in Wood-lands Edge weren't as pretty as the babies and toddlers in other homes. They were the world's unwanted: spotty, lanky, uncertain of their place in the world, and hostile. Who would want them, when even their birth parents did not?

Meg and Hannah became aware of the meetings at first.

Thomas Yates and his wife Mavis were talking to Gary in his office. Then the getting-to-know-you sessions began. Thomas and Mavis were going to adopt Hannah and Meg together. They were ecstatic at the news, hardly daring to imagine that they might finally escape from the home. Together, too. They would become adoptive sisters. They would be able to share a room again. Hannah would at last be free of the horrors of the night.

But Gary Maxwell had been waiting. He knew how to be patient. Meg was no longer under the scrutiny of the medical profession, and her post-pregnancy check-ups were over at last. The baby was gone. She was just another normal teenage girl, and it was time to remind her who was in charge. Her pregnancy had caused him some consider-able discomfort. He was hoping to be rid of her soon, along with her friend, but not before he'd fed the monster.

It had been a pleasant evening for Meg. She'd been given the all clear from the hospital. The antidepressants were doing their job and she hoped to be off them soon. They'd had a good laugh in the lounge, watching TV. It was Top of the Pops night – they'd all been getting excited over an appearance by Take That! For once Meg was a giggling teenager laughing about which member of the group she fancied most. The other girls were incredulous – how could she possibly like Mark? Robbie had the best six-pack.

Hannah knew though. Mark reminded her friend of David. That's why he was her favourite. The conversation grew raucous; there were shrieks of laughter and even some of the boys joined in, attempting to impress the girls with their renditions of 'Relight My Fire'. All the time, in the corner, Debbie Simmonds watched them. Always she was on the edges, not quite being let in. She fancied Gary, but she would never have dared to admit that, let alone get involved in the laughter. Instead she watched from her chair in the corner, wishing that she could be one of them.

Her advantageous position meant that she was able to make a sharp exit when Gary Maxwell entered the room. She sensed him before she saw him. Like a wasp coming to disrupt a summer picnic, he'd detected fun and was coming to mess it all up. He smiled at her as he entered the room, and then she left.

The laughter quietened the minute he came in, and the youngsters turned back to the TV, waiting to see what he'd come for. He said nothing, but stood in the heart of the gathered group and pretended to watch the television. All conversation ended, and one by one the kids began to drift away. Meg was one of the last to leave.

'See you later, Meg. You get to join Hannah tonight,' he said in a low voice. 'Just my way of saying thank you for the trouble you caused me. Mr Black has taken quite a shine to you. He requested your file personally. I think he likes you.'

Meg felt the energy drain from her. They were coming for her. She'd managed to avoid the night-time trips because of her pregnancy. He'd waited until the eyes of the medical profession were averted, and now the bastard was coming for her.

She wanted to run. She'd seen what it did to Hannah. Every time she was taken, it would drain a little bit of life from her. When Gary had separated her and Hannah, she'd been able to pretend it wasn't happening. They never took Debbie at night, she seemed safe from it all. What could she do? Where could she turn? She had nobody – the other kids were as trapped as she was.

Gary left the room. Meg waited to make sure that he'd gone, and then slipped into the dining room. The meals were prepared for them at the home, so she had to slip into the back area to access the kitchen. Looking around to make sure that nobody had seen her, she drew a large kitchen knife out of the drawer and tucked it carefully into the waistband of her jeans. She was still wearing looser clothes, and if she walked carefully, she'd get it to her room undetected. When they came for her, she'd go for them. They would never take her or Hannah ever again. She'd sworn to protect Hannah and now she would. She had her strength back. That bastard Gary Maxwell would regret the day he decided to come for her.

Debbie was snoring already when she got up to the bedroom. That girl could sleep. She removed the knife from under her clothes and placed it beneath her pillow. She stayed fully dressed. Although she didn't know exactly what happened when her friends were taken away in the night, her instincts told her what was going on. She didn't know the details, but she knew what was going to happen that night would be nothing like the tenderness she'd shared with David.

She waited. She dared not sleep, although she was tired. She concentrated on Debbie's nocturnal grunts; they helped to prevent her from drifting off. Then it began. It was past midnight and doors began to open along the corridor. Those youngsters who'd been chosen got hurriedly dressed and then waited on the landing. She could hear the running engine of the minibus outside.

She heard footsteps outside the door and then Hannah's voice.

'Please Gary, not Meg. Leave her, she's been through enough.'

'Wait with the others,' was all he said.

Meg's hand slid under her pillow and she clutched the knife. The door opened slowly and quietly, the light from the corridor flooding into the room. Debbie stirred and turned over, still grunting and snoring.

Gary was with another man. She'd never seen him before.

'It's time to go, Meg,' Gary whispered quietly. He was as casual as if he were asking her to come downstairs to look at her presents on the morning of her birthday. She gripped the knife tightly and took a leaf out of Debbie's book by looking as if she was still sleeping. She could see enough through her eyelids to see the other man coming towards her. He got so close that she could smell the booze and cigarettes on his breath. He waited and watched, believing her to be asleep.

'I can see why Russell wanted this one,' he sneered.

Meg felt his hand moving towards her leg. Instinctively she pulled the knife out from under the pillow and drove it into the man's hand.

'You fucking little bitch!' he screamed at her, examining his wound.

Meg leapt out of bed, pointing the kitchen knife in front of her, waving it between Gary and the other man, whose hand was bleeding badly.

'Meg, calm down, this isn't going to end well. Hand the knife to me.'

Gary attempted to defuse the situation. He was not used to the youngsters fighting back.

'Piss off, Gary. Just leave us alone! Leave us alone! I'll slit your fucking throat if you come anywhere near me!' she screamed back at him. Debbie was awake now, watching the situation as it played out in front of her. Meg had her back to Debbie. Gary and the other man would cautiously step forward then back, testing Meg's resolve, uncertain as to how far she'd go to protect herself. Meg was out of control now, furious in her anger, lashing out at both men like a small animal cornered and ready to give itself up for dead.

Her screaming was beginning to disturb the other children. Gary was keen to resolve the situation and calm things down.

'It's okay, Meg. It's okay, we'll leave you tonight. Give me the knife and we'll leave your room. Okay? Deal? Just hand me the knife ...'

Meg lowered the knife a little, wondering whether to trust these men. She'd acted in haste but couldn't see a way out of this. She could hear the commotion along the hallway. She didn't know what to do. She just wanted to stop them.

She barely registered what happened next. Debbie grabbed the knife from behind her, she was completely unprepared for it. As the knife was removed from her hand, Gary and the other man moved forward. The second man thrust his unhurt fist into Meg's stomach and she dropped to the ground.

'Vicious bitch!' he scowled at her, and then went to the sink to wrap the handtowel around his wounded hand.

'No bruises, Max,' Gary warned. 'Particularly with this one.'

'Here Gary,' Debbie smiled. 'I got the knife for you.'

'Good girl, Debs,' Gary replied. 'I'll come up and see you later when the others have gone.'

She smiled meekly at him, like a stray dog that had been thrown a scrap of rotten meat.

Gary helped Meg up to her feet and told her to join the others. Her stomach ached with the pain of what the man had done, but she knew she was beaten. There was nothing she could do now.

As she walked out onto the main landing, none of the

children spoke. The teasing and playfulness of the early evening had been replaced by the passive acceptance of what was about to happen next. Meg began to cry. Hannah sidled up to her and held her hand.

'I'm sorry,' she whispered. 'I tried to protect you. I don't know what to do. I'm so sorry, Meg.'

As they filed down the stairs, Meg caught a movement in the shadows at the far end of the entrance hall. It was Thomas Yates on the late shift watching them being guided out to the minibus in the dead of night. Boys and girls, not one of them over eighteen years of age, and two of those youngsters would soon become his adoptive daughters.

For a moment, Meg thought he was going to intervene. She really believed that he was going to come to their rescue. But Gary got there first, as he stepped out from beyond the staircase, unsure what to say or do.

'Ah, Thomas, good to see you on the late shift. You should have finished well over an hour ago, shouldn't you? Is that pipe still leaking? Make sure you finish a couple of hours earlier tomorrow. Mark it on your time sheet.'

Thomas looked uncertain. The challenge to Gary was on his lips, but it wouldn't come out.

'Get yourself tidied up and be on your way,' Gary continued. 'You'll be getting a family of your own soon, and you won't want to stay this late when you have a young family to return to. You need to put family first, Thomas.'

Meg looked Thomas directly in the eyes before she was ushered out of the front door towards the minibus. He was her only hope, the man who was about to become her adoptive father – the paperwork should be confirmed any day now.

'Yes, Mr Maxwell. I'll get cleaned up here and be on my

way. Good night, Mr Maxwell, and thank you. Yes, I'll add an extra hour or two to my time sheet.'

Gary Maxwell smirked as he closed the door behind the youngsters, releasing them to the mercies of the men who were escorting them into the darkness. By the time Yates got his new daughters, they'd both be broken anyway.

They wouldn't be back for at least three hours. Russell Black and Tony Dodds ran their parties early into the morning. He'd got time to go and see Debs. She was his special girl.

Meg walked over to the minibus, still holding on tightly to Hannah's hand, as if it were the last remaining thing that connected her to a normal life. As she stepped up into her seat, she vowed that these men would pay for what they were doing. She would have her revenge on everybody who had betrayed them. She was powerless in that moment, but there would be a time when she could take control again. And when that time came she'd come to these men of her own free will. Then she'd slit their fucking throats.

Milton Keynes looked like somebody needed to weed it. As we exited the station, all I could see was a wide expanse of concrete and paving slabs. Fortunately the taxis were close by and there were lots of them. We headed towards the small queue that had formed.

It didn't take long and we were on our way. I'd checked out the Nightingale House care home online. It was fairly rural, outside the main town area. I'd heard lots about Milton Keynes, usually in jest, but it seemed fine to me. There were certainly plenty of businesses located in its centre.

As the taxi drove off, we surveyed the imposing Victorian buildings from the outside.

'Are you ready?' I asked Alex.

'Ready!' she smiled, tying her hair back and putting on her glasses. Hopefully, they wouldn't recognise her. Glasses always worked for Superman, why not Alex Kennedy?

'Hi, we're here to see Mavis Yates,' I began.

It wasn't a good start. The middle-aged woman on reception carried on with her paperwork, not even bothering to look up.

'Do you have an appointment?' she asked.

She was one of those. Immediately keen to establish herself as a gatekeeper. We hadn't even made eye contact yet.

'No we don't,' I began. 'We—'

'Then you won't be able to see Mrs Yates today, I'm afraid.'

She must have been used to exchanges like this.

Alex saw me bracing for conflict and stepped in.

'I wonder if you'd be so kind as to look at us while you're speaking ... Julia?' she said in her posh, authoritative voice. It gave Julia the jolt that she needed.

'We've travelled many miles to try to track down Mrs Yates and we're keen to speak to her today. She is able to sanction her own guest visits, I take it? In which case, if you'd be so kind as to let her know that we're here?'

Julia examined Alex's face. She looked at mine. She clocked the scar on my face, but I sounded too educated to be a thug, so she decided to engage.

'Who shall I say wants to visit?' she asked, a little more graciously this time.

'Please tell her that her daughter's husband is here to see her. My name is Peter Bailey. She might not have heard of me, but I have been married to her youngest daughter for nine years, almost ten years now.'

'What is your visit in connection with?'

She was getting snooty again.

'Just tell her what Mr Bailey said,' Alex intervened again. 'She'll want to see us.'

'Wait here, please.'

'Nicely handled,' I whispered to Alex. 'It's easy to see why you're the TV celebrity superstar and I'm just the local radio hack.'

Julia was gone some time. I could see some of the elderly residents making their way about the place through the glass partition. It all seemed calm and quiet enough. Julia returned.

'Yes, she's happy to see you. She's getting ready now. She'll chat to you in the visiting lounge. I'll need you to sign in and to view your ID.'

She looked up at Alex as she recognised the name on her passport.

'Alex Kennedy! I love watching your show on TV. What a treat having you here. How do you know Mavis?'

Amazing how a bit of celebrity can oil the wheels. That was the last of Julia's resistance. We were in. Alex had a few scraps of paper to autograph before we were able to move on, but eventually the excitement subsided.

'You do know that Mavis is in quite a state, don't you? I need to warn you about that – some people find her appearance shocking. And she gets very easily confused.'

We made our way through the main doors and one of Julia's colleagues escorted us to the lounge. We were the only people in there. After a wait of a few minutes, we heard voices from along the corridor. A nurse walked in pushing an old lady in a wheelchair.

I saw her hands first and almost gasped when I saw her face. She looked like she'd been melted: one of her eyes was completely obscured by damaged skin, her face was terribly scarred and marked, and her hands were the same. Up until now, this had just been another news story to me, but the consequences of that fire were horrific. Even so many years afterwards, Mavis Yates was a mess.

As a journalist you become accustomed to hiding your reactions. We're impartial, we don't make judgments by giving away our emotions, but I struggled with Mavis Yates. I've never seen anything so shocking and disturbing.

'Hello, Mrs Yates. I'm Alex Kennedy and this is Peter Bailey, thanks so much for seeing us.'

Alex was so natural at this stuff. She reached out and shook Mavis's hand as if there was nothing wrong with it. Her gift, if that's what you'd call it, is that she spoke to everybody as an individual. The way that Mavis looked simply didn't matter to her.

Mavis's voice was scratchy and weak.

'So you're Pete Bailey,' she began. 'I've heard so much about you. Meg would never bring you here to see me, though. I think she was too embarrassed.'

She spoke slowly, but she was easy enough to understand. Her lips had been deformed in the fire and it was tricky for her to form some of the words, but I could see that years of surgery had succeeded in improving things a little.

I took her hand and held it, greeting her and telling her how pleased I was to meet her.

'Mrs Yates ... Mavis ... this is a difficult visit for me to make today. I don't know what you've heard about me, but I have been married to Meg for many years. She never told me of your existence. I'm so sorry about that.'

'That sounds like Meg alright. That girl was always one

for her secrets. I knew about you, Peter – you like to be called Pete, don't you? – but I never saw photographs or anything like that. She always told me you were too important to make family visits. I barely saw my own daughter as it was ...'

Mavis's voice became hoarse, and she struggled to speak.

'Shall I get you a glass of water?' the nurse asked. 'Can I get you two anything, a hot drink maybe?'

The nurse, Anna, left to get our drinks and we waited for Mavis to recover her voice.

'Do you still see Meg?' I asked. 'Has she been to see you recently? Do you have her address?'

Alex tapped her foot against mine. I was doing a Paxman, and she was telling me to cool off. But Mavis answered anyway, as Anna delivered a glass of water and went off again to finish getting our drinks.

'No, I don't know where she lives. I last saw her over half a year ago – after she was all over the papers. That's where I saw you for the first time, Pete. You're a handsome fellow. I can see why she fell for you. I could see that she was pregnant, but she denied it.'

We paused. It was that journalistic thing again. Wait long enough and they'll keep talking. She obliged.

'Meg was always troubled – after that business in the home. I loved those two girls, you know. They brought sunshine into my life. They were all I ever wanted. But that home. It damaged them. Tom would never tell me what it was about, but I'm sure that he knew. He and Meg, they kept their secret from me. Poor Hannah too. After that court case, or inquiry, or whatever it was, Meg was cross, really angry. And those men, that policeman and the social services chap ...'

'What happened the night of the fire, Mrs Yates?' Alex asked gently. 'Your neighbour told us that it was an accident. What actually happened?'

'*This* is what happened!' Mavis shouted, gesturing at her face. It took us both by surprise. Anna entered with our drinks and immediately moved to calm her.

'I'm sorry, Mrs Yates,' Alex said after a few moments. 'I know that this is difficult for you, but Meg has gone missing and we need to track her down. We're trying to piece together what happened.'

'It's alright,' Mavis sighed. 'But it ruined my life. I've been stuck here for years. The pain never goes. I have to use creams constantly, and I've had skin graft after skin graft. They think I hear voices and imagine things. They think I make it all up. But everyday I hear the ghosts of the past.'

She paused. Alex and I worked our way through our drinks, waiting for a good time to pick up the conversation.

'I loved those two girls, you know,' Mavis said at last. 'It was only after the fire that I realised how badly they were both damaged. I wanted them so desperately that I honestly didn't care how they came to us. They were my girls, my beautiful girls. But they couldn't forget whatever had happened to them in that home. It haunted them. And there was nothing I could do to help.'

'What happened, Mrs Yates? What did they do? We heard from your neighbour that Thomas might not have been killed by the fire?'

Alex was as gripped as I was by Mavis's story. We willed her to go on, but could see that Anna was getting concerned about her anxious state.

'We rowed that night, over something silly, and Tom went to sleep in the spare room. The girls shared the other bedroom – they always wanted to sleep together. Meg was the last to bed. She was cross with us, I know that. She went to bed though, I heard her. The next thing I knew, I heard movements in the house. I called for Tom, but he'd gone to sleep. I stepped out of my room and a wall of flame shot up the stairs, catching my clothes and burning my hair. I ran into the front bedroom to call for help. I saw the girls running out into the street. They just watched me. The flames were too high ... there was nothing they could do ... I had to watch my own skin dropping off my face while I waited to be rescued.'

Anna offered Mavis more water. Her face was so scarred that it was hard to gain any sense of emotion or expression, and her mouth was distorted beyond repair. But she spat those words out at us as if the fire had happened only the day before. We waited, but we could see that Anna was anxious to end this now.

'They got me out of there in the end, but the damage was done. They never thought I was going to survive. Tom died, of course. I wish we'd not rowed that night. I wish Meg hadn't been the last one downstairs. The investigation said it was the gas heater, an accident they said. I had to watch my own flesh burning, knowing all the time that my husband was trapped inside the spare room. Nobody deserved that. Nobody.'

Although they were very nice about it, we'd had all the time we were getting with Mavis Yates. We were asked to conclude our questioning and to ensure that we made an appointment next time we visited. She was quite distressed when we left her. Anna was kind enough to let us pass on contact information. She promised to make sure that Mavis got it once she'd had some time to rest.

I felt guilty about how we'd questioned her and made her relive those events, but I was grateful for the information. Anna had warned us that Mavis was unlikely to get in touch. The internet had passed her by, she struggled with the phone and she was a reluctant writer. She would still send a card to a friend in Blackpool every now and then, but that was the extent of it.

Both Alex and I were exhausted by the visit. Her story had drained us. It had been an emotional experience meeting Mavis like that. I couldn't get the image of her face out of my mind. The fire had disfigured her so badly that I couldn't even begin to imagine what her life must have been like.

So Meg had visited her, we knew that much. And Mavis had been aware of my existence, if only from newspaper reports after the murders. Had Meg ever told the truth, either to me or her mother?

'Are we staying here overnight or heading straight back on the train?' I asked Alex. 'The tickets are open, and we can book into a hotel if you want. You'll have to pay, mind you. Either that or we're looking for a hostel for the night.'

'I want to go back, Pete, don't you? Blackpool is where we need to be. I'm not sure we'll get any more from Mavis. Can you face that journey twice in one day?'

We decided to head back that evening. I agreed with Alex. It had been right to visit Mavis Yates, but I didn't think there was any further information that she could give us.

As we sat down on the train, we accessed the free Wi-Fi and checked out our emails.

'Now that's good timing,' Alex said, after scrolling

through and deleting all the adverts. 'My contact has got back to me. There's an update on the fire. The official report says that there had been a fight between Thomas and Mavis Yates. Mavis is right about the gas heater. There was a question mark about what had caused ignition though. The girls switching on the downstairs light could have done it, but it was marked as inconclusive at the time.'

'They'd have known if it was a match or anything like that, wouldn't they? They can do forensics stuff when there's a fire, is that right?'

Alex scrolled through the email, opening up the attachments one by one, and giving me a summary of their contents.

'This is interesting stuff, Pete. Guess who countersigned the adoption paperwork for the girls? It was only Russell Black. Do you think he's still alive?'

'How old do you reckon he was then – fifty or so? That was in the early nineties so he'd be in his seventies now. If we're lucky, he'll still be going strong. I wonder if he still lives in the area. We should look him up – and that Tony Dibbs guy.'

'Tony Dodds. The chief constable. His signature can be seen on a couple of these documents too. Do you not think it's all a bit—'

'Cosy?' I interrupted. 'Yes, I do. We're hearing the same names come up all the time. Blackpool is only a small place, and these guys would have had their fingers in all the pies. Everywhere we look, they're there.'

'What did you make of Hannah when you met her? Was she anything like Meg?'

'She seemed nice to me. Same as Meg: intelligent, articulate, sane – though I'm not always the best judge of that. But, come on, I've known Meg for ages. She's no psycho, not even at age fifteen or sixteen or however old she was then. Hannah neither. They're just ordinary people. That fire was an accident. Even the official report said so.'

Alex was distracted. She was reading something on her phone.

'Oi! Are you listening to me? I'm giving this my best psychological analysis and all you can do is read some nonsense on Facebook.'

'Shh, one minute!' she barked back. I hadn't expected that. It was unusual for Alex. I waited for her to finish. I could see from her face that she was struggling for a way to break something to me.

'What have you found?' I said. 'Is there something else in those papers? It had better be something good – you've really pissed me off shushing me like that. What is it?'

'I don't know how to tell you this, Pete. I set my news feed up to see all the local papers after we went to the library. I wanted to see if anybody else had covered that lollipop man story. I'm assuming you haven't seen tonight's breaking news story? I'm surprised they haven't called you in to cover it yet. Here, take a look.'

She handed me her phone. I read the headline: *Former Blackpool Top Policeman In Murder Probe.* I read down, trying to catch the bare bones of the story. It was Tony Dodds. He was seventy-seven. And dead.

They'd found him by that oak tree at the former Woodlands Edge children's home. They had a suspect under arrest already, a man who'd been spotted at the scene with a couple of others earlier in the day. The suspect was named as Steven Terry, a well-known clairvoyant.

CHAPTER SEVEN

1992 It should have been a wonderful time for the girls, but it was not. The prospect of adoption grew closer and home visits were arranged. When Hannah and Meg were away from Woodlands Edge, they at least knew that they were safe for the weekend. But their absence meant somebody else would be taken at night, so there was no consolation in that. Someone else always had to suffer.

The Yates' home was small but friendly, and when the girls were staying there they could almost forget what was going on. There were trips to the beach, family photographs, all of the things that every child craves. They were spoiled and treated, and the other families living on the street welcomed them with open arms. They looked forward to their weekend and holiday visits.

There were three bedrooms in the small terrace, but Hannah and Meg were allowed to sleep together, as they had done at the children's home. Mavis and Tom would let them chat late at night, and they'd smile at each other as they listened to the girls giggling in bed, laughing at some story or other.

But there was a cancer in that home from the minute Hannah and Meg arrived. It ate into Meg. She knew that Tom could have done more to help them the night they were taken away in the minibus. And she burned with a desire to see her baby. Is this what Mavis had felt, wanting so desperately to provide a home for the girls? This urgent maternal craving was so strong in her. She spent much of her time wondering who'd taken her child and if they loved him as much as she would have done.

Tom Yates carried the same secret, the knowledge that he'd seen something that night made him feel a sickness deep in his stomach. But he saw a change in his wife when Meg and Hannah began their overnight stays. It seemed to nourish her. She began to laugh and smile again, her joy had returned. Being a mother renewed her. For Tom, too, it made things complete. A wife, a house, a job and a family – wasn't this the way it was supposed to be? It felt good to him, and what husband wouldn't want his wife to obtain her dream?

But Tom's guilt was his albatross, wearing down his happiness, eroding the reality of their happy family unit. He'd let Gary Maxwell take the girls. He didn't know what was going on, maybe late-night parties with drink and perhaps drugs, but surely nothing worse? He'd closed his mind to the possibilities, not daring to think about them. He was only a caretaker. Gary Maxwell had the power not only to take his job, but also to take the girls from him. And Russell Black was involved too; he was as high up as they came. If Russell Black decided to interfere, they'd never be able to complete the adoption process.

But Tom knew that he should have stuck up for the girls that night, however hard, however risky it might have been. He knew it. And he knew that Meg knew it. The way she looked at him wounded him. It was as if she wanted to let herself off the leash and embrace her new life, but she remained tethered by this thing between them. She was only fifteen. What could she have done to defend herself?

Tom would console himself by thinking about how adoption would be the best thing for the girls' future. If he and Mavis could provide a loving, secure environment for them, they'd be free of the children's home and whatever it was had been going on there. That was the best solution. He had to win the war for the girls, not just the battle. He'd have to carry his wounds if it meant that he could secure their long-term welfare.

The day of the formal adoption was one of the happiest in their married lives. They'd had a good life together, but there was always something missing, and it had depressed his wife. They loved to hear the laughter of children in the house. They'd never have the mayhem of toddlers, the late-night and early-morning feeds, or the visits to the park, but they loved the girls as if they were their own, and for a short time Mavis and Tom Yates felt as if their lives were complete.

The girls arrived with one small suitcase each: two teenage lives squashed into two small cases. That's all they had. Tom had bought new posters for the girls' room. They still wanted to sleep together, even though he'd offered to decorate the spare room and make it exactly the way they wanted. Meg was pleased to see the back of her spiteful roommate in the home, Debbie Simmonds.

On the day that they arrived at number nine Tower View Street, Meg finally felt safe. They were out of the children's home, they had real parents at last, and they were together. She and Hannah, adoptive sisters, what more could she have wished for? Tom had already been like a father to them, showing them how to wire electrical sockets, replace washers in taps, and many of the other life skills that slipped through the net in the home.

Like Bob Taylor, Tom had been one of the good ones, an adult who deserved their trust. Both men were easy with the youngsters. They didn't judge them, and genuinely seemed to enjoy their company. For those two men, looking after and talking to the kids at Woodlands Edge wasn't just a job, it was a pleasure.

Slowly, Meg began to forgive Tom Yates. She knew that he was not directly to blame for the terrible things that had happened. As she began to trust him more as a father, she started to forgive him a little for not intervening. After all, what could any of them have done to stop Gary Maxwell?

It all began to unravel the night Bob Taylor knocked at the door. They'd been watching the TV together. Tom had been on the early shift that day and by seven o'clock they were all curled up on the settee watching Home Improvement. The heavy knock surprised them. It was a dark night. The football pools collector wasn't due, so it was unexpected.

Tom opened the door. The girls recognised the voice immediately. When they saw Bob Taylor standing in their lounge, they were pleased to see him, but something told them it wasn't a social call. Bob exchanged the briefest of pleasantries with Mavis and the girls, and then he and Tom made their way to the dining room, closing the door behind them. They were in there some time. The rumble of deep voices could be heard whenever there was a moment of silence on the TV.

'What do you think that's about?' Mavis had asked.

She didn't know Bob, but she'd heard the girls – and Tom – chat about him, and she knew that he was liked. She kept out of Tom's life at Woodlands Edge, but she knew that Bob had left the home after a row with his boss.

Bob left late. It was almost ten o'clock. They all remembered that because the ITN news was about to start on the TV. Tom and Mavis still had a black and white television. The licence was much cheaper – it made a real difference if you were short of money. Tom looked serious. Deadly serious. He tried to make light of it, but the girls could tell that something was up. What was the reason Bob had left the home? They knew he'd had a row with Gary – something to do with David's death. It had been heated, and it had certainly thrown Gary, whatever it was.

The girls were ushered to bed. It was school the next day and the cosy night in watching the TV together was over. They lay awake listening to Tom and Mavis talking. The voices were earnest, and there was no laughter. They were in the lounge until after one o'clock in the morning, even though Tom was on the early shift the next day.

Meg and Hannah didn't need to know the specifics of what was going on. They weren't stupid. Serious voices, weighty conversations deep into the night, and an atmosphere at the breakfast table the next day that was heavy and tense. This must be something to do with the home. This had to do with what was happening up there. It involved them.

We couldn't get off the train fast enough. Alex and I spent the remainder of the journey talking about Steven Terry and trying to find more scraps of information online.

It was a Saturday so the news teams were at their diminished weekend levels. All we got was a couple of lines of news copy lifted directly from a police statement on their news line. I even phoned into the office, but on a Saturday, once the sports team were done, there was only one person left in the entire building. Saturday was the day where they tucked the obscure programmes which weren't quite unloved enough to be relegated to Sundays. Saturday was for country music and the seventies night. Classical and gardening would wait for Sunday's programming. Either way, it meant that nobody could throw any light on what had happened to Steven Terry.

'We're going straight to the police station,' I said as soon as the news had sunk in. We'd obviously been spotted breaking into the home by some local do-gooder or dog walker. Once the body had been found, like good citizens, they'd have reported our presence to the police.

Alex wasn't saying anything, but we both knew it already. We'd seen this before. Something shitty happening – a death – and somewhere we'd only recently been. I got a bad feeling about this death, but I wasn't ready to share my fears with Alex yet. I think she was doing the same thing, working through the surely not? can this be happening? not again? type of questions.

This was too much of a coincidence. We start snooping around Woodlands Edge, we catch the scent of something not being right, and all of a sudden Tony Dodds is dead, his body left by the tree where two boys had killed themselves in the early nineties. Of course Steven Terry was nothing to do with it. We'd march straight into the police station and spend our Saturday evening giving statements and making sure that our psychic friend spent no more time in police custody than was necessary.

In fact, Steven probably knew we were on our way already.

'I bet he didn't see that one coming!' Alex said, reading my mind. We couldn't help it. For a journalist every news story is an opportunity for a dry and tasteless one-liner. Alex hadn't lost the habit, even though she'd been out of newsrooms for several years.

We grabbed some fast food on the way over to the police station and went directly to the desk when we got there. It wasn't late enough for the pissheads to have started surfacing, and we'd only just finished our burgers and chips when we got to speak to the duty officer. In a matter of minutes we were taken to separate interview rooms and assigned different officers. This was a murder investigation, after all.

I'd seen quite a few interview rooms over the past year – they were beginning to feel like a second home. This one had two plastic chairs placed on either side of a hefty wooden table. There were a couple of dog-eared posters stuck on the wall. The officer who'd been allocated to take my statement handed me one of the most disgusting coffees I'd ever drunk. I did my best to extract details about the murder from her, but she was having none of it. All she would repeat was the general information that had already been cascaded to the news outlets.

Steven Terry's words urging me to tell the truth rang in my ears as I shared every detail of what we'd been doing at Woodlands Edge. I knew that Alex would be telling exactly the same story as me; there was no need for us to get our stories straight, we just had to tell the truth and Steven's role in all of this would be clear to the police. They'd got the wrong guy.

After about thirty minutes she left the room and offered to get me another coffee before she returned. I declined. She was gone for some time, and I needed to use the toilet. I wasn't a suspect, so I decided to leave the room and use the facilities. They were only up the corridor – I'd seen them when we walked down. I could hear Alex's voice coming from the other interview room across the hallway. She was still going strong. At least I knew better than to pop my head round the door and say hello.

As I was walking back to the interview room, I heard a familiar female voice. At first I thought it was Alex, but it wasn't, it was somebody else. I knew that voice. It was DCI Kate Summers. What was she doing in Blackpool? It was only over the county border, not a million miles away, but this was not her policing patch. I knew that I'd get into trouble for it, but there was no way I wasn't sticking my head around that office door to say hello. I'd got to know Kate well as a result of all the crap that had happened previously in my life and I was certain that she'd be pleased to see me. Who wouldn't want to say a cheery hello to the man who'd left such a trail of carnage in his wake?

'DCI Summers, hi, what are you doing down here?'

I knew immediately that I should have returned to my interview room and kept my mouth shut. What's that saying about farts and space suits? Well, that's how welcome I was. I got evil glances from the small group that was assembled in the room. Some senior guy stepped straight in to have me ushered out. DCI Summers looked thoroughly embarrassed by my presence. I was escorted back to the interview room and was told, in no uncertain terms, to stay there. I heard stern voices further up the corridor and my interviewing officer came back into the room looking rattled and flustered. She'd obviously dismissed me as being no flight risk, but she hadn't realised what a prat I can be.

We got the paperwork signed off and she took me back to the waiting area. Alex wasn't done yet, so I had another fifteen minutes to kill. Her statement was probably much more literary than mine, she was always better at using the English language. The news updates online were dead. Nobody had managed to add anything useful to their breaking news stories, which just gave out the bare bones of the case: Tony Dodds found strangled ... body deposited by the oak tree outside derelict children's home ... Steven Terry being questioned by police. That was it.

At last Alex emerged.

'How did it go?' I asked.

'The coffee tasted like shit!'

I laughed. If there was ever a great deterrent to a life of crime, the police coffee was it.

'Did they ask you anything interesting?'

'No, the usual questions. I had to sign some autographs. They have a poster of me in the office apparently: my head stuck on the body of Wonder Woman. They think of me as a crime fighter according to the chap who interviewed me. Crime Beaters has quite a reputation among the Blackpool constabulary.'

Although we were laughing, this was serious. There had been a murder. Steven Terry was being held by the police and Alex and I had been at the murder scene close to the time the body was dumped. DCI Summers was away from her policing patch, embroiled in some serious pow-wow with the Blackpool police.

I was getting better at seeing death coming. It's a feeling at first, a sense that things aren't quite right. With DCI Summers on the scene, it must involve me, and I knew it would all be connected with Meg.

Sundays are a pain in the butt. I suppose they used to be worse – at least the entire world doesn't shut down these days. I wanted it to be Monday. I would be able to get to Bob Taylor then. I was very interested to hear what he had to say about Tony Dodds' death. I wanted to get more information from the police, but they'd be on press office lock down over the weekend. They'd probably call a press conference on the Monday morning. Monday again. I wanted to fast-forward Sunday and just get on with it.

Alex and I had arrived back late at the flat. The young idiot upstairs was having a noisy row with his girlfriend over even louder music. I fleetingly considered going up there and beating the shit out of him, but I thought better of it.

We went to bed early and decided to get up when we woke naturally and head to one of the local supermarkets for a Sunday morning fry-up: everything you need to hasten a heart attack and all for under two pounds. By ten o'clock we were enjoying our bacon and eggs, refreshed from our trip to Milton Keynes and ready to move things on.

'Steven Terry's out,' Alex said, looking at her phone.

'Is there anybody you don't know in the justice system?' I asked. Her contacts seemed to be everywhere.

'You get to talk to a lot of people doing a show like Crime Beaters. The police don't see us as normal press, because we're generally helping with difficult cases rather than hauling them over the coals for things that have gone wrong, the way you do.'

She said those last words smiling.

'It's all over the nationals this morning. They love this story.'

I flicked through the pile of tabloids that we'd bought – a bad journalistic habit, devouring the papers every Sunday and spending a small fortune in the process.

'They smell a rat, that's why. The tabloids love a good historical child abuse story and this one goes way back. They may still have reporters who remember the original case – if they haven't replaced them all with internet journalists.'

'Do you recognise any of the names, Alex? The reporters, I mean?'

She flicked through the papers.

I recalled a conversation I'd had with Hannah. She told me how the journalists used to refer to her and Meg as the fire sisters. That sounded like the tabloids alright. What a horrible name to use for a couple of teenage girls. But she'd also mentioned that one journalist, who'd known Tom Yates, wouldn't let it drop – kept chasing them. He was a complete bastard.

He would have been an old-style journalist, the tenacious type, the kind of guy who never forgot a story. He'd have kept on digging and digging. Since the nineties, most of them would have been pensioned off or deployed to lighter social media tasks, such as summarising complex news stories in 140 characters.

'I recognise two of them,' Alex interrupted my thoughts. I'd forgotten that I'd even asked the question.

'Two what?' I replied.

'Two old hacks in there: Patrick Eaves and Charlie

Lucas. Both old boys. The sort who would have kicked up a fuss when smoking in the office had to stop. They must be in their sixties now. Lucas, in particular, is a bit of a bastard.

'Hannah told me that they were hounded by a guy like that. A journalist, I mean. She described him as a complete bastard.'

'That's how I'd describe him too. I think he's freelance now, but if you look at the by-line you can see they've brought him in as a special reporter.'

I read how he was described in the article: 'Senior reporter Charles Lucas reported on the Woodlands Edge scandal in Blackpool 1993–1994'. There was no such description of Patrick Eaves. I wondered if Charlie Lucas was our man. I googled him on my phone.

'He's semi-retired, and they only wheel him out for the big jobs – things that require a real journalist rather than somebody who learned what to do on a podcast. He must be the guy that Hannah was talking about. Hang on a minute …'

I opened up Skype on my phone to see if Hannah was online. We'd kept in touch since I went to visit her in Spain, and we'd agreed to share any news about Meg. Fat chance of that, the way things were going. Her status was showing as away so I sent her a message instead. She'd pick it up later. I tried to remember if Spain were an hour ahead or an hour behind. Interestingly, her Skype location was showing as the UK. Unusual that. I wondered if she was back in the country again.

Hi Hannah, does the name Charles – or Charlie – Lucas mean anything to you? Check the UK papers if you haven't already. You'll want to see what's happening over here. Speak soon, Pete

I should have tipped Hannah off a bit sooner really.

She'd want to know what was going on, especially since we'd paid a visit to the home. Why hadn't I done that? I took a few moments to think it over.

Hannah's name was coming up alongside Meg's more and more. They were adoptive sisters and friends, or at least they had been, but I was beginning to wonder if she'd been telling me the whole truth. I'd stay quiet about visiting her mum and finding the old newspaper stash covering the entire history of the investigation into the children's home. I'd start to probe a bit more with Hannah, to see if what she'd been telling me was consistent with what everybody else was saying. Steven Terry's comment about there being a demon in that bedroom was troubling me. Who was he alluding to? Both sisters had slept in there – but so had many other kids.

I couldn't believe that I was writing off my wife – my estranged wife – as one of Steven Terry's demons. What a treacherous shit I was turning out to be. Besides, it was a ridiculous notion to condemn someone based on a psychic's say-so.

'I've asked Hannah about Charlie Lucas. I'll bet he's the guy she was talking about. Can you see if you can get an email address for him at the newspaper and see if we can make contact? Do you know him?'

'Yes I do know him, but we have a bit of a past. He came on the show once – it was ages ago – and we had a row before the programme went live. It's still on YouTube if you want a look. Let's just say it was a bit tense during the interview.'

'What did you fall out about?'

'He's one of those people who wind you up. It's probably great in his line of journalism, but not so nice if you're on the receiving end.'

'This could be a chance to heal old wounds, Alex. Why don't you see if you can raise him? Give him a hint of our involvement. Get his journalistic juices flowing.'

Alex picked up her smart phone and began some online research. I decided it would be better to call Steven Terry rather than send a text. I dialled his number and his phone began to ring. I didn't expect it to be picked up, and I had a mouth full of Alex's discarded bacon when he answered straight away.

'Peter – Pete – thank you so much for coming to my rescue last night.'

'Steven, hi. They let you out then?'

'Yes, as soon as you and Alex cleared things up they released me without any further questions. We have a lot of disappointed fans in town – we're trying to get last night's show rescheduled for this evening.'

'Did you pick up on anything while you were being held, Steven? Any snippets which might be useful? You can see why I'm interested.'

Alex had paused from her online research and was listening in to my conversation now. She moved closer so that she could hear his voice coming out of the speaker.

'They're very interested in this gentleman called Russell Black, the social services director. He's tied to the chief constable in some way. I heard a lot about Gary Maxwell too. And another thing, Pete, I recognised one of the women who came into the room while I was being questioned: DCI something-or-other.'

'Kate Summers! DCI Kate Summers, was that her name?'

'That's it, Pete! I thought it was unusual that she was there. She doesn't work in Blackpool, does she? She knew all about me. I've seen her on the TV talking about your case.'

'No, she's from back home, she's not local. I don't suppose you picked up any vibes while you were there? Any psychic clues or anything like that?'

'If I didn't know you any better, Pete, I'd think you were taking the mickey. No, I just get this sense of impending tragedy. I can't put my finger on it. It's all connected, Pete, but I can't see the link.'

Alex was busy on her smart phone once more. Her fingers were working furiously.

'What are the chances of you being on stage tonight, Steven? Can we come over and see you again?'

'I'm certain that it will happen. I'll get my manager to put some tickets by for you.'

'Great, Steven. We'll be along for the show tonight and catch up for a drink with you afterwards. Does that sound okay?'

I finished my call with Steven, grateful that we'd got the show to attend that evening. It would help to pass the time quicker so that we could make a start on Monday. But as it turned out, Sunday wasn't going to be so quiet after all.

'Bingo!' Alex said, as I ended my call.

'What is it?' I asked, assuming that she'd managed to find Charlie's email address at the paper. It was better than that.

'How good am I?' Alex smiled. In the time it took you to talk to our psychic friend, not only have I found Charlie Lucas's email address, but I've emailed him and fixed up a meeting!'

'In London or over Skype?' I replied.

'No, here in Blackpool. He was straight on the train last

night. He's scented blood so he's travelled up here to dig out some of his old contacts. When I told him who you were he nearly exploded with excitement. We're seeing him in ninety minutes. He's meeting us for lunch at the Old Promenade Hotel.'

CHAPTER EIGHT

1992 Meg had never had a lot of time for Debbie, but because they'd had to share a room it was inevitable that they'd be forced to get to know each other a little better.

'You don't help yourself, Debbie,' Meg had advised her. 'You should try to take better care of yourself. The kids at school won't tease you so much if you wash your hair regularly and use some deodorant. Your body is changing. You need to be aware of these things.'

Meg was too kind to dwell on Debbie's weight, but she did her best to guide her. It was another one of those things that fell through the cracks at Woodlands Edge. With no parents to lead and nurture, the children often had to act as surrogate parents to each other.

One afternoon – before that terrible night when she was taken away in the minibus – Meg went into town with Debbie.

'Let's spend Saturday afternoon in the centre,' she'd offered. 'We can buy you some hairbands and maybe some perfume. You've got a bit of allowance saved up, haven't you? I'll help out too.'

It was just the two of them. Meg hadn't particularly wanted to waste a weekend afternoon with Debbie, but she felt sorry for her. They went round the shops. They looked at CDs, but even their taste in music was disparate. It was difficult to find a way to relate to Debbie. Meg guided her through the process of buying clips and bands for her unruly hair, she tested perfumes with her in the precinct, and they stopped off for doughnuts and fizzy drinks before heading back to Woodlands Edge.

'What do you think, Debbie? Are you going to try some of these things out? If you leave them all in your bedside drawer, nothing will change.'

Debbie had a mouthful of doughnut, but it didn't discourage her from speaking. Meg winced and moved her glass to protect it from the assault of food debris coming from across the table. Debbie seemed oblivious.

'I don't mind about the others, so long as Gary likes me. Why would I be bothered with stupid teenage boys? Gary's the one who really cares.'

This was the first sign to Meg that Debbie had any kind of relationship with Gary. She'd never really noticed before. Debbie had been off her radar until they were forced into a room together. Meg had casually observed that Debbie had an easier time of things when Gary was on one of his spiteful kicks, but had assumed that was because she was always aloof from the main group.

Now she thought about it, Meg had noticed that Debbie seemed to chat more with Gary, whereas the other kids gravitated towards Tom and Bob. Meg knew for herself the children's craving for adult connection. Most of them sought approval in some way, and they found those replacement relationships among the staff, but what Debbie was saying felt intense to Meg.

'I've noticed that you and Gary seem to get on well. He can be a bit of a sod sometimes though, can't he?'

Meg never saw a face change so fast.

'Don't you call Gary a sod!' Debbie erupted, spilling her drink as her arm moved across the table. 'He's my Gary, and if he gives you a hard time it's because you're a stupid bunch of spotty teenagers. I don't need all this rubbish that you've bought me. Gary likes me exactly the way I am!'

Meg didn't know what to do. Debbie's voice was raised. It was only a small café and people were looking at them. Her face was red most of the time, but in her anger it was crimson. Coke dripped on the floor as Debbie continued her shouting. She picked up the pink striped paper bag with the hairbands inside and threw it at Meg.

'Stuff your fashion advice, Meg Stewart. I don't need it!'

She picked up the last doughnut and stormed out of the shop.

'Are you okay, dear?' Ivy, the café owner, asked.

Meg was horrified. She hadn't thought that Debbie was capable of anything like that. She was embarrassed by the disapproving looks that she was being given by the other customers and was grateful to Ivy for showing kindness when it would have been easier to scold her. Ivy mopped up the Coke, cleared the debris from the table, and offered Meg a new drink and anything that she wanted to eat. Ivy had been a teenager once, she knew what it was like.

'What was all that about, dear?' she asked, pulling up a chair and setting down her cup of tea. The café was beginning to empty. It was nearing the end of the day, and she had time to talk to this upset teenager.

'I don't know why she did that,' Meg replied, grateful to Ivy for her companionship. That day they became lifelong friends. Meg would continue to return to her café for many years afterwards, when it evolved from a soft drinks and doughnut bar to a modern coffee shop.

'She got angry all of a sudden. I've never seen her like that. I was only trying to help her.'

'Don't worry, my dear. You'll make it up soon enough. Believe me, I was falling out with my friends all the time at your age. It soon blew over. She'll be right as rain when you see her next time.'

As the customers left, Ivy stood up to clear the small tables. It felt the most natural thing on earth for Meg to help her as they continued chatting. Before she knew it, it was past half past five. Tea at the home was always at six. Gary Maxwell would make sure she went without tea and supper if she dared to turn up late.

'I need to go,' she said to Ivy, with the last tray of cups in her hand. 'I'm going to be late for tea.'

'Don't you worry, dear. My John will be waiting outside in the car to take me home, and we'll drop you off. If you ever want a little Saturday job, you're always welcome here. You've done an excellent job helping me to clear these tables. Think of it like an audition at the Winter Gardens. And you passed with flying colours!'

Meg beamed at Ivy. She revelled in the praise. It made all thoughts of what Debbie had done fade away. She would take that Saturday job, not immediately, but after the adoption was completed and she was living closer to town with Tom and Mavis.

As Meg was dropped off at the home, nicely in time for tea, all thoughts of the row with Debbie had passed. Debbie took the bag of hairbands that Meg returned to her and thanked her as if nothing had happened. Ivy was right, it just blew over.

And Meg saw no more of that side of Debbie's personality until the night that she grabbed the kitchen knife out of her hand. It was on that terrible night that she understood why Debbie had leapt so quickly to Gary's defence when they'd argued in Ivy's café. Debbie thought she was in love with him.

Charlie Lucas looked exactly as you'd expect an old newspaper hack to look. It was a long time since I'd seen the tarred fingers of somebody who smoked so much. His hair was fully grey and he had to be at least sixty-five. A navy blue cravat was tucked neatly into the top of his shirt.

We met him in the bar of the Old Promenade Hotel. It was the kind of place where they advertise free Wi-Fi and then make you ask for the password, which is something ridiculous like *password123*. It may have been doing its best to embrace the modern world, but its artwork of choice was still The Crying Boy, its preferred wallpaper floral, and its carpets dark and intricately patterned. Charlie would be lucky if he had his own ensuite. The rooms in that place can't have been costing his bosses very much.

Charlie stood up the moment we walked into the bar. He'd spotted us immediately. He gave us a wave and we walked over to his table. He'd already pulled up chairs for us – he was ready to get straight down to business. I knew how keen he was to talk to us, but he probably didn't realise that I was equally eager to pick his brains.

Sitting on the table was a spiral-bound notepad filled with neatly written shorthand. I saw Alex give me a little smile as she clocked it. We'd sat our shorthand examinations together years ago when we were trainee journalists. It was our dark secret, cheating a little in the test to make sure we both passed first time. It was ages since I'd had to use short-hand, but I could still make out the occasional word.

Charlie was halfway through a pot of tea. It was one of those metal ones that hotels still insist on using, the type which dribbles most of the tea onto the tablecloth rather than getting it directly into the cup. There was a small pile of tea-stained serviettes in the middle of the table. He spoke with a strong London accent.

'Can I order you both a tea?'

Alex and I declined and Charlie got straight down to business.

'So you were married to Meg Stewart, or Meg Yates as I knew her? She's been Meg Bailey for how long?'

He'd caught me on the back foot. He was straight in there with the questions. I'd expected him and Alex to do a bit of bonding first, but the pleasantries were perfunctory, and there was no acknowledgement of their previous altercation.

I talked him through our marriage, but he knew it already. I was just confirming his information. Charlie was good, a real quality journalist. He took shorthand notes without pause or interruption. It was a second language to him and he was completely fluent. He knew what to ask, and he checked and rechecked his facts, dropping in his questions seamlessly: Where did you live while you were married? ... Did Meg ever speak to you about the investiga-tion into the Woodlands Edge children's home? ... What did she say about life in the home?

I was beginning to feel punch drunk. I had to change the pace and make sure that I got my own questions in.

'Actually Charlie, can we have that pot of tea? I'm getting quite thirsty.'

That stopped him for a moment, and gave me the

chance to turn the tables on him. As he tried to catch the attention of the serving staff, I moved to my own agenda. I'd wait until I'd got some information from Charlie before I gave him everything he wanted from me.

'So Charlie, what was your involvement in the original case? We've seen old newspapers – it was quite a sensation in Blackpool at the time.'

'There's not much that would pique my interest these days, but this story is worth staying in a shitty hotel for. I know these people of old. It's a right old twisted mess,' he replied.

'We heard from one of our sources that you were very persistent at the time. Is it true that you called the Yates girls the fire sisters? That seems a bit cruel.'

Charlie fidgeted in his chair.

'Where's that tea? This place is like Fawlty Towers.'

He paused, but gave me an answer to my question.

'Times were different then. We had a smoking room in the office. Jimmy Savile was still doing Jim'll Fix It. Did you know Rolf Harris was on the show in 1993? How ironic is that. The world was different then. More oblivious. But there was something going on at that place. It was one of the most efficient cover-ups I've ever seen, and I've seen some major arse-covering in my career, let me tell you that for starters.'

There was another pause. It was my turn to play reporter. I waited for him to carry on.

'We did call them the fire sisters. I'm not proud of that, but you know what it's like in a newsroom. Someone starts these things and everybody has a snigger at it. They stick. It never got used in the newspaper articles, maybe in a couple of headlines. But I do regret that. It was such a great story: the investigation, the fire, Gary Maxwell. They were only young girls, it was a long time ago. I was much younger then. Your kind of age probably. When you get as long in the tooth as me you start to reconsider some of the things you've done.'

I hadn't expected that. Nor had Alex. I caught her eye, and her glance conveyed, WTF? She joined the conversation.

'Why were you all so suspicious about Meg and Hannah? As you said, they were just young girls at the time. Why did they get picked on by the press?'

'We were never really convinced about that fire. It seemed like too much of a coincidence, bearing in mind all the bad blood in Blackpool at that time. You know, my marriage ended because of that case. I spent so many weeks up here that my wife pissed off with the kids and took up with some new bloke that she'd met. Absent father she called me. I think a lot of us got a bit obsessed with it.'

Again, another meeting of the eyes with Alex. Charlie Lucas was in confessional mode.

'When the Yates' house burned down so close to the investigation being concluded, we were looking for blood. We originally thought it was going to bring down the entire hierarchy in Blackpool. The chief constable was implicated, the head of social services Russell Black, Gary Maxwell, Ray Matiz, they were all in there, but nothing stuck.'

I hadn't heard the name Ray Matiz before. That one was new to me. I didn't want to steer him off course – he was in full flow. I thought I'd got him where I wanted, but I should have known better. Charlie Lucas was an old pro and he was just softening me up for a blow to the head. He left the pause longer than was comfortable, even for me, and then came straight out with it.

He took some photographs from his shirt pocket and

spread them out on the table. There were three of them, clumsily cut out from a computer printout. Where the fuck had he got those? I didn't even know that they existed.

A picture of me with Ellie Turner, the first woman I'd cheated with, taken from a CCTV image in the bar where we'd met. Another grainy image, this time with Becky Jarvis, the woman who'd tracked me down to the holiday camp where I was living, leading to the sexual encounter which started the violence all over again. And then, the thing that I thought was over. I thought this was dead and buried, hidden forever. Somehow, he'd got a still from the sex film that Becky had made. How the fuck had he got his hands on that? I thought we'd erased any copies.

He drew a final set of photographs out of the back pocket of his trousers. These were set of photos showing Alex walking along the street with a variety of men. And there was a business card too: *Ultimate Discretion Escorts - Soho, London.* The bastards, they were even onto Alex. Probably biding their time until they released the story. Bastards.

'Now, Mr Bailey ... and Alex,' he smirked. 'I've a couple more questions that I need to ask you.'

I felt sick after our encounter with Charlie Lucas. What the heck was I thinking? There was no way I was going to end up top dog after that. He wouldn't tell me where he'd got the images, but the police must have had those shots on file. CCTV video would have formed part of both murder investigations I'd been involved in. The camera hadn't been working in the hotel the night I cheated with Ellie, but we'd met in a pub over the road. I hadn't even thought about that. The photo with Becky, that was trickier, but the arcade area had a closed-circuit security system, and they'd caught a shot of us kissing outside the arcade windows.

The leak had to have come from within the police. And that video – I thought we'd sorted that out. Alex said the digital forensics team probably lifted it. It could have been deleted from a smart phone, but there was still a chance it might not have been permanently deleted from the main server.

The bastard, he stitched me up good and proper. He asked me all sorts of details about our marriage – what Meg had been like while we were married, what she'd told me about the past. He pushed and pushed. He even wanted to know every detail about our discussion with Mavis Yates and the ladies at the Methodist church. Violated is the only word I can use to describe how the encounter made me feel. I felt grubby and dirty after we'd spoken. I was completely deflated by the experience.

'I'll be in touch if I need anything else,' were his last words.

He tucked the photos back into his top pocket. We got the message loud and clear.

We walked out of the hotel in silence. As the swing door closed behind us I spoke.

'That's why you resigned from Crime Beaters. You knew that was coming.'

I'd had one of my rare moments of insight. The minute Charlie had dropped those photos of Alex on the table, I knew what had happened.

'They've got you in a tabloid sting haven't they, the fuckers?'

Alex's face reddened. We crossed over the road and

took a bench in one of the wooden shelters which populated the promenade. She sighed as she sat down.

'Okay, hands up. You're right. I've known this was coming for some time. I was pretty well sacked from Crime Beaters. They couldn't see me out of the door fast enough. Those shits from HR, you'd think they'd show a bit of loyalty. Instead, I had to sit through a load of bollocks about brand identity, family viewing and positive role models.'

I held Alex's hand. I couldn't remember seeing her so angry.

'It's made me rethink everything, Pete. Why did I ever want to be on TV anyway? The intrusion and lack of privacy is appalling.'

'I take it you've spoken to lawyers?' I asked, knowing already what the answer was likely to be.

'Yep, that's the only reason they've held off this long. I'm not very interesting really. I'm not married or in a relationship. We got statements from the four escorts that I used, confirming that no sexual activity took place in their visits. Can you imagine how humiliating that is, Pete? It's nobody's fucking business but my own. You remember all the libel stuff we did at college? I never thought I'd get to learn it all so well. I confided in HR and they showed me the door. Bastards.'

'What are we like?' I said, deciding to lighten the mood. 'There's me with my sex tape and you with your escorts. Who'd ever have thought this is how we'd end up?'

'There has to be a mole in the police somewhere, Pete. Someone leaked those pictures of you. Charlie will have his contacts all over the place, but that's come from police evidence.'

The thought of my sex tape with Becky being leaked in any way horrified me.

'I don't think he'll publish that tape, Pete. He's using it to get you to speak to him. He's trying to write a story – they have a paper to fill tomorrow morning. Recording that video was against the law. If they publish a piece of revenge porn, they'll get hauled over the coals.'

Alex sighed.

'I'm sorry I didn't tell you the full truth, Pete. I was going to, honestly, but I needed to deliver the news in instalments. It's so humiliating.'

I squeezed her hand again.

'I know what it's like to be lonely. That's why I slept with Becky. When you've been in relationships all your life, it's hard to go back to a single bed. I desperately missed the company.'

'It was you I missed, Pete. You and me is all I've ever known as a steady relationship. It was good, wasn't it? Why did we fuck it up?'

'It was losing the baby that messed it up, Alex. We were young, we had exciting things happening in our careers. But we stayed friends, right? Something good came out of it.'

'You know how I feel, Pete. If you're ever ready to give it another chance, there's never been a better time, let's face it. Once your sex tape knocks Paris Hilton's off the top of the charts and my escort pictures launch my career in porn, nobody else will want to touch us anyway.'

I snorted at that one. My stomach churned just thinking of all my colleagues at the radio station gathering round to watch my video on somebody's PC, tittering at the sight of my arse bobbing up and down. The humiliation of it.

'How much will this mess things up for you on telly, Alex?'

'I think we can say goodbye to Crime Beaters for the foreseeable future, but my agent reckons it will only take a well-timed appearance on a reality show to make everybody forget it. Maybe I could tell my version of the story on a chat show, shed a few tears, and the tide could turn back in my favour.'

'Can you face all that?' I asked.

'Not really, Pete. In many ways it's been the kick up the behind I needed. These photos are just part of a bigger problem. How can I build serious relationships in an environment of constant intrusion? I can't.

'And I want to have kids, Pete. I want to have a life with someone else. I can't do that if I'm on the telly all the time. It's not fair to put anybody through that.'

We sat in silence for a while, watching the trams as they made their way up and down the promenade. My Sunday hadn't turned out to be quite so boring after all. And there were still surprises to come. Steven Terry's performance was only four hours away, and that would turn everything on its head once again.

CHAPTER NINE

1992 The story was all over the newspapers. First the local and then the national newspapers picked it up.

'They seem to be convinced that something was going on at the home,' Mavis said to Tom as she examined that day's paper. Were you aware of any of this? It seems incredible.'

Tom maintained his silence, pretending to have a problem opening the marmalade jar. This was going to be tricky for him. He had to think of the welfare of the girls. They were safe, the adoption was complete, but that wouldn't stop social services coming for them if there was a whiff of a problem.

The allegations were vague as it involved children, but most readers with any experience of the world could fill in the blanks.

'Why was Bob Taylor here that night, Tom?' Meg asked. They still used Tom rather than Dad. Meg wasn't certain that she was ready to call him Dad.

The question caught Tom unawares. He'd thought that he had managed to brush the topic away.

'Have one of the children said something? Did Gary Maxwell get called out at last? That bastard!'

'Meg! Enough of that language!' Mavis scolded.

Tom shuffled in his seat and made a big deal of finishing a mouthful of toast. He paused for a moment, but figured that the game was up. It was in the newspapers now; there was only so long he could keep it quiet. They'd want to interview the girls anyway. Mavis would need to know everything.

'I didn't tell you everything about that night,' he said, looking sheepishly at his wife. 'I wanted to protect you as long as possible, but it's going to hit us eventually.'

'What is?' Mavis asked, already annoyed that he'd not told her everything about Bob's visit.

'Bob and I have agreed to tell them everything that we saw at the home. Bob has been thinking about it for a long time, but he's finally decided to do something. He made an official complaint. When we're called to the inquiry, we're not going to hold anything back—'

'And just what is it that you saw?'

Tom looked across the table, first to Meg, then to Hannah. The girls had barely discussed it between themselves. It was a part of their life that they compartmentalised. How could they even begin to articulate it?

'Gary Maxwell is not a nice man,' Tom continued. 'I do know that he can be a nasty piece of work. I've also seen some things ... things that, um ... things that didn't seem right to me.'

'What?' Mavis asked. 'What did you see, Tom? Are you caught up in this? Please tell me this doesn't involve the girls.'

'I had nothing to do with it, love, but I am going to have to give evidence. When Bob came that night he wanted to be sure that I'd be backing him up. He thinks that Maxwell was up to something with the older children. I saw ... I possibly saw some evidence of that.'

Meg glared at him across the table.

'The girls will need to speak to the inquiry as well. They'll need to explain what they saw and what they knew. There's no getting out of it.'

'And what do they know? What happened there, girls? Did that Maxwell man hurt either of you?'

How do you talk about something so horrific that you can't even admit it to yourself? How do you share a shame that poisons your entire body, right down to your blood and bones? Meg and Hannah looked at each other. It was an unspoken terror, but they were safe from it now.

'Gary Maxwell was a horrible man, but he never hurt us ... directly,' Hannah began, 'but there are things that we can say about Gary that won't look good for him. We'll talk when our turn comes, won't we, Meg? We'll tell them.'

Meg nodded. This was their chance to avenge David's death and to get justice for Jacob. They'd tell them everything. But not now. They'd do it when they had to. They couldn't talk about it yet. It was too raw. They still weren't sleeping through the night. They were still waiting for the bedroom door to open in the darkness, to be taken away in that minibus.

Meg stood up and left the table.

'Excuse me,' she said, rushing up the stairs for some solitude. She wanted this inquiry, but she almost dared not take part in it. It was going to be a huge struggle. When the time came could she say what had happened? She had to. Hannah too. Would they believe her? There would be a lot of intimidating people there. They had to find the strength to tell the truth, to make sure it never happened again.

The girls were relying on Tom to say what he'd seen. They were just two young girls. Meg had been sleeping with David. She'd had a baby. They'd want to talk about that. Had Hannah been sleeping with Jacob? She didn't even know. They were best friends – like real sisters now – but some things they didn't talk about. Most of the youngsters in the home started sexual relationships young. It was the closeness they craved. They wanted to be close to someone who understood. They'd want to talk about all this at the inquiry. They'd call her a teenage mother. The suggestion would be that she was a slag. Everybody would know about her and David.

As she sat on the lid of the toilet, locked in the bathroom, Meg wondered if she'd have the courage to speak up. Would Tom and Bob be able to say enough to stop what was going on at the home? Would they stand up for the youngsters there? What would the other kids say? They'd be as terrified as she was.

The girls were right to be worried about how they'd be handled in the inquiry. The press were digging up dirt on everybody involved. It was a scramble to see who could discredit the young people fastest. Details of sexual activity among the youngsters, mild drug use, petty crime, and even prostitution made their way into the tabloids. There was information in there that even Meg and Hannah didn't know. It seemed extremely unlikely that Gary Maxwell could survive.

Russell Black was seen on local and national TV vowing to review procedures within the home to ensure the wellbeing of the young people in care there. But he was at pains to point out that the children involved were mostly over fifteen years of age, and that afforded them certain freedoms in life. It wasn't a prison, after all.

Debbie was referred to in press coverage as Child A. They all knew who it was, even though the papers couldn't identify her. It wasn't long before stories began to come out about Child A. Apparently Debbie Simmonds had been involved in a small way in prostitution. She'd taken money or drugs in exchange for sexual favours to men of various ages. A stash of cannabis was even found taped behind the wardrobe in the bedroom that she and Meg had shared. Meg found that unlikely. The wardrobe was old and heavy, and it was difficult to move. Debbie wasn't a strong girl and, in any case, they hid things behind the drawers in their bedside tables if they wanted to conceal things from staff. She still had a packet of condoms taped to the back of her drawers from when David and she had been together. A fat lot of good they had done her.

According to the papers, Debbie was known in a couple of the local shops for shoplifting. Out of kindness, the shop owners had never reported her – they knew she was troubled – but they were happy to share the revelations with the papers for a small token of financial recognition.

Debbie was being discredited. She'd not even had time to speak formally to the inquiry and already they were painting her out to be somebody she wasn't. Is this what they'd do to her and Hannah?

A lot of senior people had their necks on the chopping block in this inquiry. Meg was too young to appreciate what that might drive them to do to protect reputations, marriages and incomes. But she was about to find out just how far they were willing to go to preserve the status quo.

Alex and I were feeling unsettled by our encounter with Charlie Lucas. There was a feeling that something ugly had entered the room. What would he uncover next? Or threaten?

We easily managed to kill the rest of the day, wandering up and down the seafront, watching the sea, admiring the tower and sitting in a café for an hour or so. Before we knew it, it was time for Steven's show.

I hadn't looked at my phone for some time, but as I entered the Winter Gardens, I remembered to make sure that I had the sound switched off.

I'd missed a couple of messages.

'Hannah's got back to me on Skype. She's suggested we catch up for a chat asap.'

'I think that would be a good thing,' Alex replied. 'Maybe it's time to push her on what happened. I don't think she's giving you the full story.'

'DCI Summers has texted me too. She's a bit pissed at me for walking into that meeting when I was at the cop shop. She's down here for a few days and is suggesting that we meet somewhere in town for a coffee and a catch-up. What do you think? Is tomorrow okay?'

'Yeah, you bet!' Alex replied. 'I'd love to know what she's doing down here. It happens all the time, cops helping other cops on cases which travel. I wonder why she's down in Blackpool all of a sudden.'

'Oh bollocks, I've missed one from work. It's from Mark, my new boss. I'd better call him before we go in. How are we for time?'

'They've started ringing the bells to say the show is starting soon. I'd make it quick if I were you.'

'I dialled Mark's work mobile and he picked up straight away.

'Hi Pete, sorry to call you while you're off. I need you in tomorrow. Can you do an interview for me?'

'Is it the murder? Who have we got?'

'Tony Dodds' wife wants to speak to us. And it's only us that she's doing an interview with. We have to get the audio ready and share with the other media outlets, but it's our exclusive. We get the credit. I want you to do it.'

'Yes, sure, but is nobody else around to do it?'

'I want someone senior on it, Pete. No youngsters. She needs handling properly. This interview is going to TV and the nationals. I don't want it screwed up.'

'No pressure then!' I laughed. 'What time is it?'

I thought about Bob Taylor. We wanted to catch him early the next day. Most exclusive interviews were saved for the breakfast show.

'Ten o'clock, at her home. Just you and one engineer can go in. I've asked Pat to do it – he'll be there from nine to get the satellite vehicle set up. It's live into the ten o'clock news. You get ten minutes, and then it's done.'

I was relieved that she hadn't gone for an early slot. If we got to Bob first thing on Monday morning, I'd be able to make my way to the interview, and then catch DCI Summers afterwards. I wanted to talk to Tony Dodds' widow. That was access I was very happy to have.

'Not the breakfast show?' I asked Mark.

'No, we pushed her, but she said 10 o'clock. She'll have a legal adviser there too, so expect to be leant on over the questions. Save anything controversial until the last few minutes, and make sure we at least get five minutes of usable audio from her for syndication.'

'No problem. I'll be there in plenty of time before ten.

Can you text me the address? I'm about to go in for a show at the Winter Gardens.'

I ended the call.

'It's already started,' Alex said. 'We'll have to creep in.'

'Sorry,' I said, scanning the address that Mark had texted. It was Lytham St Annes, the posh part of town. Tony Dodds must have been loaded – he was a former chief constable after all.

I tucked my phone into my back pocket and we made our way through the fire doors into the auditorium. Poor Steven, it was full enough to warrant doing a show in there, but he'd done the sensible thing and asked the audience to move into the front seats, rather than having to perform to a theatre where the entire audience was patchy and spread out. The lighting had been changed from the first show we saw. They'd left the empty seats at the back dark and the front seats were lit up. He saw us coming in and looking for a seat and gave us a short wave to acknowledge our presence.

'Ladies and gentlemen, this is all rather cosy, don't you think? It reminds me of the more intimate shows that I used to do before my book came out and things started to get really busy. I want to thank you all for your support tonight, after the story in the press. And I want to apologise to you all for having to reschedule this show ...'

He was good. A real pro. The lighting and the rearranged seating worked really well; it felt as if we were in a smaller venue. He'd acknowledged the news story, dealt with it and dismissed it. Then he got on with the show. I was liking Steven Terry more and more as I got to know the man better. I was embarrassed to recall how quickly I'd dismissed him as a charlatan when we'd first met.

Steven walked to the edge of the stage, and then sat down with his feet dangling over the side.

'I want to talk a little more about the events in the newspapers this weekend,' he said, 'because I know that they will hit this community hard. And also, I sense that there are people here tonight who came specifically because of my involvement with it.'

Now this was getting interesting. I'd assumed he'd mention it and then move on, but he was going to make a big deal of it. He jumped up and ran to the side of the stage, walking down the steps towards the audience. The spotlight followed him as he looked into the crowd.

'You, sir!' he shouted. 'You were not intending to be here tonight, were you? But you were drawn to this place. May I ask why you came? You are closely connected with this news story ... I think you were even involved. Is that correct?'

The spotlight was shining on the man. Even in that stage lighting I could see that he was uncomfortable with what Steven was doing. It was par for the course in a Steven Terry show, but this appeared to be unwelcome.

'I can feel that there are others here who have also come tonight because of what happened at the Woodlands Edge children's home. Are you happy to make yourselves known to me?'

Two hands went up in front of me, and two women and a bloke hesitantly raised their hands behind us.

'You people were involved in the home in some way. Madam, you were a cook there. Sir, I can sense a terrible sadness in you. You were a child there. And madam, you too were a child there. You knew each other, I think ...'

The audience members were not sitting together. They'd come with their partners. They were looking around, trying to figure out if they knew each other. It had been many years since their time in the home. There was a buzz among the audience. This was an interesting story. We were all wondering where Steven Terry was going next.

But it was the audience who took the initiative, rather than Steven. Like me, the people whom Steven had identified were looking at the first man that he had picked out. The reluctant one. I was certain that I'd seen his face before, but I couldn't work out where. One of the audience members put me out of my misery.

'That's Ray Matiz!' he shouted.

Damn it, yes, that's who it was. I'd not really taken much notice of the name until he'd been mentioned by Charlie Lucas earlier, but I recognised him straight away. He'd been one of the men photographed in the old newspapers that we found at the home. He'd lost his long hair and moustache. His head was close shaved now. The glasses were deceptive as well. He was wearing a pair that were much more understated than those in the old newspaper photos from the nineties. But it was definitely a much older Ray Matiz. And he was looking extremely uncomfortable.

'You bastard, Matiz!' one of the women shouted. 'You stole our innocence!'

'This man is a bloody criminal!' the man shouted from behind me. Ray Matiz stood up and started making his way along the row of seats, trying to get out. A man stood up as Ray tried to pass, hitting him in the stomach. Steven Terry tried to restore calm. It had all got away from him in a matter of seconds. It was turning into a brawl. It felt as if the entire audience was shouting at Ray, although it must have been just a vocal minority.

His face was bloodied by the time he made it to the end of the row. Steven was doing his best to calm things down, and eventually Ray made his escape out of a fire exit at the back of the auditorium. I'd never seen anything like it. Alex was speechless too. Never in my life had I seen a crowd turn so ugly so quickly. What a terrible night for Steven. A second terrible night for the poor guy.

Steven was trying to take the heat out of the situation, and the police arrived shortly afterwards, prompted by the Winter Gardens staff. I tried to clock the people who'd been shouting at Ray Matiz, but it was a sea of unfamiliar faces. Some of those people would have known Meg.

The show was over. It had degenerated into a complete mess. The police wanted to speak to people in the audience to get an idea of what had gone on. Steven made himself available to talk to audience members and sign autographs. It was the best anyone could do, given the circumstances. He'd lit a firework, Steven must have known that, and it had gone off in his hand.

He was trying to smile and be as genial as he could, but I could tell as I looked at him from across the theatre that he was worried. At last the crowd dispersed. Alex and I had been hanging back, waiting for him to see off the last fan.

'I'm so sorry, Steven. You're not going to want to do a show in Blackpool again!' I said as we walked over.

He looked tired.

'I'll take the words out of your mouth, Pete. I really didn't see that one coming.'

It was a joke that I didn't want to make. It had been amusing the previous day, but not now. I didn't want to kick the man when he was down.

'This is terrible, Pete. And Alex. I have just killed a man. Not with my own hands, but that man is going to be dead by the end of the day.'

'Come on, Steven. You're tired. He's fine, he got out

okay. He probably went straight back home and closed the door.'

'No, I saw a darkness in him. He came tonight to see what I knew. He was scared – of me and what I might reveal. I didn't understand that, not when I first spoke to him. It's my mistake. I just killed that man.'

Alex and I did what we could to console him, but Steven was having none of it. And sure as anything, the first thing that I heard on the radio when my alarm went off the next day was that former nightclub boss, Ray Matiz, had been found strangled. His body had been dumped by an old oak tree outside the former Woodlands Edge children's home.

Alex and I had slept in the same bed. Nothing was going on, it was just a habit we'd fallen into. We were so familiar with each other, we'd not bothered with the usual niceties of one sleeping on the sofa. The radio alarm had turned on to the local news at six o'clock. We were up early to make sure that we caught Bob Taylor on his lollipop-man shift. It would be a close run thing. I had to be at Lytham for 9.30. If I missed the Dodds interview I'd be toast.

'Shit, did you hear that?' I said to Alex.

'Bloody hell, Steven was right. And the body found at the same tree too. There's something going on here, Pete. Someone is killing off all these old buggers who were implicated in that scandal. I'd be shitting bricks if I was Russell Black!'

'It's unbelievable, Alex. Why would it all surface now – after all these years? I can tell you something though, I want to talk to Bob Taylor even more now.'

'Do you think Tony Dodds' widow will still do the interview? What's her name ... June? Do you think she'll cancel?'

'Who knows?' I replied, hoping that she didn't. 'I suggest we carry on until we hear otherwise.'

We got showered and breakfasted, picked up our phones and headed for the door. It was quiet. There had been some music coming from a flat above until midnight or thereabouts, but some other tenant had banged on the door, threatened whoever it was with violence, and the music had stopped. So classy. There would be none of that in Lytham St Annes when I paid a visit to June Dodds.

We got in the car. The windscreen was misted up, and I could barely see out. I passed Alex a rag and she began to wipe the windows. I tried to start the engine.

'Shit, it's damp,' I cursed as the engine turned over but didn't fire.

I tried again. The third time, it caught.

'Bloody car. I thought it was going to die on me there. Maybe I should just let them repossess it.'

It didn't take us long to drive across town to Sandy Edge Primary School. It was quite a large school, red brick, Victorian probably. We were waiting outside by eight o'clock, in plenty of time to make sure that we caught Bob.

Before long one or two kids began to make their way to the school. These were the ones who'd been thrown out of the house by working parents. They waited in a nearby bus stop. It was too early to go into the school, and if they had a breakfast club there they'd have to pay to access that warmth.

'What should I ask June Dodds?' I asked Alex. 'I need a killer question. He's dead now, no libel, so I can say what I want about him. But I don't want to piss her off so she never talks to the radio station again. Mark will kill me.'

'Ask her if she knew,' Alex replied.

'Knew what?'

'Leave it like that. Nothing else. Ask her if she knew and let her fill in the blanks.'

I was looking for something more damning than that. A car drew up along the road. An older guy with a grey head of hair got out. He messed around in the back of the car for a bit, and then took out a fluorescent yellow mac.

'They used to be white when we were kids,' Alex said.

We watched him as he fastened the coat, put on the matching hat, and took out the distinctive lollipop pole.

'No bugger's going to knock him over. They can see him from London!' she added.

'You, me or both of us?' I asked.

'I think I might be a distraction,' Alex answered. 'You start and I'll come out if you signal to me. He might need a bit of celebrity to help him along.'

'Bob Taylor?' I asked as I walked up to him. The flow of children and parents hadn't begun yet, so he had a few minutes to talk.

'Yes, can I help you?' he asked. He was on his guard. He'd probably heard the news and thought I was a reporter. I was, I suppose, but I was there on personal business.

'Pete Bailey ...' I extended my hand.

'Ah, Peter Bailey, I know you. You're interviewing Tony Dodds' wife later, I hear. They won't stop talking about it on that radio station of yours.'

'Yes, that's right. I'm pleased to meet you. Congratulations on your long career. I saw it in the newspaper.'

'Thank you. But that's not why you're here, is it? Is it about Matiz and Dodds? It has to be, surely?'

'It is and it isn't,' I replied. 'It's about Meg Yates. You may remember her as Meg Stewart.'

Bob paused a moment. He needed to think this one through. A couple of kids walked up with their parents. It gave him an excuse to walk away and cross them over the road. The kids chatted to him and he laughed with them and the adults. He had an easy way about him. I could see why he was popular in the job.

'Now that's a name I haven't heard in a while,' he said, as he walked back up to me. 'How do you know Meg? What became of her?'

'She is ... was ... She's my wife. We've been separated for almost a year now.'

This time it was me who paused. It was almost a year to the day. I hadn't realised that. A year to the day since I cheated on her and our lives had started to unravel.

'You don't seem sure,' he smiled.

'We are married. You must have seen the story in the papers – the cathedral murders?'

'I saw the stories but I didn't clock who was involved. That wasn't Meg was it? She's okay, isn't she?'

'Yes, she's fine. She's living in Blackpool again. I'm trying to find her. Our relationship is ... complicated.'

I hated that word. It made me sound like a teenager on Facebook. But that's what it was. Complicated.

More kids came, more people to cross over. This was going to be hard work. I looked at my phone. He'd be finished when school started. I might get twenty minutes uninterrupted then.

'It's going to get busy, I'm afraid,' he said, looking along the path at the next set of kids about to swarm around him.

'How about we meet over there in the café when I'm done? If you know Meg, I'd love to talk. I knew her father too.'

I went back to the car to update Alex and we walked across the road to get a hot drink while we waited for Bob.

'He seems nice enough,' I said. 'I think he'll talk.'

'I've been thinking,' Alex said. 'I'm going to leave you after we talk to Bob and walk into town. There's no point me coming over to June Dodds' with you. You're working. I'll keep out of your way and catch up with you later. You should see DCI Summers alone too. I don't want to tag along to everything. They'll think I'm your shadow.'

'Fair enough,' I said. 'I'll text you when I'm done with Kate. That works well – we'll both be in the town centre. Good idea!'

Bob joined us a little after nine o'clock, and I got him a coffee. He recognised Alex straight away. They chatted as I got Bob's drink. I kept an eye on the time. I'd have maybe ten to fifteen minutes with Bob, and then I'd have to be on my way.

'I'll have to keep things brief, Bob,' I said, handing him his coffee. 'I need to leave shortly – the big interview. But you know about that already. I'll cut straight to the chase. What's going on, Bob? This is all connected to the home, isn't it?'

His face straightened and he shifted gear from his conversation with Alex.

'It's entirely to do with that, Peter. That situation was never going to go away. I've had to watch Tony Dodds, Russell Black and the others swan around this town as if nothing had happened. How do you think I ended up doing this job? I love it, don't get me wrong, but it wasn't my career aspiration. It was those guys who messed it all up for me.'

'Is Gary Maxwell still local?' Alex asked.

She got in there before I did.

'What about Ray Matiz?' I followed up. 'We saw him last night at the Winter Gardens.'

'Gary Maxwell went to prison. Eventually. He's the only one who did in the end. He must be out by now, but I don't know where he is. Ray Matiz sold up several years ago and moved away when his wife left him. I was surprised that he'd dared to come back here when I saw that he'd been murdered.'

'But what happened at the home?' asked Alex. 'You seem to be one of the good guys. Nobody has told us otherwise.'

'Yes, I hope I was a good guy. I tried to be. But with all that pressure on, when push came to shove, I was forced to back down. I had to take care of my own family. I always felt that I let those kids down. I still do.'

I sneaked a look at my phone.

'Look, I'm so sorry, I'm going to have to leave you both,' I apologised. 'I can't miss this interview. Anything I should ask her, Bob? I need to be quick, but you can talk to Alex. Alex knows what to ask you. Is that okay?'

They both nodded.

'Ask her why she stood next to Tony all these years. She must have known what they were doing with those kids. Ask her that.'

I made my excuses and was away. It was a terrible day. The wind was blowing off the sea and there was a biting chill. Again the car wouldn't start. It took four turns of the key to coax the engine back to life. I revved a couple of times, made sure it wasn't going to stall on me, and then drove away towards Lytham St Annes. I was looking forward to my interview with June Dodds. I was keen to see how evasive she would be. There'd be a lot of eyes on this interview. At least Charlie Lucas would be pissed off that I'd got the exclusive.

I knew that Alex would know what to ask Bob. It felt as if we were finally getting somewhere. The story was coming together. People were beginning to step out of the shadows now. However, the next time I got to catch up with Alex, it would be in a hospital.

CHAPTER TEN

1993 One of the things that Hannah and Meg liked to do on their own was to visit David's grave. He was the father of Meg's child, after all. However light the adults might have made of that relationship, Meg had believed herself to be in love.

Jacob had been buried hundreds of miles away in the town of his birth. His had been a troubled childhood, passed from pillar to post. Although he'd ended up in Blackpool, his final resting place was in Devon. It was beyond Hannah's resources to get to the graveyard in Tiverton, so she had to make do with her memories. It helped to visit David's grave with Meg. It made her feel closer to what had happened.

The girls would make a day of their monthly visit, ensuring that they always marked the anniversaries of Jacob and David's deaths. It was a decent walk for them from home, but they enjoyed the time to chat, away from the adults. They'd remember the boys and the fun they'd had in the home, and then their thoughts would turn to sadness and reflection as they neared the cemetery entrance.

'This might sound ridiculous, but have you been watching that car?' Meg said suddenly. Hannah had been wondering if she'd get tearful again, as she usually did when she saw the grave.

'It's the blue one. Look. It keeps passing us, pulling over, and then moving ahead of us again. I'm sure it's following us.'

'You've been watching too much X-Files,' Hannah teased. 'You're convinced everything's a conspiracy since they started showing it on the telly.'

'No, I'm serious,' Meg replied, in no mood to be mocked. Sure, the X-Files was like nothing she'd seen on TV before. It had captured her imagination alright. But she was certain the car was tailing them. Most likely it would be some creepy guys from school, nothing more.

'Don't look,' Meg said as they walked past the car, which was parked on the other side of the street. 'But you watch. It'll start again and then move further up the road. Sometimes it pulls round a corner, but they've been with us since we left the house.'

'Okay, okay, I'll watch,' Hannah replied, humouring Meg. She tried to get a good look at who was in the car without turning her head. It was two men, as far as she could see. Well-dressed. Nice coats.

The girls walked by and as they neared the end of the street the car began to drive on, passing them, and then pulling up towards the end of the next road. It was far enough to be out of the way, but not so far that they couldn't be viewed in the car's mirrors.

'You might be right,' Hannah conceded.

'Let's take this side street up ahead and loop back to the main road. See what they do.'

The girls walked on, as if they were going to walk

straight ahead, and then took a sudden turning into a side
street. They made a few turns, using their sense of direction to guide them, and came out on the road that they'd
been heading for in the first place. Parked opposite the
junction was the Vauxhall Cavalier. Meg tried to clock the
registration number. It was K-registration, she saw
that much.

'You see! They're following us, I'm sure of it.'

'I think you're right, Meg. Should we find a phone box
and ring Mum? Maybe they're police or something. It might
be to do with the inquiry.'

Meg wasn't so sure. They'd already had some prelimi-
nary chats. They'd always been handled in open environ-
ments with a trusted adult in attendance. This was
something different.

'There's a phone box near the cemetery. Let's see if they
go first. Mum will do her nut if she thinks we're in trouble.
She might stop us coming on our own. We won't be alone in
the cemetery, there are always people up there. Let's wait
a bit.'

Hannah seemed confident enough, and Meg was
pleased that she was taking her seriously. As they began to
make their way up Stocks Road, the car hung back until it
disappeared from sight.

'They've gone, I think,' Hannah said. 'They might have
been lost.'

Meg looked behind. She couldn't see them. Besides,
they'd spot them from a mile off in the cemetery. And there
were speed bumps all over. If they did follow the girls in,
they'd be able to shake them off.

'Is the office open on Saturdays?' Meg asked. 'We could
ring Mum from there if they are following us.'

Hannah looked back.

'We're fine, Meg. They've gone. Another X-File is closed!'

Meg resented that. She still had a bad feeling about the car. It was new, posh too. None of their schoolmates could afford anything like it. They were all driving bangers if they even had access to cars at all.

'Okay, let's go in,' she said reluctantly.

She was alert, looking ahead and behind all of the time. She couldn't see anything out of the ordinary. There was a young couple in the children's area. The tiny graves were decorated with small toys – dolls, cars and the like. Occasionally, balloons were attached to vases, indicating the ages that the babies would have been, had they lived.

Meg thought about her own child, and tears formed in her eyes. It had been like a bereavement for her. She'd given birth and her baby had been taken from her almost immediately. She'd seen him: a boy, a lovely boy. She knew she was too young, but she loved that baby from the moment she saw him.

How was what she'd experienced any different from that young couple? She was crying, and he was comforting her, crying too, inconsolable about the death of their young one. It was a fresh grave. It was still raw for them, but it felt raw to Meg too. After the baby had been taken, her body recovered fast. Physically it was as if nothing had happened, but she had lost part of her soul. The home had already stolen her innocence. There was not that much of her left.

They walked past the graves. They knew the path well. Before reaching the headstone, Meg removed the cellophane from the flowers that they'd brought with them and Hannah filled one of the watering cans which were stood next to the taps. They always brought scissors to trim the flowers. They'd learned that trick early on.

'You're young to be in here, my dears. Are you visiting your granny or grandpa?'

An old lady, maybe in her eighties but still sprightly, walked up them, throwing her own rubbish into the bin. They had this a lot. People were often wary of two teenage girls unaccompanied in the cemetery. Someone usually did a quick check.

'Yes, we're putting some flowers on the grave,' said Hannah, sounding as polite and reassuring as she could.

'Poor things, but it happens to us all I suppose. I'm seeing my Ted. He's been gone for five years now, but I miss him every day. I'll be with him soon, I'm sure. I won't go on forever!'

She laughed, squeezed Hannah's arm, and was on her way. The girls walked over to David's grave, slowing as they approached.

'Oh no!' Meg gasped. 'What's happened?'

David's gravestone had been sprayed with red paint. The words *Gone To Hell* could be made out, though the paint had run, making a complete mess of the stone. David's flower vase had been thrown across to the opposite grave, and the dead flowers from their previous visit were strewn across the grass.

'This paint is still damp!' Hannah said, touching it and then wiping the paint from her fingers onto the grass. Meg was sobbing. Who could do this to David's grave? The surrounding graves were untouched. It didn't appear to be random vandalism. That would have been bad enough, but this seemed to be targeted. Hannah put her arm around Meg and they stood there, looking at the painted message, wondering if it would wash off with water.

They stood there a few minutes, absorbed and upset. Hannah was aware of the movement first. Then Meg saw them approaching: two men in smart coats and shiny shoes, both wearing driving gloves. One of them hung back. He was wearing a hat, and it was hard to see his face.

'Hello Megan, Hannah. Good to see you.'

'Who are you?' Meg asked.

'Let's just say that we're both interested in your welfare. We wouldn't want something terrible – like this – to happen to either of you, would we?'

Meg felt Hannah tense. She moved her arm from where it had been resting across Meg's shoulders.

'What do you want?' she asked.

This man was cold and used to speaking like this. He understood how to scare people. He knew what to do to control them. This was like what happened at the home on those horrible nights. Hannah wanted to run. Meg was pinned to the spot, terrified. They knew men like this already. She knew *this* man, but couldn't place him.

'You need to think very hard about your time at Woodlands Edge. I'm certain that when you think really hard about it, you'll understand that they were perhaps the happiest days of your life.'

Meg felt a sickness deep in her stomach, and Hannah's face was white. The man with the hat stepped forward. The girls were petrified. They wanted to claw out his eyes, beat him to death and spit on his corpse. This was one of the men who had taken them in the night. He was one of the men who ... They hated him. They were paralysed in his presence.

'Hello Megan, Hannah. Good to see you again. We've missed you at our little parties. We'd love to see you again. Feel free to drop in at any time. In fact, depending on what you say about your time at Woodlands Edge, we might be getting acquainted again.'

Meg was actually sick. On David's grave too. She couldn't help it. She looked around for somebody to call to. All she could see was the old lady who'd chatted to them earlier. She had her back to them. She was talking to her dead husband probably.

'Oh Megan, Megan, that's not very nice, is it? And on your boyfriend's grave too. You know that I know who has your baby? In fact, I rubber-stamped it personally. He's not so far from Blackpool. You might even walk past him some days without knowing it.'

Meg wiped her chin, looking at the man with hatred in her eyes. Hannah took her arm, sensing that she might do something foolish. The man with the hat spoke again.

'How old are you now, girls? Sixteen and seventeen? You must be about that now. Still young enough to be wards of court if, say, your new mum and dad were found to be doing something nasty to you ... Even if it was just an allegation made by, say, some interfering neighbour. You might even end up back at Woodlands Edge. Maybe only six months or so for you, Hannah. Much longer for you, Megan. But long enough for both of you.'

Hannah went to move this time. Meg took her hand and squeezed it. They had to get through this as they had all those times before. Shut it out. Think of something else. It would pass. The other man spoke.

'Life can be sweet, girls. You need never see us again. But you know what you have to do. Make sure you do the right thing – for the sake of your mum and dad too.'

The men turned to leave. The man in the hat looked back towards the girls.

'Somebody ought to do something about the vandalism

in this cemetery. It's appalling. I must remember to mention it to the police.'

As they walked away, the one wearing the hat stopped to exchange pleasantries with the old lady who'd been tending her husband's grave. He even put his arm around her, giving her a reassuring hug.

The girls stood in silence, barely daring to move. They didn't know what to do. Who could they speak to? Nobody would believe them. They'd be written off as two silly girls who'd been in care. But they'd both recognised the men. They'd worked out who the one in the hat was straightaway. It was Russell Black, the social services man, the one who was in charge. They'd seen him in the home. He had power. He really could return them to Woodlands Edge.

The other man had taken a little longer to identify. They'd seen him, but didn't know his name. One thing was for sure, his face had burned an imprint on their minds. They would never forget either of them. The second person was Tony Dodds, the man who ran the local police.

They'd felt this fear before. It was the helplessness of being at the mercy of others, of having no ability to influence a situation. But as they stood there watching those two men casually walking off into the distance, both girls vowed that someday, somehow, they would have their revenge on those monsters. However long they had to wait, they would have their revenge.

I cut it a bit fine getting to June Dodds' house. I could see that Pat Green had the satellite van connected up outside the property and ready to go on air. June's house was gated so I had to park along the road. It was the usual media scrum: newspaper reporters, TV camera teams, radio journalists, the lot. This story had real legs now that Ray Matiz's body had been found. The press had caught the scent of blood. And, for the moment, that scent led them to Tony Dodds' former residence.

I walked up to the gates and the assembled reporters began shouting for my attention. A couple handed me pages torn out of notepads on which they'd written the questions that they wanted me to ask on their behalf. The media hate arrangements like this one, where one outlet gets the exclusive and has to ask questions on behalf of everybody else. These guys needed to get me on their side, but they also hated me for landing such a great gig.

'Pete, Pete, ask her if she knew about her husband's secret property deals.'

'Peter, push her about Russell Black and his cronies. She must have known Black's wife socially?'

'Look guys, wait a minute!' I shouted out. 'If I don't get through those gates sharpish, none of us is getting anything out of June Dodds. I've heard your questions. I know the story. I'll do my best.'

Charlie Lucas was there. Of course he was. He leant into me and spoke quietly in my ear.

'Make sure you ask this one, Peter. Ask it on behalf of me, please. It will help me to fill the column inches which might otherwise have to be used for some other story – perhaps an exclusive about a TV presenter and her bad habits, or maybe one about a local reporter who likes things a bit spicy in the bedroom. Say these exact words and nothing else: "Are you still in the black?" Just ask her that. Not on air – ask her that, and then make sure you tell me her answer. Understand?'

I nodded. I wanted to punch the little shit, but I had

more than myself to consider. I had to think about Alex.

I walked up to the gates, which were guarded by two police officers. I showed one of them my radio station ID and she let me through.

It was a long gravel drive. Pat heard me before he saw me.

'You cut it a bit fine,' he said. 'They're shitting bricks back at the station.'

'It's okay, Pat. We've got ten minutes. Where's Mrs Dodds? How is she?'

'Considering everything that's happened, she seems remarkably calm. A warning though – it looks like she thinks she's coming out to do a prepared statement. I don't think she's expecting an interview.'

'Bollocks. Has she been nobbled?' I said, thinking aloud rather than asking for Pat's opinion.

A well-dressed woman walked through the front door, which had been partially ajar. She looked professional and severe. Lawyer, I thought.

'Hello. Mr Bailey? I'm Mrs Dodds' representative, Evelyn Scott. She's going to give a short statement, and then you can ask a maximum of three questions. Do you know what you're going to ask yet? I'll need to vet them beforehand.'

This was a journalist's nightmare: controlled questions. It was a stitch-up. There would be no journalism required. I reeled off three simple questions. I didn't want to frighten the horses.

'How are you coping after your husband's tragic death?'

The insertion of the word tragic indicated empathy on my part. That would play well.

'Your husband was a very well-respected leader in this

community. Do you have any idea who might have wanted him dead?'

Again, the respect and reverence was always good, with a bit of a probing question sneaked in at the end. She'd just say something boring, such as her husband would have made many enemies keeping Blackpool safe from the criminal element ... blah, blah, waffle, blah. I'd heard it a million times before.

I needed to come up with a final question, something which would offend.

'How confident are you that you'll get the support of the police in hunting down your husband's killer?'

That would be another blah, blah, blah answer. The guys in the office would play word bingo with that. Some smart arse would bet a tenner on her saying the words 'I have every faith in' and make some easy money off the younger reporters who hadn't worked out yet how the world spins.

Evelyn made a note of my questions and then returned to the house to run them by June Dodds. Pat handed me my headphones and a microphone and I spoke off air to the technical operator back at base.

'Hi, this is Peter Bailey reporting live from the Dodds' residence in Lytham St Annes ... How's that for sound level?' I asked.

'All good!' came a chirpy voice over the talkback. It was Sue. Good. I liked Sue, she knew what she was doing.

'What's the betting like on word bingo? Did I get beaten to my favourite phrases?'

'Sorry, Pete. All the good ones are gone. I'd hang onto your money if I were you!'

'I want you to keep recording, Sue. Okay? Even if you think the interview is over, get it all recorded.'

'Will do!' came the voice in my headphones. 'We're all

set to go here, Pete. They're going to news as normal, and then your cue line is "Reporting live now from Lytham St Annes, here's Peter Bailey". Got it?'

'Good to go!' I replied. 'Mrs Dodds is coming over now.'

June Dodds looked very poised, considering her husband had just been murdered. She was a chief constable's wife. She'd probably known her husband since he was on the beat. There wasn't much that June Dodds wouldn't know about real life, however posh she looked now.

I introduced myself, expressed my condolences and talked her quickly through what I'd be doing, while keeping one ear on the radio station's output in my headphones. I heard the news jingle being played and held up my hand to indicate to June that I'd need to listen – my cue was coming. The news was introduced, I got my cue and I was away. I knew that the press pack at the end of the drive would have it blaring out on a car radio. They'd all be urging me on to ask their questions.

I stuck to the plan. I let June read her statement. I'd done so many of those in my career that I knew exactly how it would play out: 'Shock ... horror ... respected member of the community ... dear husband ...' June used them all. I made sure that I was respectful on air, of course I did, but I knew how to rattle a guest and get a good answer out of them. First, I had to make sure that we got a few questions in the can. I'd be lynched by the reporters outside the gate if I didn't get some quotes that they could use.

I watched Evelyn tense and move closer to June as I linked between her prepared statement to my own questions. I'd seen this many a time before. The hovering adviser waiting to end – or sometimes even spoil – the interview if they lost control of it.

I started with the first question, as agreed, word-for-word. That helped to lull Evelyn into a false sense of security. I was playing nice, sticking to the script. I got a good, full answer. Great.

With question two, I reworded the phrasing that I'd agreed with Evelyn. I saw her tense as I began to speak, but she relaxed once again when she realised that I'd only changed the order of the words.

June had given me two good answers. We'd got plenty recorded back at the radio station to go straight into the special live news bulletin. Sue whispered in my headphones.

'We're getting this all loud and clear. Squeeze what you can out of her.'

Now was the time to take my chance. I began by asking the question, as agreed, and watched Evelyn as she looked away, thinking that this was now simply a case of coming into land.

'How confident are you that you'll get the support of the police in hunting down your husband's killer?' I began, exactly as agreed. Then I slipped in an extra question. 'Because it seems very likely, Mrs Dodds, that your husband was involved in some small part at least in the scandal at the Woodlands Edge children's home in the nineties. Are the deaths of Ray Matiz and your husband linked in any way to the alleged cover-up in the Woodlands Edge inquiry?'

I caught about thirty seconds of June Dodds hopping about on the proverbial hot coals. She blustered away, but had been caught entirely off her guard.

Evelyn Scott intervened the minute that she realised what I'd done.

'That's enough now, Mr Bailey. Mrs Dodds is in a very distressed condition ... Please stop now, Mr Bailey ... Mr Bailey!'

She tore the microphone out of my hand and pulled out the cable. Sue laughed afterwards that the last words that you could hear in the interview were June Dodds saying, 'Will you please leave my property now, Mr Bailey!' and then an electronic thud as it all went quiet.

'Classic!' I heard Sue laughing over the headphones. 'Absolute classic, Pete! Everybody's happy here. It's all recorded. Better get your arse off Mrs Dodds' property!'

Pat was lowering the satellite dish already. He'd realised that we'd overstayed our welcome and would probably be escorted out by the police. Much of this is par for the course when you're a reporter. You get used to people getting stroppy when they can't get it all their own way.

Evelyn was flustered and June was irate but I still had one more question to ask. Evelyn put her arm around June's waist and began to steer her towards the front door.

'Mrs Dodds, one more thing!' I called after her. 'An additional question from Charlie Lucas: "Are you still in the black?"'

She stopped dead and turned around. She looked as if she'd seen her husband's ghost.

'Fuck Charlie Lucas!' she replied. 'Tell him he can go to hell!'

I don't think I've ever seen Pat Green pack up a rig so quickly. We must have been off site within five minutes. I walked up to the gates alongside the satellite van and waved him off at the gates. My adrenalin was running high. I was used to tossing in grenades like that, but you never knew what the fallout was going to be.

I was met at the gate to shouts of 'Nice one, Pete!' and

'Well done for sticking it to her, Pete!' My performance seemed to have met with general approval. They'd all get their headlines from that final question. *Widow of Murdered Police Chief Refuses to Rule Out Involvement in Child Abuse Inquiry!* That would help to keep the story alive. I could see that Charlie was waiting for me to stop chatting so he could find out how June had reacted to his question.

'So?' he asked, with that horrible snarl of his.

'There's no love lost between you and Mrs Dodds, is there?' I teased.

'What did she say? Spit it out.'

'Fuck Charlie Lucas!' I repeated her words. 'That's from her as well as me, by the way. You happy now? Got what you wanted?'

He walked off, saying nothing. He would know June Dodds of old from the inquiry – maybe not directly, but he'd have had dealings with her husband. I wondered what he'd meant by those words. He'd used the word 'black'. Was that a veiled reference to Russell Black? I hadn't got a clue. It was between June and him, probably something that went way back to the original case.

I needed to pick up my car and head back to town. I had an appointment with DCI Kate Summers to keep. It was chucking it down again – we'd been lucky to get some respite during the interview, but it was a dull, grey day, not nice at all. I climbed into the car and turned the key. No response. I tried again. I was getting used to the drill now. Twice. Three times. A fourth time. It was dead. I kept trying, but the engine sounded as if it had given up.

Damn it. I was going to be pushed to get to DCI Summers in time. I opened the door and checked for parking restrictions. I was fine. I could leave the car for now.

I wouldn't get a ticket. I'd need to catch a bus. They pretty well all passed along the promenade. I'd be able to get to the town centre that way. I checked my wallet. No notes, just change. I'd been relying on Alex, and I'd let myself run short. I'd top up in town – if the machine would keep paying out, that is.

I walked up the road looking for a bus stop. I hadn't a clue what the routes were from Lytham. I waited for a few minutes before a single-decker bus drew up.

'Do you go along the front?' I asked.

'You're pointing the wrong way, mate. I terminate at Saltcotes and then come around again. You can jump on if you want to, but it'll be a long wait. Use the stop across the road. They should be regular enough from there.'

I walked across to the new stop, grateful for the shelter it was giving me. I had a ten-minute wait, and then an open-top bus drove up. The doors opened. I was thankful to step out of the rain.

'How much to the town centre?' I asked.

It was more than I had in change.

'How far can I get on £1.60?'

'If you get off a couple of stops along the way, you'll have a ten-minute walk. I'll give you a shout to let you know when to get off, alright?'

'Great, thanks.' I counted out my coins into the tray.

'Do these things get wet through when it rains?' I asked. 'They're not very practical on a day like today.'

'This one will stay in the depot when I get back if this doesn't clear up. There are still a couple of people up there in rain macs looking at the view. I guess if you're on holiday here, you want to make the best of it!'

I moved towards the middle of the bus. It wasn't packed, and I got a seat to myself. The windows were steamed up and I wiped my hand across the glass to clear an area so that I could see where we were. I was fine for time. It was tight, but I wouldn't miss DCI Summers. I cursed my car. Another bill that I couldn't afford. If I was lucky, it would just be a damp issue which would sort itself out when the weather improved.

The bus seemed to take forever. It was quite handy as a journalist to travel along some of the back streets that I didn't know very well, but it helped me get my bearings when I saw the tram depot up ahead and knew that we were getting close to my stop. As we stopped at the tram depot, I wiped my window again to get a better view. I loved the trams. They were a great feature for a seaside resort.

Then I saw her. It was Meg. She hadn't changed a bit. Maybe her hair was longer. She was getting on a tram. A young guy was helping her with the pram. They were chatting and laughing. It was Meg. At last. I jumped up out of my seat. The bus driver had closed the doors and begun to drive off.

'Stop the bus!' I called.

'This isn't your stop yet, mate. You've a fair bit to go yet.'

'I need you to stop the bus!' I shouted at him.

'Now steady on, sir. There's another stop five minutes up the road. I can't stop wherever you want me to.'

'Stop the bus, please. It's my wife!'

'Look sir, please sit down and stop distracting me. We'll pull up again in a couple of minutes.'

'Damn you!' I shouted. I considered my options. It was an open-top bus. It wasn't too high. I couldn't miss this chance. I was too close to her now. I had to speak to her.

I ran up the stairs to the top deck. A retired couple were sitting up there in waterproofs, absolutely drenched. They seemed surprised to see me. I looked up the road to see

Meg's tram drawing away. Damn, I had to catch up with it. If I ran fast enough, I'd be able to follow it. The trams were slow. It would stop and start all along the promenade. I had to catch her.

I looked over the edge of the bus. If I climbed over the side and hung on to the rail, I could let myself down to the pavement. I was going to do it. I think the old guy sensed what was happening.

'Hang on a minute, mate ...' he said, as I cocked my knee over the edge and lowered myself along the side of the bus, hanging onto the railings. I was on the path side. When the bus stopped, I'd drop to the ground. I worked out which way I'd have to run. I was already out of breath from the exertion of throwing myself over the side of the vehicle.

I wasn't sure what happened next. The bus driver must have seen me dangling there in his mirrors and stepped on the brake. Whatever happened, I remember an abrupt stop. It caught me off-guard and my grip loosened on the side railing. I wasn't ready for the fall. It wasn't too high, but I landed, then stumbled, careering across the pavement trying to find my balance. From nowhere some idiot on a bike smacked directly into me. He was cycling on the pavement. I went flying and my head made a horrible thud as it hit the paving slabs.

The next thing I knew, Alex was sitting beside me and I was in a hospital bed.

CHAPTER ELEVEN

1993 Meg and Hannah walked home from the cemetery in silence. They didn't know what to do. They had no way of defending themselves against these men. Their power seemed unassailable.

The thought of returning to Woodlands Edge was unthinkable. They were safe with Tom and Mavis – they no longer needed to fear the night. Would they be believed? They thought it unlikely.

As the girls approached their house, Meg spoke.

'Should we tell Tom and Mavis? Will it make things worse?'

'Who's going to believe us? They'll make us out to be two silly little sluts. There's nothing we can do, Meg. We have to let it go, for now. We can't risk going back there.'

They never spoke about what had happened to them during the night-time visits. It was too painful, too shameful for them. But they knew. They understood what they were running from. They knew that they couldn't go back.

'I want to kill those bastards!' said Meg, punching the

front door of one of the terraces as she walked by. It drew blood, but it felt good. She had to let it out.

'Me too. I know,' Hannah replied. 'But we can't do anything now. One day they'll be old and we'll be adults. There's no sell-by date on revenge, Meg. We can get them later. For now we have to survive. We have to stay with Tom and Mavis. We must keep out of that home.'

They reached their front door.

'Say nothing,' Hannah warned. 'Don't let Tom and Mavis know what happened. It's our secret. Bob and Tom can still give evidence at the inquiry. They'll be believed.'

Although Hannah was much wiser than she should have been in the ways of the adult world, she was naive enough to believe that Tom and Bob would not be threatened. It didn't even occur to her or Meg. They assumed that they'd been bullied in the cemetery in the same way that Gary Maxwell would humiliate and intimidate the young people at Woodlands Edge. It was how life was for them. They had no stake in it – their lives were defined by the will of adults.

Tom was on a late shift that day, and Mavis looked unnerved when they walked through the door.

'Are you alright, Mavis ... Mum?'

Meg was getting there, but she still didn't quite believe that having someone to call mum was permanent.

'Something happened while you were out, just before your dad left for his shift. We had a visit from Russell Black, the man from the social services. He had somebody waiting for him in the car. I don't know who it was.'

The girls looked at each other. They must have headed to the house immediately after threatening the girls in the cemetery. What were they up to?

'What did he have to say?' Hannah asked, aware that her face was reddening.

'Nothing really. It was odd. He said that he'd run your dad to work. It would give them a chance to chat. Tom was surprised too. He went with them. It wasn't that long ago.'

'Did he mention us?' asked Meg, daring to probe a little further.

'He seemed very interested in how you were doing. He asked if you were behaving and how the adoption was suiting us. He mentioned that social services don't just leave us to it. It was funny how he said it, though. Like he was warning us. "We can get involved in the welfare of the girls at any time," he said. He was smiling when he said it. It was really odd.'

The girls knew exactly what he meant. They wondered what Russell Black and Tony Dodds were saying to their father in the car. They'd kept Mavis out of it, but they would, no doubt, be leaning on Tom too.

Tom was going on a slight detour on his way to work. Tony Dodds and Russell Black were about to give him some career advice.

'Do you enjoy your work at Woodlands Edge, Tom?'

Tom wasn't certain which way the conversation was going. He knew that Russell Black could make life very uncomfortable for him.

'I really like it there,' he replied cautiously. 'I love working alongside the kids. They're a good bunch.'

'And how is life with Megan and Hannah? Is life as a father suiting you?'

'Yes, Mr Black, it's wonderful. We're so grateful for

being able to adopt the girls. They've made our lives ... wonderful. That's the only way I can describe it, really. Things are wonderful now.'

Tony Dodds spoke up. They'd made Tom sit in the back, like a child.

'In my line of work, it's terrible how quickly life can change. I see it everyday. One moment you can happily be going about your life and the next – bang! Something terrible happens: an accident, a murder, an unprovoked attack. It can all be snuffed out in an instant.'

'What's your take on this inquiry, Tom?' Russell Black picked up. 'Anything in it?'

Tom did not like the way this was going. He couldn't put his finger on it. They were being very polite. Why did he feel so threatened?

'Where are we going?' he asked, aware that they'd entered the motorway.

'You're going to be a little delayed this evening,' Tony Dodds said, 'but don't worry. They know that you're going to be late into work.'

'Is that what this is about? The inquiry? Are you worried about what I'm going to say?'

Tom couldn't believe that he was talking to these men in this way.

'What do you think it's about, Tom?' Russell asked. 'You might think it's about the inquiry. Perhaps it has more to do with those girls of yours and that wonderful new family that you have.'

'Are you threat— What's this about? Where are you taking me?'

'Pull off at this exit,' Tony Dodds said.

Russell indicated and the car took the Kirkham turn-off. They pulled off the road into a secluded spot.

'Get out of the car!' Tony Dodds was shouting now. It shook Tom. He did as he was told.

'Climb into the boot!'

Tom looked between the two men. He was terrified. He'd never experienced anything like this.

'What are you going to do?'

As if they were going to tell him. Tony motioned towards the boot. Tom climbed in and they closed the lid.

The drive was forty minutes or so. Tom tried to work out where they were going. It was hopeless, he hadn't a clue. There was no attempt to make it a comfortable ride. It felt as if Russell were throwing the vehicle around corners on purpose.

Eventually they came to a stop. The boot opened. It was fully dark now. Both men carried torches.

'This is Denham Quarry,' said Russell Black. 'You can see Blackpool Tower from here on a good day.'

'It's a bit too dark to see at the moment,' Tony Dodds said, 'but it's a long way down there. People use this place for climbing now. Personally, I think it's too dangerous. You could really hurt yourself if you fell.'

Tom could barely see their faces. He knew that he was alone and miles from home. They were the only people there. They could push him over the top and nobody would have a clue who'd done it, except his wife, who'd do her best to blame the two men. And what then? Would she join him?

'We want to have a little chat about the evidence you intend to give at the inquiry,' Russell Black began.

'And I'd like to offer you a little legal guidance,' Tony Dodds continued. They worked together like a double act. Only this was more like the Krays than Morecambe and Wise.

It took half an hour of threats and intimidation before Thomas Yates finally acquiesced to the demands of the men and agreed to withdraw from the inquiry. In return, he was promised the safety of his precious new daughters. At least Meg and Hannah were safe with him; he could protect them if he did what the men had commanded. He'd finally made that decision as they'd pushed him right to the edge of the quarry and Tony Dodds was about to boot him over to take his chances on the rocks below.

That same night, hanging from the top of Blackpool Tower, as he was held by the ankles by two hired hands, Bob Taylor had made exactly the same decision.

It took me a few minutes to figure out what was going on. My head felt heavy, as if it had been filled with concrete. It was sore too, really painful. The room was bright. I had to wait for my eyes to adjust. I opened them, just a little at first, and saw Alex sitting in a high-backed chair next to me. There was some old bloke in a bed a few feet away. Hospital.

I shuffled, trying to get up, but wasn't ready yet.

'Woah, steady!' Alex said, jumping to her feet and encouraging me to lie down again.

'You've had a nasty knock. How are you feeling?'

I did a swift body assessment.

'Like crap,' I replied. 'What happened?'

As I said the words, I recalled the events that had led to my waking up in this place.

'Meg,' I began. 'I saw Meg!'

'Pete, take it easy for a moment. Don't move. I'll get a nurse and tell her you're with us again.'

I don't know where she thought I might be going. My body felt as if it was pinned to the bed. While Alex was out in the corridor, I did a pain audit. My head was sore and uncomfortable. That seemed to be the centre of the problem. My right leg had plasters stuck at various points along it and I felt a bandage and cotton-wool dressing on my left knee. I also appeared to have damaged my elbow, as that too was dressed.

Nothing was missing or broken. I thought back to what had happened. I shuddered as I recalled the bang to the head. No wonder things were feeling fuzzy.

The old man opposite me was in a bad way. He was wheezing loudly and unsettled in his bed. I looked around. It was a small ward, National Health, five men in there, one bed empty. It was visiting time as far as I could see. The old man had nobody with him. There was a younger guy there, who was being visited by a lovely-looking wife or girlfriend and a wriggling baby. The other chaps were middle-aged. One was on his own, the other being visited by a wife and two children. I was grateful for Alex being there. I would not have wanted to wake up alone in that place.

Alex was back, followed soon afterwards by a nurse and a doctor who shone a torch in my eyes, asked me to look up, down, left and right, asked a few questions, checked my dressings, and scribbled a few notes on the clipboard at the side of my bed.

'All fine, Mr Bailey. A mild concussion, nothing worse than that. No broken bones. You'll be able to leave tomorrow morning. We'll monitor you for the night.'

With that, she was away. The nurse told me that they'd be round with the meds after visiting time and that I should tell them if I experienced blurred vision, a feeling of sickness, or difficulty speaking. She moved over to the old guy to try to make him more comfortable.

'I've got one of those bloody gowns on, haven't I?' I attempted to smile at Alex.

'I didn't want to mention it, but your arse has been poking out all afternoon. It's why the guy in the next bed is so disturbed.'

I tried for a second smile. My face wasn't working yet. The family across from us were trying to take selfies with Alex in them. They were doing a poor job of concealing that they'd spotted the TV celebrity in the room. Alex was either ignoring it or hadn't noticed.

'What happened, you idiot? It sounded like you'd done some James Bond manoeuvre from the top of a bus, or more like Johnny English by the look of it.'

I made a third try at a laugh. A little cough came out this time around. I decided to give humour a rest for a while.

'I saw Meg!' I began. 'She was getting on a tram—'

'So you jumped off the top of a bus? What were you hoping to do, Pete? What were you thinking?'

'I'd have been alright if it wasn't for that bloody cyclist. The speed of him. Did anybody catch him?'

'No, like a good citizen he went racing off, according to the ambulance crew. Nobody appears to have seen what happened.'

'What if I'd been an old dear or a child? Would the bastard have stopped then? These cycling buggers act like they own the place. He was going pretty fast.'

'Are you sure it was Meg, Pete? Did you get a good look?'

I thought it through. Yes, I knew my wife, even from a distance. The way she moved, her smile. She'd looked happy. She was at ease with the young guy. Had she found somebody else?

'It was Meg,' I answered. 'Without a doubt. She looked good. Happy. She had a child with her and she was with a young guy. He was helping her onto the tram with the pram. They were chatting, and she was smiling.'

'Well, at least we know that much. She's definitely around. It's only a matter of time until you run into her again. Hopefully it won't involve stunts next time.'

'I've hurt my leg again, you know. It's where I messed it up last time. I can feel it playing up. I thought it had healed properly, but it's painful again now. I hope it's not going to start giving me aggro – I thought I was done with that.'

'I've got some news of my own,' Alex said.

I could see that she was eager to share what she'd found out. She'd been hanging onto it, no doubt urging me to wake up.

'This is where Meg had the baby – in the maternity wing. While you were sleeping I went exploring and got talking to a nurse down there. He came up to me – he recognised me from the programme. It was handy. He was speaking to me as if he knew me. I did a bit of probing. It turns out he was on shift that night. She was here as Megan Stewart; she's using her birth name again. He clocked Meg because he thought he knew her – he'd seen her picture in the papers. It's a boy, apparently. He hadn't been given a name, not one that he could recall.'

'Wow, you've done well. So she has a boy. I wonder if he's mine. Was the baby prone to accidents and extremely good-looking? If he is, he has to be mine.'

I was attempting humour again, but I actually wanted to cry. Meg had a baby, though I knew that already. The past came surging back. Was he my child or Jem's? Jem, my best friend, who'd drugged my wife, then had sex with her. He was dead in the ground now, but it all came back when Alex mentioned the baby: the hatred for Jem and the loss of my best friend at work; the frustration and anger about what had happened to Meg, and the pain of the past year. So much had happened. I tried to make light of it, but it was taking its toll. All I wanted was to see my wife again, and I wanted to know if I was a father.

I could feel my eyes reddening. I forced back the tears. I'm not prone to crying, but I felt overwhelmed. I'd been so close to seeing Meg, yet she'd slipped through my fingers again.

'Sorry, I thought you'd be pleased to hear that, Pete.'

'I am,' I replied. 'Honestly, I am. Did they give me any drugs? I feel really emotional.'

'Not that I know of. I can't blame you if you're feeling upset though. Are you ready for a bit more news? You might want to steel yourself first.'

'Is it about Meg?' I asked.

I tried to settle down. I was anxious to hear her news.

'My chat with Bob was fruitful. He and Tom were leant on heavily. I mean, big time. They were under a lot of pressure to rescind their claims. In the end, they did.'

'What do you mean? You're talking about the inquiry now, yes? Who did the leaning?'

'Bob said it was horrible. It was Tony Dodds and Russell Black. They got to Tom first and threatened him over the girls, told him they'd make some horrible accusation about Tom abusing them. They'd say he was using the inquiry to cover it up and place the blame elsewhere.'

'Those guys are a piece of work,' I said. 'What did they do to Bob?'

'Let's put it this way: he escaped with his life and got

the job as a lollipop man as a consolation prize. They had him grabbed off the street one night and dangled from the top of the tower. Can you imagine how scary that was?'

'Who did? Not Dodds and Black, surely?'

'No, a couple of hoodlums is how he described them. It was right in front of his wife too. He said a car drew up, two guys got out, threw him in the back, and left his wife standing on the pavement. They must have had access to the tower – it was late at night. He says they each held an ankle and hung him over the edge. They told him to keep his mouth shut and follow Tom's lead. When he got home, his son had been arrested on suspicion of stealing school property. He got the message. He dropped his claims and the inquiry collapsed. His son was let off with a caution.'

'All this happened in Blackpool? It's unbelievable. Those guys must have owned the town back then.'

'They did. Bob said that if it hadn't been for his son, he'd have carried on. But once they got to his kid, he was terrified. He knew there was no beating them. They offered him the job on a school crossing patrol and he kept his mouth shut. He hates himself for it, Pete. Every day, he said, he curses them for what they did. He was pleased that Tony Dodds and Ray Matiz had got their comeuppance – he'd have liked to have strangled them himself.'

I was allowed out of hospital the following morning, after the doctors had done their rounds. I felt as if I'd been there forever. Alex had returned for the evening visiting session too. She'd booked into a nearby hotel to save taking taxis across town.

'You'll have to stop buying your clothes in Blackpool,' I

laughed at her. 'This is the second time I've seen you in an I Love Blackpool T-shirt.'

'Yeah, only now it's a sweatshirt because it's so damn cold out there.'

I was sore, but fine. The worst thing about being discharged was keeping my arse in the gown that they'd given me while I walked along the corridor. Why do they do that? Can't the NHS get someone like Stella McCartney to do a makeover on those gowns? My trousers were torn and bloody. I'd have to go home to get changed. I looked like a tramp. Alex took the mickey. I'd have expected nothing less.

I was told to take it easy for a few days and given a list of symptoms to be wary of. It was good to be out of that place. I'd seen far too many medical professionals in the past year.

Alex and I sat in the hospital grounds. She called a taxi while I turned on my phone. I couldn't remember the last time I'd gone twenty-four hours without checking it. I'd turned it off while doing the radio interview with June Dodds. The battery was still fine, so I could at least catch up with events while we waited for our transport.

'I'll have to get my car sorted out,' I said, remembering for the first time that it was abandoned at Lytham St Annes.

'It can wait for now,' Alex said. 'You're not running off over there to mess around with your car. Leave it. It'll be fine.'

She had a point. I waited for my phone to find the signal and then the messages started to come in.

'Oh shit. DCI Summers is pissed off with me because I didn't turn up for my meeting. I'd better let her know what happened. Hannah has been in touch too. There are several Skype messages. That's interesting – they still have her Skype location as the UK. Is that determined by your settings or does it follow you round wherever you are?'

Alex shrugged.

'What am I, an IT expert? I don't know. I've never paid much attention. I'll see if I can find out online.'

She tapped at her phone and I read my messages. Hannah seemed keen to know what was going on. She was anxious for a chat over Skype. She'd tried me several times.

Are you online, Pete?

Hi Pete, you're showing as offline, are you there?

Hi Pete, keen to chat, let me know when you're connected. Hannah.

I'm in the UK on business atm. Keen to catch up. Where are you living now?

That was a lot of messages. I tapped in a reply telling her that I'd get connected asap, and letting her know that I was in Blackpool. I thought I'd told her that already in one of our occasional catch-up chats, but I didn't want her booking rail tickets to the wrong place. It was only fair that I told her about Meg. She'd want to hear that news.

'I have to call Mark at work,' I said. 'Did you tell him what had happened? They need to know where I am.'

Alex looked sheepish.

'No, sorry, I didn't think. They're journalists. If they'd wondered where you were, they'd have known to make hospital check calls.'

I was on the phone to work when the taxi finally arrived. My interview with June Dodds had caused a bit of a sensation. Our altercation was all over the papers. Mark was very excited by it. I was the hero of the hour, and they'd had good feedback from the other press outlets. He wished me well and told me to take a couple of days off to recover.

'If we get more exclusive interviews, I might need you to limp back in though. You're a bit of a celebrity round here at the moment. Can you do an interview from your deathbed?'

It was good to know that my colleagues were so concerned about my health.

Alex and I got in the taxi and didn't talk on the way home. I had too much running through my mind; I needed to get it all straight. We pulled up outside the flat. I got a sinking feeling at the thought of being home. You're not supposed to feel that way about the place where you live. I promised myself that I'd hand my notice in. Perhaps I could take a loan and shuffle my finances around.

'I've just remembered. It's a year to the day since I last saw Meg. I can't believe it,' I said. 'Ever feel you're being punished for something?'

There was a large brown envelope among the post pile addressed to me. It was full of letters. The estate agent was still forwarding my mail from home.

'At least the phantom post-opener didn't get to it first,' I said. I tore open the envelope as we walked up the stairs and took a quick look through it.

'Usual rubbish. Why do they keep sending this shit?'

My leg was sore after the climb up the stairs, so I sat on the settee and took a second look at the post. I spilled the contents of the larger envelope to my side and sifted through the contents. There was a postcard in there, from Blackpool. It was a picture of the tower of all places.

I turned it over. Meg's handwriting. She'd sent it to the house. Of course she would. She didn't know where I living. She'd have known that it would have got to me if she sent it there. I looked at the postmark. Damn, it had been sent over a week beforehand. The estate agent had hung onto it before forwarding the pile of mail. I read the message. I hardly dared to look at the words. I was terrified of what news they might contain. I'd waited a year for this, now it had come, I almost didn't want to read it.

Pete, I hope you're well. I saw what happened. The police spoke to me. I'm sorry I didn't reach out, I wasn't ready. Things have changed. We need to speak. Can you meet me at Ivy's in the town centre, next Wednesday at 11am. I need to introduce you to somebody special. I'm sorry Pete, I really am. Meg x

My eyes began to well up. Had they given me something in that hospital? I'd been really emotional over the past day.

'What?' Alex asked, sensing that something was up. 'What is it, Pete?'

'It's Meg,' I said, looking up at her. 'She's got in touch at last. She wanted to meet me in town last Wednesday. This postcard took so long to get to me, I've missed it. Now I'm no further forward.'

CHAPTER TWELVE

1993 Thomas Yates didn't return to work. He was driven back to Blackpool in the dead of night. Tony Dodds and Russell Black chatted between themselves as if he wasn't there.

Tony Dodds was expert in the art of intimidating without evidence. He knew the police procedures in intricate detail. Thomas Yates had experienced a draining evening of violence and aggression, but he'd barely been touched. He'd got the message alright. He'd feared for his life while dangling over the top of that rocky ledge. He would be no good to Meg and Hannah if he died – he couldn't protect them then. He had to stay alive, buy time and think it through.

It seemed to take an age to reach the M55. Thomas had never travelled much. Flights abroad were expensive, not for the likes of him and Mavis. He was happy in Blackpool. He'd been born and grown up there and had no desire to travel further afield. The sight of the illuminated tower in the distance comforted and soothed him as they drove into the outskirts of the town.

Thomas was let out of the car along the promenade. There was no door-to-door service for him, and no further conversation. Tony Dodds looked up into the rear-view mirror as they pulled up along the seafront.

'Remember what we said. This is your first and only warning. Get out!'

Thomas stepped out into the road and moved to the side, out of the way of the traffic, mainly taxis running up and down the seafront. It was late at night. There were still people around, many of them drunk. Thomas walked along the road a little way, unsure what to do next. He heard a revving behind him and turned to see the reverse lights of the car. It took a few seconds for him to realise what the men were doing, but he turned to run the minute that he did. The clutch was released and the car shot backwards, hurtling towards him at speed. He thought it was going to hit him. He hadn't yet made it to the pavement – he couldn't make his legs work fast enough.

The sound of heavy revving was replaced by the screech of brakes. The car boot bumped him, but not enough to send him flying. Thomas crumpled to the ground, his heart ready to explode with the shock. The car had stopped short. They'd only intended to scare him.

They drove off slowly, like a Sunday driver. A taxi sounded its horn at Thomas, who was now sitting in the road, and swerved to avoid him. The driver pulled up alongside and opened his window.

'Get out the bloody road, you pisshead!' he shouted, before driving off.

Thomas stood up with difficulty and headed over to a nearby bench. He sat down and checked himself for cuts and bruises. There was nothing. He was fine. It was inside his head that the damage was done.

He watched a couple kissing across the road in a shop entrance. The man had his hand up the woman's short skirt and even from that distance Thomas could see that he was working her knickers down, ready for a knee trembler on the seafront. He stood up and walked to the next bench. He didn't want his soul-searching to be punctuated by the grunts of a couple who'd got lucky in a local nightclub. Neither did he wish to be a spectator.

He looked at his watch. It was way past midnight, closer to one o'clock. Being out of season, it was quieter than it would have been in the summer months. Would there be witnesses? It wouldn't matter. Tony Dodds would stifle any complaint that he dared to make. How do you complain about the police if your complaint is about the man who runs them? Thomas wanted to cry with frustration. He saw himself headed off at every pass. And he could lose the girls, that much was clear.

What had been going on at the home? Did he really know? He'd seen them taking the children out that night. It was too late to be any regular activity. He'd seen Meg and Hannah. They'd been like animals going to slaughter, accepting their fate because there was nothing that they could do. He'd heard Gary Maxwell talking to Meg after she'd fainted. Not every word, but he'd got the sense of it. He didn't need to hear the words to know that it had been threatening.

But the girls would say nothing. He knew they were happy living with him and Mavis. It was obvious that they didn't want to go back into care. If he did give evidence with Bob Taylor, there would be more of this. He could lose the girls. If they went back to the home, whatever had happened to them, whatever they were doing to them, would it continue? He sensed what was going on. He hadn't seen it first hand, but something terrible must have driven those poor boys to kill themselves.

Thomas was not a brave man. He'd never been exposed to this level of threat before. The last time he'd felt remotely intimidated was back at school when the classroom thug had cornered him and stolen his dinner money. What Tony Dodds and Russell Black were doing was something completely different. These men could wreck their lives.

Thomas got up and walked along the promenade in the direction of his home. The man and the women had finished and the woman was hooking her knickers over her left foot ready to walk away from the scene of their romantic encounter. Thomas waited until he was well clear of them, and then crossed the road, ready to make the winding journey through the streets and back to the house. Mavis would be awake, worried, but assuming that he'd got delayed by some boiler problem or leaking pipe that had taken him over his shift times.

He couldn't bring himself to talk to her when he returned home. She was dozing with the bedside lamp still on.

'Hi luv, you're late. Did you have a problem?'

'Just the boiler again, dear. You know what it's like. Sorry for not calling you. I was up to my ears in boiler parts. It was hard to get away.'

'It's alright, luv. Come to bed and we can chat tomorrow.'

She was asleep within seconds. Thomas got undressed and slipped into bed, putting his arm around her. It wasn't only the girls that he had to think about. Mavis would never forgive him if they lost them now. He'd seen how she'd flourished since they'd moved in. He hadn't realised how sad it had made her over the years not having their own kids in the house. Meg and Hannah had changed everything. Did he really want to put all that at risk?

He kept thinking back to Meg's face that night in the home. She had been pleading with him to intervene and he'd done nothing. Was he going to do nothing again? He didn't know, he needed to sleep.

Morning came too soon. He was awoken by Mavis. She was dressed already – he must have slept in. That was unusual for him.

'There's a phone call for you. Says it's important. Bob Taylor, I think.'

Thomas got out of bed and rubbed his eyes. He hadn't had enough time to think it through yet. If Bob wanted to talk to him about the inquiry, he'd need to keep quiet about his doubts for now.

'Hi Bob, it's Tom.'

'Hi Tom. Sorry to ring you first thing on a Sunday but it's important. It's about the inquiry.'

Of course it was. Thomas said nothing, just gave an uh huh to confirm that he was listening.

'I've been, um, thinking it over,' Bob began. 'I've ... er ... I've changed my mind.'

There was a pause.

'I ... I think we're doing the wrong thing, Tom.'

He cleared his throat.

'I think we've ... I've been too ... hasty. Yes, I've been too hasty.'

'Did they get to you too?' Thomas asked.

Bob ignored him.

'Look Tom, I know I came to you and said ... Look, I know it was my idea to start all of this. But I think it was wrong ... I didn't actually see anything ... I shouldn't have started it. I was annoyed with Gary ... I let it cloud my judgment ... I'm not going to take part in the inquiry.'

'They came to see you last night, didn't they?' Thomas said.

'Look Tom, I know I set the ball rolling with this. But I think it has to stop here, before it goes too far. Think of your family, Tom. The girls ... think of the girls. The children are the most important people in all of this. We've gone far enough. Whatever ... whatever it was they were doing – and I don't know, I'm only guessing – whatever they were doing, it'll stop now. Now they're being watched. The children will be okay now ... won't they? But we have to stop, Tom. Please.'

Bob was going to betray the children. They'd got to him too. He hadn't got the courage to face his bullies. Thomas didn't know what to do. He listened to the hum of the line as he heard Bob Taylor stifling his tears at the end of the phone. They were going to abandon the youngsters at the Woodlands Edge children's home. They were going to become forgotten children.

'Where's Ivy's?' Alex asked.

'I'm not sure,' I replied, running the names of the various cafés through my head. They were not something that was on my radar in any particular way. I tended to stick to the chains.

'I'll take a look on my phone,' Alex said. 'Hopefully they'll be online.'

I turned the postcard over in my hand. Meg had written this. She'd touched it, thinking about me as she wrote it. She was ready now. It must have been my birthday that made her send it: the anniversary of me sleeping with Ellie, the event that started everything.

We could talk at last, move on with our lives. And she wanted to introduce me to somebody. That had to be the baby. Was it my child or Jem's?

Immediately my thoughts began to taunt me. If it was my child, she'd have contacted me sooner. Why wouldn't she? The only possible reason for delay had to be her finding out that it was that bastard Jem who'd fathered the child, forcing himself on her without consent. I still struggled to say the word 'rape', it was too painful. But that's what he'd done: drugged and raped my wife. My best friend.

I looked for clues on the postcard. Meg wouldn't have known that our post was being collected and forwarded by the estate agent. She'd have expected to post it first class to arrive the next day. She wasn't listening to the local radio station either, or she'd have known that I had followed her down to Blackpool. Blackpool was only two hours drive from the home that we used to share, she would have known that I would drop everything to attend that meeting with her at Ivy's.

Damn, she'd think I'd ignored her intentionally. Why didn't she just send an email or something like that? A postcard. Only pensioners still use those. There was no address. Just a date, her note and signature. She'd added an X too. Was that her reaching out to me? I've never got used to the younger generation adding rows of Xs to notes and emails. It was something I saved for people I love.

'Ivy's is in the town centre,' Alex said, looking up from her phone. 'Shall we go? They might be able to help us, and at least we can leave a message for her there.'

The doorbell rang. I went over to the window to see

who was standing at the door below. Surely it wasn't my friend from the finance company again? We'd paid him, he should be happy. Damn, I'd forgotten about the car. We'd have to do something about that or I'd lose a fortune paying for taxis.

'I can't see who it is,' I said to Alex. The bell rang again. 'I'll go down. Probably some time-waster.'

'I'll go,' Alex said. 'You need to rest. You're going to screw up that leg of yours if you're not careful.'

Alex soon returned, chatting happily to our guest. It was DCI Kate Summers.

I went to stand up to shake her hand, but got a terrible pain in my leg as I did so.

'God, that hurt!' I winced. 'Sorry DCI Summers, you'll have to settle for a hello.'

She laughed.

'I see you're busy messing everything up again,' she smiled at me. 'Not content with a trail of carnage in your home town, I see you're intent on making an impact in Blackpool.'

'It's beginning to feel like that. Look, I'm sorry I barged in on your meeting like that. I'm sorry if it embarrassed you. I know it was wrong. I was just so surprised to see you down here.'

'Well, seeing as you stood me up yesterday, I thought I'd better come and see you first. And explain.'

'How did you find me here?' I asked.

DCI Summers laughed again.

'You're a police officer's dream,' she said. 'You leave a trail of crap wherever you go. Your fight with a bus was recorded in the log, and I did a check call to find out which hospital you were in. I got your address from the radio station. So here I am.'

'Great detective work,' I said. 'It makes me feel safe just knowing you're here. But why have you come?'

'You're not going to like this, Pete, and I'm sorry to be the one to tell you, but they're investigating your wife, Meg.'

I collapsed back into the sofa. Here we were again. Meg. I looked at Alex. She'd sensed how I was feeling.

'What now?' I asked, after a silence.

'I can't give you all the details, Pete, but it's why I'm down here consulting with the local constabulary. Meg is the connection – and, in a roundabout way, you too.'

'Is this to do with the deaths?' Alex asked.

She was always on the mark with her incisive line of questioning.

'Yes,' DCI Summers replied. We know that Meg lived at the Woodlands Edge children's home for a couple of years. We know that someone is killing off the old guys who were involved in an inquiry there in the nineties. She has to fall under suspicion.'

'Does she know I'm here in Blackpool?' I asked.

'Look, Pete, you know I won't tell you her address and I won't be telling her yours. You know I can't do that.'

She paused before continuing.

'I'm speaking to you because your name keeps coming up. Whoever we talk to, your name is usually in there somewhere: Bob Taylor, June Dodds, Steven Terry, Charlie Lucas, every one of them has mentioned your name. What's going on, Pete?'

I sighed and rubbed my hands across my face. Alex stayed quiet, looking between me and DCI Summers.

'Where do I start?' I replied. 'As you say, it's all about Meg. I've been trying to track her down. You know that. She's done a great job of hiding from me. I've used all of my journalistic tricks, but she didn't want to be found. I've been trying to get to know her a bit better. She kept a lot of secrets from me about her life before we met. We've been digging, and the more we dig, the more we find.'

'Anything I need to know?' she asked. 'Last time you didn't fill me in ... Well, both of you know how that ended. You two are like the two members of the Famous Five who never retired. You need to promise to let me know if you find anything. This is a murder investigation. You know how that all plays out, right? People get killed. You've seen it before. Twice already. Don't bite off more than you can chew.'

'Do you have any leads on the murders?' Alex changed the subject. 'I'm assuming they're murders. They can't be suicides?'

'No, they're murders alright,' DCI Summers said, 'and whoever is involved must have been connected with that home in some way. Did you know that Meg had a boyfriend who killed himself at the home, Pete? She must have told you that.'

I felt ridiculous.

'No, she never told me.'

'You need to be careful, okay? Meg has a ... Look, Meg's only involved because she was in care at the home. We're working through anybody that we can trace who was in Woodlands Edge at the time. I'm down here because she got flagged on the computer system due to what happened last year. I'll be heading back home after tonight and I'm not expecting them to need me again. My advice is to let the police do their job. Seriously, Pete, and you, Alex. You know how this ended last time. You know how it ended the last two times. Keep your noses out of it and let the police handle things. Okay?'

'Okay.'

'Sure,' said Alex, looking at me with a straight face.

'You buggers!' DCI Summers said, looking between both of us.

She knew as well as we did that we had no intention of backing off. We'd keep pushing and pushing until we got our conclusion. However things turned out.

Alex and I were keen to get over to Ivy's and speak to the staff there.

'It's almost a week since I was supposed to meet with Meg. I'm really pissed off about that postcard taking so long to reach me. What would you think if somebody was a no-show?'

'I'd think you were a wanker!' Alex teased. 'Actually, I'd probably do exactly what you're doing now: look at all the angles and figure out that I'd screwed something up, or convince myself you didn't want to see me again. She says she knows what happened to you after she left. She must know that I was staying with you at the time; the papers will show her that. What did you tell her about us, Pete? I know I was always a touchy subject for Meg.'

'You can say that again!'

I stopped for a moment and thought. I'd felt embarrassed when DCI Summers had exposed how little I knew about my wife. Yet I hadn't told her the full truth about my own past. She knew Alex and I were close. However, I'd missed out the bit about the pregnancy – and the miscarriage – and the living together. I'd convinced myself over and over again that it was irrelevant. Alex and I were history. We were still friends; we hadn't had some spectacular break-up, but it was in my past. The past is the past.

Maybe that's what Meg had thought. Perhaps I was being too tough on her, expecting her to trawl up the unhappinesses of her childhood. Maybe I had been her chance to move on.

'Did you ever talk to anybody about us?' I asked Alex. 'You know, the baby and everything?'

'No. I think about it a lot, but I don't talk to anybody. Why would I? I buried it. I didn't deal with it at the time, and the longer you don't talk about something like that, the harder it becomes.'

'Do you think it affected us more than we thought?' I asked. 'Do you think we skimmed over it all too lightly? I wonder if we should have carried on with the counselling.'

'I think the answer is probably yes, Pete. But it's too late now. It's done. It was a different time and we were different people back then. And you might have a child already. I know you've convinced yourself it's Jem's, but what if it is yours? What if you are a dad? You'd still be a lucky devil, if you ask me.'

I did have a tendency to focus on the negative. Alex was right, this could all work out well for me. Once again, it depended on finding Meg. She wanted to get in touch with me now, and that was good.

'Shall we get a taxi?' I asked.

'Yes. And I'm taking care of the fare!' Alex replied.

As we walked down the stairs to meet the taxi, we passed the little shit from the upper floor.

'Was that the pleece?' he asked, not even bothering to say hello. 'I know the pleece when I see 'em. Was she askin' about me? What did the stupid bird 'ave to say?'

I felt as if I'd walked onto the set of EastEnders. I'd never heard him speaking at a normal level. Shouting was his default volume.

'Yes, she was from the police,' I said, and then the devil in me made me follow up with a little lie. I wanted to piss off the little git.

'She was responding to complaints from the neighbours about shouting. There are concerns about somebody getting a bit physical with their partner. I didn't say anything, of course. I don't need to say anything, do I?'

I hoped I was doing his girlfriend a favour. Even if he played a bit nicer for a few days, it might help her.

'Fuckin' pigs!' was all I got, and he stomped up the stairs.

'You shouldn't have said that,' Alex said. 'That poor girl has to take control of the situation herself. She'll have to walk away from it. There's nothing you can do. She'll keep going back to him until he finally grinds her down.'

I knew she was right, but I wanted to help her. Short of kicking the shit out of that guy, any attempt at which was unlikely to end well for me, I'd just have to let it run on.

I'd passed Ivy's many a time but I was completely blind to it. Now a coffee shop, it looked like it had started life as a run-of-the-mill café. It wasn't the kind of place that I'd frequent, so I'd blanked it out.

'Shall we get a drink?' I asked Alex. 'My leg is hurting after being crammed in the back of that car, and I could do with a sit down.'

We placed our orders and looked around the place. The proprietor was called Ivy Davies. I wondered if she was an absent owner or if she actually worked there. The girl that had served us was young, eighteen or nineteen maybe, she seemed a bit vague to be of any help.

I checked my phone.

'Can you see a Wi-Fi code anywhere?' I asked.

'There's a sign by the counter. You have to ask for the code,' Alex replied, pointing to the location of the poster.

I walked up to the counter, my leg still sore, and asked the girl for the code.

'I'll have to check,' she said.

She poked her head around the swing door to the kitchen.

'Ivy, there's a man out here wants to know the password for the internet. What is it?'

I heard a 'Just one moment, luv!' from the kitchen, and then a much older woman, probably in her mid-to-late sixties, stepped out of the kitchen, wiping her hands on a cloth.

'Are you the gentleman wanting the Wi-Fi password?' she asked.

I nodded. She beckoned me over and whispered the password conspiratorially.

'It's P-A-S-S-W-O-R-D,' she whispered, 'but keep that to yerself. We don't want any of those cider criminals hacking in or whatever it is they do.'

I almost burst out laughing, but managed to keep a straight face. I suspected that the Russians would have already managed to infiltrate the coffee shop's security systems.

'Are you Ivy Davies?' I asked, eager to get back to the table to share my new password anecdote with Alex.

'Yes, that's me. Can I help you?'

'I was supposed to meet a lady called Meg Bailey here last Wednesday. You might know her as Meg Yates. Do you know her? Is she a regular here?'

Ivy looked blank for a few moments. Then her eyes lit up.

'You mean Meg Stewart. Yes, I know Meggy. I've known Meggy since she was a teenager. You're not the reason she was so upset last week, are you?'

'I think I might be. We were supposed to meet here last Wednesday, only I didn't get her message. Do you know where she lives? I want to get in touch with her.'

Ivy's expression changed.

'You're not one of those reporter fellows who come round here fishing for information, are you? If you are, you can buzz off now. I don't want you troubling Meggy anymore. She's had quite enough of your type!'

'No, honestly, I'm Meg's husband, Pete – or Peter. Did she mention me?'

'I learned a long time ago not to pry into Meggy's private life, and if you ask me, a lot of folks these days would do well to follow her lead. But she didn't mention any husband. What did you say your name was? Peter, was it? The only person I ever heard her talk about that that young David, the poor boy who hanged himself. That was a terrible business. And her so young, too.'

I nodded. I hadn't a clue what she was talking about, but thought it was probably one of the lads who'd died at the home, perhaps even the boy that DCI Summers had mentioned.

'Would you be prepared to give her a message from me? If I leave my address and contact details, would you pass it onto her?'

I leant over the counter to grab the pen left by the waitress and scribbled my details onto a paper napkin. I handed it to Ivy who studied it.

'Ooh, that's a rough spot if you're living there. Full of unemployed people who don't want to do a day's work. I'm not so sure I'd want her walking around there with that new baby of hers. Gorgeous little thing he is.'

I sensed Alex looking over in my direction. She was clearly dying to know what we'd been talking about.

'What's the baby's name?' I asked.

'Tommy – Tom, she called him. After her father. Now that was a sorry affair too. Poor girl. I hope you're not going to be causing her any trouble, not now she's found that young man and all?'

'Who's that?' I asked, suddenly jealous and concerned. Had Meg moved on? Already?

'Some lovely young fellow. Local he is. Doing very well for himself. He's a lawyer or a solicitor or something legal like that. They came in here holding hands only a few weeks ago. She looks so happy with him. I love to see Meggy happy. She's had so much go on in her life.'

'It's really important that I speak to Meg, and please, believe me, she does want to speak to me.'

Ivy placed the napkin in one of the pockets of her apron. I hoped it wasn't about to end up in the bin.

'You don't know where Meg lives now, do you?' I asked, trying my luck one last time.

'No. I know it's out of town – she uses the trams to come in and out of the centre – but I don't know her address. I wouldn't know that kind of thing. Mind you, I've known Meggy ever since she was a young 'un and had a big bust up with that fat girl. I never saw that one in here ever again – she didn't half upset little Meggy that day.'

I thanked Ivy and limped my way back to the table. The pain in my leg was intermittent, but I'd been standing on it for ten minutes while we chatted. I was pleased to be sitting down again.

'Anything useful?' Alex asked.

'I'm not sure,' I replied. 'I keep getting glimpses into a life that I knew nothing about. Ivy has known Meg since she was a girl. How can you be married to someone so long and yet know so little about them?'

'I saw you give her your contact details. I take it she doesn't know where Meg lives?'

'No, Meg is just a customer that Ivy's known for ages. I know the name of the baby though. Tom. Same as her dad. Doesn't that strike you as unusual? I got the impression from speaking to other people that she was angry with her dad. Why would she give the baby his name?'

'Who knows, Pete? Not much of this makes any sense to me. She's a cagey one alright, your wife. I'm as caught up in all this as you are ... What's wrong? She told you something else, didn't she?'

I paused a while. I wasn't even sure what I thought about it yet, let alone being able to articulate it to anybody else. I took a sip of my drink, my mouth was dry.

'I think I know why she wants to see me now. I think she wants to move on. She's found some new guy down here. Ivy was talking about him. It looks like they've made a life together. I saw him with her on the tram. They looked like a couple. They were chatting and laughing. I think it's over, Alex. I'm sure she wants to tell me that we're over.'

CHAPTER THIRTEEN

1993 Tom thought long and hard about the threats from Tony Dodds and Russell Black. He'd never experienced a level of violence like that in his life. He kept out of the way of Mavis, Meg and Hannah for the rest of the day. It wasn't difficult. Meg and Hannah had made themselves scarce too.

'What was that about?' Mavis had asked when he put down the phone. 'Sunday morning's a funny time to call.'

'It's nothing, just an update on the inquiry. I'm not really sure why he rang.'

'Something's up,' Mavis probed. 'You were twisting and turning all night in bed, and it's not like you to lie in so late on a Sunday. It's like having a third teenager in the house!'

Tom laughed at that one, deciding that being non-committal was the best course of action.

'Will you sort out that pilot light on the gas heater, by the way? It's a devil to light. I've been using matches. I hate the way the gas whooshes when you light it – I'd rather the pilot was fixed properly.'

'I'll take a look. It's getting chilly again, so it's going to be on a lot more now. I'll get to it after my bath.'

Whichever way Tom framed it in his head, he'd be letting the girls down. If he ignored the threats and gave his evidence anyway, they'd stitch him up and take the girls away. If he followed Bob's course and withdrew his claims, he'd be letting down all the children in the home – he'd be letting his own girls down. But what was the alternative? Sending them back to the children's home, where it could happen again?

The truth was, without Bob's evidence, the case would be flimsy anyway. What had Tom seen? Nothing, really. He just had a feeling that things were going on. There was a real danger that they'd laugh at him.

Back at work on the Monday, he sneaked off at his break to enjoy a cigarette in the den. He'd given up smoking a long time ago, at the request of Mavis.

'When we have children in the house, I don't want you blowing that disgusting smoke all over the place. And think of your health!'

It had been tough quitting, but he never regretted it. However, with the stress of the responsibility now resting at his feet, it had seemed as natural as anything to buy a packet of ten Embassy from the newsagent when he picked up his morning paper.

He'd been looking forward to this all day. To reach the den, he had to climb over the fence into the wooded grounds behind the house. The woods still belonged to the property, but they were largely unused. It was the children who'd first told him about the den. They confided in him. He loved that. He knew that they'd sneak off there to be alone, to meet with boyfriends and girlfriends, to have a smoke. He kept their secret; they were in that home all day, and everybody needs a bolthole. Besides, it was part of the grounds, it wasn't as if it was hidden.

When he'd first found out about the den, he'd taken his toolbox over there after his shift ended to make sure that it was safe for them. It was an excellent place for children, a small Victorian redbrick structure built in the middle of the woods. Time had taken its toll, but it still had a roof on it, albeit one which was struggling to combat the ivy that was creeping all over it. Tom assumed it had been built for whoever managed the woodland when the children's home was an imposing family house. It was probably kept for saws, axes, barrows and the like. The Victorians knew how to do things properly; it even had a small chimney and iron stove.

Tom had checked the slates on the roof, inspected the woodwork and replaced the old wooden door with one that had been discarded in the home's workshop. He swept out the brick floor and even placed some old chairs and settee cushions in there to make it as comfortable as possible. It was a little gift to the children, a safe place that they could call their own, a den to play in when out in the woods.

Three years later, he was using it as his own retreat, a place of quiet where he could figure out his next move. Whatever he did next would cause repercussions, whichever way the wind blew. Tom lit his cigarette, took a long, deep drag and closed his eyes. He scanned the den. He'd been naive when he made that place so hospitable. He'd assumed that it would be used as an HQ in children's imaginary games or a mini youth club for the older kids. As he surveyed the collection of blankets and the old mattress that was propped against the wall, he realised that this was probably where Meg's child had been conceived.

Tom pondered about the baby for a moment. If they'd managed to adopt the girls earlier, he and Mavis would have loved to have had that baby in the house, and Meg wouldn't have been railroaded into giving up her child. It would have been lovely: two teenage girls and a baby in the house. What a perfect family. Not quite the order that it should have come in, but who cared?

He wondered how Meg felt about the baby. Poor girl. She was young, but she must have thought about the child. They never talked about stuff like that. They were still all getting to know each other. It was difficult with teenage girls. They were growing up, and they had their right to privacy. They didn't have the father–daughter relationship they'd have built up if they'd been Tom and Mavis's own kids. It was a day-by-day process; the trust was gradually building up.

Tom took another drag on the cigarette. There had to be a way through this which allowed him to keep the girls and to protect the children in the home. Tony Dodds and Russell Black had a lot to lose. It's why they were turning the thumbscrews and scaring the life out of anybody who could expose them. Would they negotiate?

Tom shuddered, thinking through how they'd threatened him at the quarry. He'd almost given himself up for dead. He pictured himself with his head dashed on the rocky floor below. He'd never been so scared in his life. He'd been convinced that they were going to drop him down there.

Then he saw it. There was a way that they could all get what they wanted from this: Gary Maxwell. They needed a fall guy. What if Gary Maxwell took the hit? Tom thought it through. The kids hated him. Tom wasn't sure what was going on at night but whatever it was he knew it was Gary Maxwell who was facilitating it. If Gary took all the blame, the inquiry would have its man – and Dodds and Black would walk away.

Would Dodds and Black go for it? He hardly dared to consider even talking to those men again, but it would protect the kids in the home. The new woman in charge was great, popular with the youngsters. It had changed the atmosphere in the home immediately.

What if Gary Maxwell never came back? That would give everybody what they wanted. It would protect Meg and Hannah from being taken back into care. It would protect the other youngsters from whatever was going on. And at least one of the shits who'd hurt the children might end up in jail. But Dodds and Black would be off the hook. Could he live with that? Tom took a long drag on his cigarette. It felt good to be smoking again after so long. Mavis would give him a hard time if she ever found out.

He'd need something more on Gary Maxwell. He hadn't seen Gary going out at night, so that might be a problem. It was time for a talk with the girls. Tom needed to find out what Gary Maxwell had been saying to Meg that night in the sick room. With any luck, they'd be able to find enough rope to hang him.

'He might just be a friend,' Alex suggested, doing her best to put my mind at ease.

'He looked very familiar to be a friend. The way he was helping with the baby and everything, he looked like he was installed to me.'

I looked at my smart phone. It's the curse of modern life, to be so attached to the darn things, but every bit of news that I received came through this small device.

'How did we ever do without smart phones?' I asked.

'When you and I were together, we couldn't even afford a home computer.'

Alex smiled, using the mention of phones to check out her own messages.

'It's my agent. I've got an offer of a new TV series. Bad Boys Gone Straight it's called. They want me to interview former gangland bosses and see how they've reformed. They reckon it will be a great vehicle for me after Crime Beaters.'

'Sounds more like a job for Ross Kemp to me. Are you going to take it?'

'They're offering a shedload of cash. They want to meet me for talks. What do you think?'

'It's nice to have people chasing you with work. It's up to you. I thought you were considering staying in Spain.'

'I am. I'm tempted, but I want to see how things work out here first. I'm not going to pretend, Pete. You know I want us to get together again. You were the only guy I ever loved ...'

She'd said it. I looked at her, searching her face. She meant every word. I could see that. My phone made a sound and it gave me the excuse to look away. Why confront the issue when it can be avoided?

'It's Hannah,' I said. 'She's in Blackpool. Wants to meet with us. She's suggesting Blackpool Zoo.'

'That's a bit odd. It's out of town, isn't it? It seems an unusual place to arrange a meeting.'

I tapped a reply into Skype and Hannah got straight back to me.

'She says she's staying out that way and doesn't have a car. She's nervous about the press coverage over the bodies. I hadn't thought about that. It's fair enough, I guess. She was in that home with Meg. I might be jittery about being spotted too.'

'Okay, but your car is still parked up over the other end of town. Can we walk it from here? When does she want to meet up?'

'It's no more than an hour on foot and we can go through Stanley Park. You'll love that, it's great. Although my leg is still playing me up – I'm not sure if I'm up for it.'

'What time can she get there?' Alex asked.

'She's saying two o'clock, so we've got some time to kill. How about we take our time walking and if my leg gives me too much aggro we'll call a taxi? The doctor told me I should exercise as much as I can.'

'Okay, let's do it!' Alex said, getting up and leaving a ten pound note on the table as a tip.

'That will make sure that Ivy remembers us,' she smiled. 'The minute Meg comes back here, we need to know about it. It feels as if we're so close now, Pete. She can't hide forever in a town this size.'

We made our way through the town centre and were soon walking through the grounds. Alex loved the Italian gardens and the Art Deco styling. I had to stop for a moment. My leg was sore and I wasn't sure I'd make it beyond the limits of the park.

'You know what you said earlier?' I ventured, as we watched the water cascading in the fountain.

'I meant it, you know. We've known each other long enough now to be honest. It was the worst thing I ever did heading off to London. It may look glamorous and it's helped me put some money away, but it's all meaningless. Without someone to share it with, it's pointless.'

'You know I've always loved you, Alex.' This was rare

exposure from me. 'We always got on – we still do, but you do understand that I have to deal with Meg first?'

'How do you feel about her now?' Alex asked, running her hand through the water in the fountain.

'It's difficult. I don't know if I'm in love with the memory of being in love or if I really do still love her. We haven't seen each other for a year. My life has adjusted to being without her. I need to see her to sort out the mortgage and our finances, but it's not just that. And there's the baby. I have to know if the baby is mine. If nothing else, we were in love when the baby was conceived.'

'I get it. I understand. I'm here for you, always. I know we can't just pick up where we left off, but it feels as ... comfortable ... It feels as comfortable as it ever did between us. You must feel that?'

'Of course I do. I love us being together, but there have been two loves in my life and I can't easily separate the two. Meg is my wife and if she wants us to get back together – if the baby is ours – you know I owe it to them both to try again. It's difficult to see how we can step beyond all these things that have happened now. And ...'

'What?' Alex asked.

'It's nothing, I was just thinking about something.'

'Tell me,' Alex urged. 'Remember what Steven Terry said: you need to start being more honest.'

'You know after Jem and Sally's deaths?' I began slowly, wondering if I should share this information with Alex. 'I met Meg one last time in the graveyard. It was after the funeral. She knew she'd find me there.'

'You never told me this,' Alex replied. 'What did she say? I thought you'd gone your separate ways when you were released from hospital.'

'Not quite. I saw her one last time. She wanted to tell

me something – something she wanted me to know, because she trusted me.'

'Go on. You've got to tell me now, Pete. You can't just tease me with that information.'

'Remember Ellie's stalker, that Tony Miller guy? You know that all of the deaths were attributed to Sally?'

I think that Alex could sense where I was going.

'It was Meg who killed Tony. She admitted it to me in the cemetery. The police assumed Sally had done it; there was so much blood in the house at the time. But it was Meg.'

'And the police didn't figure it out?' Alex asked.

'No, how could they? All the witnesses were dead, the crime scene was messed up by yours truly, and both Meg and Sally were covered in Tony's blood. Meg told them Sally had made her help her to move the body onto our bed. It was an easy cover.'

'Why did she do it? Did she tell you that?'

'He'd tried to sexually assault her. He didn't do it, but he'd started to put his hands in places where he shouldn't ...'

I stopped for a moment, suddenly filled with rage. I felt angry that he'd dared to do that to my wife. The fucker deserved to die. I'd have probably done it myself if I'd been there.

'So it was self-defence then?' Alex asked.

'Yes, of course,' I replied. 'He'd been touching her up and making threats. She'd already seen him kill that poor lad in the hotel. She grabbed the kitchen knife while he was having a pee and stuck it in him. She made certain he was dead – I saw the body. There was no way he was getting up again.'

'They said it was a frenzied attack at the time, didn't they? Meg might have a problem using self-defence if she made a mess of him like that. Do you think that's why she hid it from the police?'

'I don't know,' I said, thinking it through. 'Maybe it was easier to misdirect the police to make them think that Sally had done it. It's really shitty for Sally's kids. It's enough to know that she killed their father and Jason Davies ... Sorry, I know you're still sensitive about that one.'

'Less so now we've met his brother and I've had time to explain myself to him. I'm getting over it. It's not every day you send a man to his death, you know.'

I only just made it to the edge of the park before I had to admit defeat and call a taxi. There wasn't even that far to go to reach the zoo, but I was beginning to think better of my decision to walk.

'So much for doctor's orders,' I cursed as a spasm shot through my leg.

'Serves you right for being an arse and jumping off the top of a bus. Leave the tough guy stuff to the superheroes.'

She had a point. I wasn't cut out for all the leaping around and daredevil stuff. I was relieved to get in the taxi and take the weight off my leg at last.

'You won't believe the news!' the taxi driver piped up.

Oh no, a talker. I'd hoped he'd leave us in peace. I looked at Alex to help me out.

'What's going on?'

'There's been another death. They're not saying it's a murder, but if you ask me it's all connected.'

My ears pricked up immediately.

'There,' he said, pointing to an A-board outside a corner shop.

Third Woodlands Edge Death Shock it read.

'Who is it?' I asked.

'That lollipop man. Bob whatever-his-name-is.'

I skipped a breath, and felt a sickening feeling in my stomach.

'You're kidding.'

'No, they just flashed it on the radio news. You're that Peter Bailey fella, aren't you? I recognised your voice straight away. I have the radio on in here all day. I knew it was you as soon as you started speaking. And you're that Alex Kennedy off the telly, aren't you? I recognised you too. I love that *Crime Beaters* show.'

'What happened?' Alex asked. She was as shocked by the news as I was.

'Hit-and-run driver!' came the reply. 'Don't you listen to that radio station of yours, Peter? They had all the details on the one o'clock news. It was early this morning that it happened, before the kids started coming to school. Poor bugger got hit while he was getting ready for work. Killed instantly he was.'

'I was only talking to him yesterday,' Alex whispered. 'You know this involves us now. Do you think it was an accident?'

'Normally I'd say yes, but with my track record recently, I'd say it's connected to the murders. You saw Bob yesterday, he's on and off that road all morning. If you wanted to knock him down before the traffic picked up for the morning rush, it'd be easy.'

'Are the police linking it to the other murders?' Alex shouted over the crackling radio.

No!' the driver replied. 'They're saying that he used to work at the home, but it's an accident they reckon.'

210 PAUL J. TEAGUE

We were only a few minutes in the car. Alex paid our fare and tipped the driver.

'I will pay you back for all this,' I said. 'When I get sorted with Meg and the money is flowing again, I'll treat you to something to say thank you. I appreciate it.'

We'd been dropped outside the zoo. We didn't have to pay to get in, I'd arranged to meet Hannah at the cafeteria by the entrance.

'I'm not really up for a walk around. Are you okay if we sit here?' I asked Alex. 'I'm shocked at Bob's death. There's no way that's a coincidence, not with Tony Dodds and Ray Matiz dying too. Someone has been settling old scores. The police must know that. I'm going to text Kate Summers and see if she knows anything.'

I sent a message to DCI Summers, hoping she'd pick it up and play ball with us. It wasn't her case, so perhaps she'd be willing to talk more freely about it.

'Is that Hannah?'

Alex tensed suddenly. She'd been resting her legs too. She'd been looking along the long walkway which served as a way into the zoo, watching for somebody who might be Hannah.

'Yes, that's her. Who was she talking to?'

'I can't see. Some older guy by the look of it. Probably asking her where the loos are. They seem quite chatty.'

Hannah approached us. She recognised me straight-away. I greeted her and then introduced Alex.

'This is my friend Alex Kennedy,' I said. 'She knows all about you – it's high time you two met.'

Hannah sat opposite us at the table.

'What brings you back to the UK?' I asked to get the conversation going.

'I had some, er, money things to deal with. I still bank over here. The exchange rate has been suffering a bit recently. I needed to sign some paperwork to shuffle a bit of money around. You know how it is.'

I nodded, but I didn't know how it was. I had no money to shuffle around. Hannah looked paler than usual. The last time I'd seen her, she'd clearly been benefitting from the brightness of the Alicante sun.

'You look like you've just suffered through a British summer,' I observed. 'You're barely more tanned than I am.' I laughed at my own joke, but it appeared to annoy Hannah.

'I've heard from Meg at last,' I said to break the awkwardness. 'I'm finally going to get the chance to catch up with her. You've come here at the right time. I'm certain she'll want to see you.'

Hannah perked up at this news. Have you met with her yet? What did she have to say?'

'We missed her,' Alex chimed in. 'Pete got the postcard too late and we're trying to rearrange a meeting. He saw her too. That's how he messed himself up like that.'

'I can see you've been in the wars,' Hannah replied. 'Though to be honest, Pete, you don't seem to be able to stay out of trouble.'

I decided to venture onto delicate territory.

'Have you seen the murders that have been taking place? You must have spotted the story: Tony Dodds, Ray Matiz, and now Bob Taylor. They're all connected with the home that you and Meg lived in, aren't they?'

I watched as Hannah's face changed. There was still pain here for her, and anger too by the look of things. She modified her expression and tried to look calm.

'I've seen it, yes. It's a terrible business. Bob Taylor

particularly. He was a nice guy. I didn't know the others. He must have been quite an age.'

'What do you think is going on?' Alex asked.

'Who knows?' Hannah answered, keen to get off the topic. 'I'll be pleased if I never hear of that place again. When do you think you'll see Meg?'

'As soon as possible. I've left my details at Ivy's coffee shop in town. It was – is – a favourite haunt of Meg's apparently. She's in there quite regularly, so in the next day or two, I hope. Are you around long enough to catch her?'

'I'll stay as long as it takes,' Hannah replied. 'I haven't seen Meg in years and I'm desperate to catch up with her again. She just disappeared off the face of the earth. I'm as excited as you are to see her again.'

'Where are you staying?' I asked. 'So I know where to find you when I finally reach her.'

Hannah shifted her weight on the plastic seat.

'I don't remember the name of the place, but it's ten minutes' walk from here. This seemed the best place to meet. Blackpool has changed so much, but you can always rely on the zoo as a landmark. Skype me if you hear anything. I'm always around.'

'What are your plans now you're here?' Alex asked.

'I've done what I needed to do, so as soon as I find Meg I'll be out of the country again. I'll fly from Manchester to Alicante.'

'The minute we hear from Meg, I'll let you know,' I promised. 'Are you sure you can't remember the name of your hotel? Is it part of a chain?'

'No, I'm sorry, I just checked in off the street. It's got some weird name, something like Seaside Retreat. I'm sorry, I didn't even notice the name of the road. I lived here long enough, I ought to remember things like this a bit better.'

'Okay, look, it's good to see you again, Hannah. I'm sure that it's going to give Meg quite a shock to find out that we're all gathering here on her behalf. As soon as I hear anything, I promise I'll be in touch.'

Hannah said her goodbyes, and then headed off back into the zoo.

'You know the exit is this way, don't you?' I asked.

'Oh yes, I know. I'm going to have a look around. I ... um ... used to know somebody who worked here. I want to see if he's still here.'

'Okay, see you later,' I said, getting up to leave.

'Mind if we get home now, Alex?' I said. 'I want to spend the evening sitting on the sofa watching TV.'

'She dyes her hair, you know,' Alex said suddenly.

'What?' I asked. 'Does it matter? That's a bit catty for you, isn't it?'

'Just an observation. You'd never notice something like that. I bet you can't even tell that I dye the grey away either, can you?'

I looked at Alex's hair.

'I hadn't got a clue,' I replied. 'I don't notice that sort of thing unless it's done badly or is a weird colour. We're all getting on a bit – she's entitled to dye her hair, you know.'

My phone rang.

'Can you call a taxi while I'm answering this?' I asked. 'It's Kate Summers.'

Alex nodded and stepped well away from me so we wouldn't interrupt each other's conversations.

'Hi, DCI Summers. I didn't expect to hear from you so soon. Are you back home now?'

'Hi, Mr Bailey. No, I'm still in Blackpool. If my kids ever see me again it'll be a miracle.'

'Mr Bailey, that's a bit formal. Is something up?'

'Yes, Pete, it is. I asked you to keep out of trouble, didn't I? And yet here I am calling you on police business again. It's a good job I was down here or you'd have every bobby in the place looking for you.'

'Oh hell, what have I done now? It's nothing to do with jumping from the tram, is it?'

'If only!' Kate replied. 'It's nothing to do with that. Have you seen that there's been another death related to the children's home? They only just released the information to the press. They're not officially calling it a murder ... yet.'

'I know about it, yes. What's it got to do with me?'

'I said I'd call you in for questioning. You don't half land yourself in it sometimes. Every person on the street has pointed the finger at you. Your car has been parked near June Dodds' house for the past two days. You were spotted talking to Bob yesterday. They've got you marked out as a potential suspect.'

CHAPTER FOURTEEN

1993 It was Meg who provided the opportunity that Tom was looking for. It didn't arrive in the way that he would have liked, but it gave him the result he wanted.

Tom was working on the gas heater in the living room. Full central heating was something they still aspired to in their terrace, but much of the downstairs space could be kept at a tolerable temperature by leaving the gas heater on during the day. He was used to getting his tools and fixing household appliances. He'd do anything to avoid having to replace them from new.

He could tell that Meg wanted to say something. Mavis had gone to the corner shop and Hannah was upstairs in her bedroom listening to music on her headphones.

'That was Mr Taylor on the phone earlier, wasn't it? Why do you keep talking to him?'

'That was a private conversation, Meg. How did you hear what was being said?'

'I was sitting at the top of the stairs listening. The phone woke me up. What did he have to say?'

'Nothing much. He was calling for a chat.'

Tom busied himself with the repair. He could see that the pilot light was causing problems again; he'd patched it up several times now. Eventually the heater would need to be replaced, but if he could just nurse it through one more winter.

'I could tell from the tone of your voice that it wasn't nothing!' Meg shouted at him. 'Don't lie to me. What did he say? You're backing down, aren't you? They got to you too and you're backing down!'

'What do you mean, they got to me *too*? Have they spoken to you? What have they been doing?'

Tom felt a sharp burst of anger and helplessness. He was taken aback by the sight of a furious teenager screaming at him. He'd seen the girls in sullen moods before, and sometimes they could be offhand, but he'd never had to deal with this.

Meg quietened. Her eyes began to redden as she fought back her tears of frustration.

'Of course they threatened us! It's what they do, it's what they always do. That's how it works. Don't you get it? We can't touch them. They do what they want to us and we can't touch them!'

Tom put down his screwdriver and stood up. For the first time he saw his fiery daughter for the vulnerable young girl that she was. The girls had developed a cocksure way about them in the home. It was a defence mechanism, geared to pushing everyone away and keeping a distance. It was the natural consequence of never knowing what changes were going to disrupt your life next.

'They've messed up my life. They took my baby. They did those ... they did those things to me. I hate them. They've got to pay for what they did. They can't get away with it!'

It was Tom's eyes which teared up now. Meg had never opened up to him like this. As he watched her standing at the bottom of the stairs, he knew that these had been no harmless parties. He'd hoped that perhaps it had only been a bit of fun – underage drinking and maybe some gambling. But as he looked at his adopted daughter, her face flushed and tears now streaming from her eyes, he finally understood the gravity of the decision that he would have to make.

'Come and sit on the sofa with me, Meg.'

She moved over from the stairs and they sat on the settee, one at either end.

'We're going to have to withdraw our claims. Bob Taylor was scared off. I ... I was threatened too. They're powerful people, Meg. They can take you and Hannah away from us. Russell Black has the power to do what he wants, and he's got the back-up of that bastard Tony Dodds. I don't know what to do, Meg. Tell me what you want me to do.'

She stood up again and shouted at him.

'You're supposed to be my dad! You're supposed to protect me! What can I do? I'm just a bloody child – nobody has ever listened to me. I want you to kill those men. I want them dead. That's what I want!'

Tom considered trying to calm her down, but thought he'd probably exacerbate the situation. She needed to let this out.

'Don't just sit there. I know you saw what was going on. I know you heard Gary Maxwell that night when you were shuffling around in the store cupboard. And you let them take us. You watched them as they took us. I'll never forgive you for that. You could have done something and you just watched!'

Meg was screaming now. Tom had known that

teenagers could be a handful – they'd been guided through the issues before they adopted the girls – but he'd never seen anger like it. She moved over towards the heater and began to kick at the tools and parts that were scattered on the floor.

'Meg, I need you to calm down. Look, there's a way out of this. I need to know about Gary Maxwell. Is there anything you can tell me about him? I think we can make him pay, at least.'

'I want all of them to suffer! They took my baby, they did those horrible things to us – they killed David. They didn't hand him the rope, but they might as well have. I loved him! We didn't have much to love in that bloody place, but he made it better. He made it bearable for me. And they killed him!'

Signs of affection were still rare between Tom and the girls. It wasn't that he didn't feel a growing love for them every day, but they were young women, and he was still uncertain of his place as their father. He desperately wanted to put his arms around Meg, to hold her tight and to help to take the pain away. But he couldn't. He feared she'd reject him. If he'd been their natural father, he'd know the girls, they'd trust him, and they'd have grown up knowing him as point of safety in their lives. But as it was, they were still learning to be comfortable with each other.

He tried again.

'Meg, what can you tell me about Gary Maxwell? Is there anything that we can say to get him permanently removed from the home?'

She kicked the pipework by the heater several times. It was as if she were exorcising some demon which had taken residence in her body: the shame, the powerlessness and the inability to even begin to express what had happened to her.

She thumped the wall and her knuckles began to bleed. She quietened, the physical pain distracting her from the agony that she had bottled up inside.

'Come here. Sit down and let me look at that.'

Meg grew calmer and sat closer to Tom this time. She held out her bloodied hand. Tom went into the kitchen and returned with some cotton wool which he'd soaked in cold water. He dabbed gently at the broken skin. She let him take her hand as he tended to her wounds.

It was a small thing, but he cherished that moment. She was letting him in, just a little way, but she was allowing him to help her. She wasn't ready to treat him as her father yet. She didn't know what that was like, she'd been in care so long, but she was sore and upset and in that moment she accepted his help.

As Tom applied antiseptic cream gently to the broken skin, Meg began to speak.

'Don't ever talk to Mavis – to Mum – about this. It would kill her. This has to stay between you and me. But I want you to get Gary Maxwell. I hate that man. He took my baby and he drove my boyfriend to his death. He made our lives miserable. He was the one who let them take us. Without that monster, they couldn't have done anything. They couldn't have harmed us. I want them all dead, but I want him punished most of all.'

Tom let her speak. He hoped that Mavis would not return home. If she did, Meg would clam up once again and this moment would be over.

'I can't talk about this. Please don't make me tell them what happened. I'm too ashamed. I hate myself. I should have fought back. I could have done more, but I let them take me. I was so scared. I didn't know what to do.'

Tom squeezed her hand now. Meg let him.

'When I was sharing a room with Debbie Simmonds, Gary Maxwell would come in at night. I'd have to pretend to be asleep while they ... while they ... did what they did. She wanted it. But she's a child, we're all just kids. It's not right. Debbie Simmonds was the one that he liked. Everybody else thought she was fat and a bit ugly, but she and Gary Maxwell ... it was horrible. I can't speak about the other stuff, but if I have to, I'll tell them that. I'll tell them what he was doing with Debbie Simmonds. That will hurt him, won't it? They can sack him for that?'

Tom wanted to cry for his daughter. She wasn't ready to think of him as her father yet, but as he held her hand he knew that he loved his adopted children and that he would do what he could to protect them and keep the family together.

He was too insignificant, too powerless to confront Tony Dodds and Russell Black on his own, but if he could at least stop Gary Maxwell he'd have given his daughters some form of revenge. And he could prevent it happening again at the home.

The front door opened and Mavis walked into the house with two carrier bags packed with groceries. She put them down in the hallway and walked into the lounge. Immediately she saw the red streak of blood on the plain wall where Meg had hurt her knuckles. She looked between Tom and Meg and at the mess on the floor where tools and parts had been kicked around.

'Is somebody hurt?' she asked. 'We'll need to see if we can make that better.'

I'd spent far too much time in police stations in the past

year. I'd be grateful to never step inside one again. But I wasn't concerned about being called in to account for my whereabouts and the reason that my car was parked along the road from June Dodds' house. Of course they had to interview me. DCI Summers had already been called in because of the loose connection with Meg through the children's home. This still didn't feel like my problem. In spite of the three deaths, I had convinced myself that it only had a cursory link to me. I was so wrong.

My car had been towed away. It looked as if Alex would be paying for taxi fares a while longer. It would be released to me eventually, but for now it was impounded while they did whatever checks they had to do.

I was grateful to DCI Summers who came to meet me at the desk in the police station and accompanied me to an interview room. This wasn't her case so she had to stay out of it, but it was nice of her to see me and get me a decent cup of tea before we began the questioning again.

It's no problem being questioned when you have nothing to hide. I thought back to when I'd slept with Ellie and I'd had to avoid giving the full truth. I'd been terrified that Meg would get to learn of my infidelity and I was desperate to hide what I'd done, through shame as much as fear.

This time it was a simple case of explaining why we'd been talking to Bob Taylor. They knew I was a journalist, and Alex came with me to corroborate my story. We were done in an hour and DCI Summers was waiting for us after we'd given our statements.

'Are you ever going to get back to that family of yours?' I asked as we began the walk down the long corridor.

'Not at this rate,' she replied. 'I've had to stay on another day.'

'That doesn't sound very good,' Alex chipped in. 'You're only here because of the connection with Meg, aren't you?'

DCI Summers stopped and turned to face us.

'Come on, Alex, Pete. You know I can't discuss case details. Let's just say that I'm needed down here for a while longer. And please stay out of trouble. I've known criminals who keep a lower profile than you two.'

We walked to the end of the corridor and she opened the door to the waiting area. There was some altercation going on, but it wasn't with a yob or a drunk. The guy who was protesting was tall, had well-cut hair and was dressed in a suit. His voice was confident and authoritative, and he was actually scolding the police officers who were escorting him into the building. He was there voluntarily like us – there were no cuffs and no force was being used. I marked him out immediately as a pompous, arrogant arsehole.

'I'd like a coffee please, and none of that machine crap. Get me a double espresso with brown sugar, not white!'

He had an air of power and authority about him. He was used to being listened to and obeyed. The accompanying officers looked flustered, out of their depth, even servile in this man's presence.

'Yes, Mr Black, we'll do what we can. If you'd be kind enough to step this way.'

They exited through the same door that we'd come through. With the man now gone, it felt as if there was a vacuum in the room.

'Was that Russell Black?' I asked.

'It was,' DCI Summers replied, looking around to see who was in the waiting room. She moved in close.

'And what a right little twat he is!'

I was taken aback by the language. She'd been so professional in her dealings with us, but she'd let her guard down.

'DCI Summers, I do hope that you don't use language like that in front of those children of yours?'

'He's a nasty little man. He's been in a few times. He's semi-retired and part of the inspectorate these days. Part-time work for five times the salary, you know the sort of thing. He has this aura about him. I've dealt with some hard cases in my time, but this guy is something else.'

'I guess we don't need to ask why he's here,' said Alex. 'Don't tell me ... you can't discuss case details.'

'It's fairly obvious, isn't it? With all the deaths related to that children's home. Let's say he's helping them with their enquiries. If ever there was a case for police brutality in the cells, that's it. Please don't quote me on that. I need this job and I have mouths to feed.'

'Your secret is safe with us,' I smiled. 'I don't think I've ever seen anything like that. It was as if Cruella De Vil had walked into the building. And he was the head of social services? God help us all.'

We said our farewells to DCI Summers and took a seat in the waiting room.

'Okay if we go home now? My leg is killing me,' I said. 'We'll need to call another taxi. We might as well wait in the warm.'

I took my phone out of my pocket and powered it up. I'd had it switched off during the interview.

'Bollocks!' I cursed. 'I missed a call from Meg. She's left a voicemail. Damn it!'

I keyed my PIN into the phone and played back the message.

The waiting room was empty so I put it on speaker. There was hesitation at first. Meg and I hadn't spoken for a year – where do you begin?

'Pete ... hi ... I'd hoped I'd get through to you directly.

Look, I know you're in Blackpool. We've got to talk things over. I'm sorry I disappeared like that, but I ... I had things to do. Things from my past. I had to sort stuff out.'

There was another pause. I could hear a man's voice in the background and a baby gurgling happily. Whatever was going on, he was making the baby laugh. I cursed him. That's all I needed, some new man on the scene, getting in the way, making things even more complicated. She might have held off until we'd had time to talk, to get things sorted out.

'This is difficult, Pete. Look, we need to meet up. Ivy gave me your details. If you get this in time, I'll be in town until closing time – I've got some things I have to do. I'll be at Ivy's at five-thirty. If you can make it, meet me there. If you can't, call me back. See you soon, Pete ...'

There was a hesitation. More silence. Then she ended the call. I looked at the clock which was hanging on the wall above the reception desk. It was 5:10pm. If we rushed, we'd make it to Ivy's in time.

***

'You need to go alone,' Alex said after the message had finished playing in full. 'I'm not coming with you.'

'Yes, you're right. That's all we need at my grand reunion: the woman I spent five years of my life with and who was almost the mother of my baby. That's a great way to smooth things over with Meg. See? I am learning.'

'You need to stop making wisecracks and get over there fast, Pete. Don't miss her again. I'll call two taxis and you take the first one that comes.'

We moved out to the front of the police station. It was a twenty minute jog to the town centre, but my leg wasn't up to it. I'd have to take my chances with a taxi. I looked at the clock on my phone. Five minutes had passed already. I couldn't miss Meg again.

'How long did they say they'd take?' I asked Alex, agitated now.

'Up to twenty minutes. It's the end of the day, Pete – a terrible time to get a taxi.'

At that moment a cab came along the road. I couldn't see if it was full or empty.

'Fuck it!' I said and ran out into the road, putting my hand up into the air to show him I wanted him to stop – as if he was going to plough straight through me.

'Jesus, Pete!' Alex screamed at me from the safety of the pavement.

The driver had passengers, a young couple. I took a chance and opened the door.

'I have to get to the town centre before five-thirty. It's an emergency. I'll pay the full taxi fare for me and this couple, and I'll add a ten pound tip. That's how much I need to get there. Okay?'

'Get in!' the young woman in the back of the car said, smiling. I'd gambled on them being young and broke.

'Where to then?' the taxi driver asked, 'seeing as this appears to be a hijack?'

'Ivy's coffee shop. It's in the town centre.'

I slammed the door shut and we drove off. I could see as we departed that Alex was trying to get my attention. She was waving a couple of ten pound notes at me. Shit, I didn't have any cash. I had no intention of revealing my financial status to the taxi driver before we arrived at our destination. It would only be twenty or thirty quid. I'd pay it back as soon as I could.

We seemed to hit every red light on our way through

town. I watched the time ticking away on the dashboard clock. If my leg hadn't hurt so much, I'd have got out and run the rest of the way.

It was 5:28pm. I was exasperated and was getting ready to start swearing. I'd been stupid. I tried to ring Meg's number so that I could let her know I was on my way. I looked through my missed calls log. Damn it, it was a with-held number. She'd called from her house by the look of it. It wasn't a mobile phone that she'd used to get in touch.

I'd changed my phone since I'd last seen Meg. The crappy model that I'd had previously had been partly responsible for all the problems we'd had communicating after events unravelled the first time. I didn't have her new mobile number. I'd called the old one several times after I'd seen her for the last time, but that ship had sailed already.

An elderly couple crossing in front of us was the final straw. I try to be patient with old people. I always imagine it's my mum and endeavour to be kind, but I was all for running this pair down.

'I can't wait any longer!' I announced, opening the door.

'Hang on a minute, mate. You owe me a taxi fare!'

'I'll have to pay you later. I'm sorry, I have to go ...'

'Oi, come back here, you tosser.'

I threw my phone into the car.

'Take that as security. I'll come back and pay you, honestly!'

I ran off as fast as I could with a leg that felt as if it was about to drop off at any moment. I'd regret handing over my phone later, but I was making it up as I went along. At the time I didn't know how much I'd come to curse that impulsive action.

People were leaving work. The shops were emptying and my route along the pavement kept getting blocked. It had to be past five-thirty. How long would she hang on for me?

I needed to stop. I cursed my leg and my luck. What an idiot I'd been leaping off that open-top bus. What had I been thinking of? I was paying for my bad decision now. In fact, I'd been paying for my poor decisions for the past year.

I could see the light from Ivy's coffee shop in the distance. Almost there. I had to push through the pain in my leg. It was getting dark, the nights were closing in. If Meg disappeared into the darkness, I'd never find her. I was so close. I desperately wanted to see her. I could wait until the next day, but I'd had enough of the missed opportunities. This meeting had to happen now.

I stopped on the pavement across the road from Ivy's and I could see Meg standing outside by the window. She was still there, thank God. She hadn't changed. She was alone, with one hand on the pram handle, looking up and down the pavement. Was I about to meet my child? Or was this Jem's baby?

I became aware of a black car pulling out into the road and at the same time a taxi pulled into the vacant space. The car had a rental sticker in the back window. The driver did a dangerous turn in the road and pulled up right beside Meg. I was aware of somebody approaching me from behind. It was the taxi driver whose fare I'd just avoided paying.

'Oi, wanker, you can stick your phone. I want my fare or I'm calling the police.'

'Meg!' I shouted, but she couldn't hear me. I started to run across the road, regardless of what the traffic was doing. I didn't care.

A man got out of the black car, walked up to Meg and grabbed her by the arm. She let go of the pram handle and I could see her protesting. He manhandled her into the back of the vehicle before she realised what was happening. I ran up to the car as another vehicle swerved to avoid me. I banged on the window.

'Meg! Meg!'

He drove off at speed, ignoring me completely. I couldn't see much inside the car, the windows were tinted, and it was impossible in the poor light. But I did get a look at the man. I'd seen him before, but I couldn't place him. And I heard Meg screaming for the baby.

As the car drove off, I was about to run after it, in spite of the searing pain in my leg. I was stopped by a hand which would not release its grip.

'You owe me thirty pounds, wanker!'

CHAPTER FIFTEEN

1993 The gas heater on the living-room wall never did get properly fixed. What with the distraction of Meg's outburst and Mavis's inconvenient arrival back at the house, the mess was cleared up quickly and the job got put on hold for another time.

Tom and Meg never spoke about the details after that day. There was an understanding between the two of them about what had happened. The specifics didn't need to be discussed. It was too painful for Meg. She was embarrassed and ashamed, and she blocked it out until she was forced to think about it.

When she did remember what had happened in the home, it came washing over her as a rush of anxiety and for a moment she would feel as if her life were spiralling out of control. Then she would think about Hannah, Tom, Mavis and their new home. They were a family now and she was safe from that place. If they could punish Gary Maxwell and spare the other children in the home from his return, then at least some good might come out of things.

First Tom had to meet with Russell Black and Tony

Dodds. When they'd wanted to find him it had been simple enough, but for him to get a meeting with them was almost impossible. They were surrounded by gatekeepers and cronies. A man like Tom Yates, a handyman, had no sway.

So Tom found another way to get attention. It was playing with fire, he knew that. But there was only one way he could make the deal. When Bob Taylor withdrew from the case, claiming that he'd been mistaken and no longer wished to give any evidence, Tom held firm and said that he would continue, even though the likelihood of legal success was now slim. He knew that Dodds and Black would hear this news immediately and know that he'd ignored the warnings. It would result in the inevitable intervention. Tom prayed that the men would not simply grow impatient with him and arrange for an accident without further dialogue.

Sure as anything, the day after Tom had confirmed his willingness to proceed with his claims about what had been going on in the home, he was met from work by two shadowy figures. Tom had expected to be visited by Tony Dodds and Russell Black, but they'd sent two other men to do their dirty work.

'Thomas Yates, you need to get in the car,' said a man who was twice Tom's size and who had healing scabs on his knuckles.

'Who are you?' Tom asked. 'Have you been sent by Tony Dodds?'

'Just get in the car,' said the second, smaller man. Somehow he was more threatening. The bigger man looked as if he was the muscle, but the smaller man was the one who could hurt him most.

Tom had been caught off-guard. He'd expected Dodds and Black to do their own dirty work.

'Where are you taking me? I wanted to speak to Mr Dodds and Mr Black. I couldn't get an appointment. I needed to speak to them.'

Silence. They were driving him towards the seafront. At least they were public there. It wasn't too late, people were still about, but not many. It was a stormy, windy night, and the sea was wild and high, the waves powerful and deadly. They headed for Bispham and Cleveleys. It would be quieter there. Tom wondered how many places they had like this where they would take people who needed to be intimidated, away from the gaze of others.

They pulled up at a quiet spot on the beach. It was dark and Tom could hear the crashing of the waves. Another car was parked there, a black one. Tony Dodds and Russell Black stepped out when they saw that Tom had arrived. They were dressed for the cold. Both wore scarfs and warm woollen hats. Tom had no such protection, and the air from the sea was biting cold.

'We did ask you politely, Mr Yates,' Tony Dodds shouted over the howls of the wind, 'yet you persist in pushing forward your claims.'

'I'm afraid that it's time to end this now,' added Russell Black.

'By the way, we picked up another friend of yours,' Black continued, walking to the boot of the car. He opened it up. Meg was inside, her hands locked in a pair of police cuffs and her mouth covered with a strip of grey tape. Tom saw the terror in her eyes. How had they ever thought they could beat these men? In the safety of their living room, they had felt so sure. Yet here, in this deadly situation, they were nothing, they could do nothing.

'This ends tonight,' Tony Dodds said. 'You've taken up far too much of our time.'

He nodded at the bigger stooge, who walked over to the car boot and picked up Meg with one arm and dropped her to the ground. She flinched, but stood up and steadied herself on her feet.

'Such a shame,' Russell Black said, looking at Meg. 'A teenage daughter meets her father on the seafront to watch the crashing waves. The father walks too close to the sea, getting caught by the waves. The daughter, seeing her father in trouble, rushes to help, but is overpowered by the force of the sea. A tragic waste of life, but there have been so many warnings by the council to stay away from the sea when it's like this. And Simon here saw it all, but arrived too late to save either of you. Isn't that true, Simon?'

The smaller man nodded.

'It's a tragic waste of life. I tried my best, but the force of the sea at this time of year is just too dangerous. I called the police to help, and two officers arrived who commended my efforts to save you. Alas, there was nothing I could do.'

Meg struggled and Tom began to plead. This had gone terribly wrong. It wasn't how it was supposed to play out. He should have heeded Bob Taylor's warning, and now he'd involved Meg in all of this.

'Stop, listen. I only wanted a meeting with you. It's the only way I could get your attention. I want to make a deal.'

'Too late!' said Russell Black, and waved his hand towards the beach.

Simon took Tom by the arm. He tried to pull away but was stopped dead.

'If you struggle, we'll make it slow for your daughter. And we'll make you watch.'

He despised Russell Black. The man was evil.

What could he do? They were going to die, there on the beach. They were marched over towards the sea. The waves were wild and the noise was deafening. Tom was freezing, and Meg's face was white. The second thug removed the tape from Meg's mouth and unfastened the cuffs, handing them back with the key to Tony Dodds. He put them in his pocket.

'Send the girl in first,' he said to Simon. Simon nodded and the bigger man picked her up and threw her into the waves. Water splashed over Meg as she tried to steady herself and stand up. The waves crashed over her and she disappeared for a moment. The sea almost reached their feet and then drew back out, pulling her deeper into the water.

'No, stop!' Tom cried. The sound of powerful crashing water was so great that he could barely be heard. He tried to run towards the sea to save his daughter, but Simon restrained him, getting ready to thump him across the face.

'No violence!' Tony Dodds shouted. 'No bruises and no markings. This has to be an open-and-shut case of death by drowning.'

Still Tom struggled. He desperately looked out to sea to watch Meg flailing among the dark grey waves. She was struggling, fighting to stay upright. It was deathly cold. She'd been fully immersed, she had taken water into her lungs. It couldn't be long now.

Tom was shouting wildly at the men, desperate to do anything to save his daughter.

'We can sort this out, I'll do anything. Please, get her out of there. Please, I'll do anything!'

Meg looked like a scrap of rag bobbing about in the water. She couldn't survive much longer.

Tom was beginning to resign himself now to what was going to happen. He loathed himself for thinking that they could come up with a plan to stop these men. He let out a long, agonised cry as he watched Meg drop below the waves for the third time. The tears streaming from his eyes were immediately washed away by the force of the wind and the spray from the sea. It was as if the sea didn't care what he felt.

He thought it was over. He could feel Simon beginning to move him towards the waves. Then something happened that he could never have anticipated – something that would immediately turn the situation on its head.

'Look, will you just give me two minutes to sort myself out here?'

I could see that Ivy was turning off the lights in the shop and getting ready to lock up. The baby had been abandoned in the pram. It was in no immediate danger, but it was a little more pressing to me than that bloody taxi fare.

I'm not proud of what I did next, but I didn't feel that I had much choice at the time. The taxi driver would not let go of my arm. He was hanging on for dear life. It was thirty quid for Christ's sake. How bad could it be?

I'm not a violent man, but I pushed him to get his hand off my arm. He wasn't expecting it. He stumbled and fell into the path of a white van which screeched to a halt but hit him anyway.

In the confusion that followed, I slipped behind the gathering crowd to the pram where the baby lay asleep, tiny and wrapped up warmly in blankets. There was a little blue bunny toy resting by his head. He was beautiful. I could love that child, if he was mine or not.

I rushed over to Ivy who had just taken the key out of the door.

'Ivy, Ivy, it's me, Peter Bailey. Meg's in trouble. I need you to take the baby!'

She examined my face. I think she thought she was being mugged. I could hear the crowd at the accident scene growing restless. A tide of anger and indignation was beginning to surge through them.

'Who does he think he is anyway?'

'If it wasn't for scum like him, Blackpool would be a better place.'

I could sense that things were about to get even more difficult for me. My damn leg. It hurt so much.

'Ivy, look it's me. Take the baby. Look after the baby. And if you can, please play that taxi driver his fare. I'll come back and put all this right, but I have to go.'

I took one more look at the baby and then ran off into the crowd.

'He's trying to get away. Somebody stop him!'

'Call the police. Who got a good look at him?'

I got lucky. The town was full of shop and office workers heading home. I mixed in with the flow, doing my best to hide my limp, and soon felt safe enough to sit down on a bench.

I needed to call the police. This was an abduction. Shit. I'd given my phone to the taxi driver. I looked around for a phone box but I couldn't see one. I had never cared about the disappearance of call boxes on our streets until I needed one. Desperately.

A police car raced past me, its lights flashing. It was followed by an ambulance, no doubt for the taxi driver that I'd just thrown into the path of a passing vehicle.

I had to think fast. What had happened to Meg? She'd been snatched off the pavement right in front of everybody. You don't expect things like that.

Who was that man? Where had I seen him? It was recent, really recent, but I couldn't place him. Yes ... yes, it was the zoo. He'd been talking to Hannah at Blackpool Zoo. Who was he? How did Hannah know him?

I wondered if I'd been mistaken. Was Hannah in that car too? Had they been picking Meg up? No, they'd left the baby. She'd been snatched – by someone who knew Hannah, or at least had spoken to her. Had he been setting her up at the zoo? Perhaps she was in danger too.

I had no money, no phone and no bankcard, although there was no point me carrying a bankcard since the bank had stopped letting me draw out cash. I'd been sponging off Alex for the past few days and now my human cash machine was gone.

My leg hurt so badly that I didn't know if it would take my weight anymore. And to add insult to injury, no taxi in the town would touch me with a bargepole now. They'd all get my description on their radios in a matter of moments. And the police would be after me too. Again.

My options were limited. I could walk on, away from town, and find a phone box, but I had no money. I could hand myself into the police and tell them about Meg, but it would take so long to get past the fare-dodging-taxi-driver-wounding matter that it would use up valuable time cutting through all the crap.

For a moment I felt lost. Where had they taken her? What did they want with her? She was an innocent person standing on the street – with a baby, for God's sake. They even left the baby.

Then the penny finally dropped. This was all connected. Whoever had come for Tony Dodds, Ray Matiz and Bob Taylor had now come for Meg. Somebody was clearing up a mess that had been made at Woodlands Edge.

Meg was next on that list. She'd been in the home and was involved in the big investigation that went on there at the time. These people were dying because of something that went on at that home, something which Meg had never had the courage to tell me about.

I don't get many breaks in life, but I got one then. I wondered afterwards if it was fate, but it was probably simply the fact that I was sitting on a bench and people usually sort out pockets, handbags and change when they're sitting down. It was a pound coin. Right underneath the bench. I thought it was a bottle top at first and was about to ignore it, but something made me pick it up. It was covered in crap, but it was a pound coin. I felt like I'd won the lottery.

I had two choices. I could find a call box and phone Alex, or I could hop on a bus, get as close to my place as possible, and see her there. We hadn't agreed where to meet up, but I assumed it would be back at the flat. She had the spare key; it made sense.

Tentatively I put weight on my leg. It stung with the pain, but I pushed through it. I wasn't so far from the seafront. There would be a phone box near the tower. I'd be able to get lost in the crowds too. I had to speak to Alex before going to the police. It would take me several hours to explain what I'd seen and to convince them that we couldn't wait twenty-four hours before reporting Meg as a missing person. I knew where they were taking her. It had to be to the home, where the others had been killed.

I found a phone box before I reached the seafront. I didn't know Alex's mobile number. I'd texted and called several times, but I hadn't got a clue what it was. I rang home. Please, Alex, be back at the flat.

It rang. Twenty times I let it ring. I pushed the button

down and got my pound back, terrified that it would be swallowed up. I heard the metallic sound of the coin falling down to the coin-return tray.

I pushed it straight back into the slot and dialled again. I let it ring. I counted again. Eighteen ... nineteen ... twenty ...

'Hello? Alex Kennedy speaking.'

She sounded out of breath.

'Alex, it's Pete, we've got to be quick.'

'Damn it, Pete. How did you sort out the taxi fare? Didn't you see me—'

'Alex, I don't have time. Look, Meg has been abducted by somebody. Remember the man we saw talking to Hannah at the zoo? Him.'

'What's going on, Pete?'

'I've got to speak fast. I don't know how much time I get on this pay phone. We need to get to Woodlands Edge as fast as possible. Can you come in a taxi for me?'

'Where are you, Pete? Shouldn't you call the police?'

'I can't. I got into some trouble earlier on. The police are looking for me. If they find me, we'll never get to Meg. I'm on Talbot Road, near the florist. Come as quick—'

I heard a beeping sound and the phone went dead. It was ages since I'd used a pay phone and I couldn't believe how little time I got for my money. I heard the coin fall down into the chamber below. That was it. I was out of money. If Alex couldn't get to me fast, who knows what would happen to Meg. And then I realised. We had an ally. DCI Summers was still in Blackpool. I wouldn't have to explain anything to her; she'd believe me and summon the cavalry. Only I hadn't thought of it soon enough and now my pound coin was all used up.

Alex did well. She arrived in no time at all. It felt like an eternity to me, but she said it was no more than twenty minutes.

'Shall I ask the taxi to wait?' she asked, getting out of the car and giving me a hug.

I didn't reply. I was looking at the carrier bag in her hand.

'What's that?'

'It's the walking stick you bought for me when I fell through the floor at the home. Use it, even though you won't want to.'

'You couldn't have brought it at a better time. My leg hurts like crazy.'

'Are you paying, luv, or what?' the taxi driver shouted.

'Shall we jump in?' Alex asked. 'I don't see that we have any choice, do we?'

We got into the car. I hoped that the taxi driver wouldn't realise who I was. She was studying me in the rear-view mirror. If she did rumble me, she'd probably drive us directly to the police station.

'What are we going to do?' Alex asked, speaking low so that our conversation wouldn't be heard above the car radio. It was tuned into my radio station which was playing something melodic, Cliff Richard I think.

'Here, I bought you one of your painkillers from the flat. I haven't got any water so you'll have to do your best to swallow it. I figured you'd be grateful for that.'

What would I do without her? Alex was patching me up, and I needed it. If we were going to find Meg I'd have to press on and forget my pain.

'The other bodies were found at the home. If they're planning to do what they did to Ray Matiz and Tony Dodds, we have to go to the tree first.'

'Woodlands Edge Children's Home please,' I called across to the taxi driver. 'Drop us as close as you can, thanks.'

She was still studying me in the mirror.

'You're Peter Bailey off the radio, aren't you? I recognised your voice. And your friend is Alex ... Alex ... Docherty off the telly?'

'Alex Kennedy,' Alex corrected. 'Pleased to meet you.'

'I heard your report with that Dodds lady on the radio. My best friend used to live at that home. It was a terrible place. All sorts of horrible things were going on there. Is that why you're going there now? Is something up?'

Alex and I looked at each other. I chose to tell the truth – this lady seemed to be on our side.

'I have a friend ... my wife ... was abducted a short time ago. I don't know why and who did it, but she used to live at the home too. I think it's connected. I think she's in danger.'

'Jesus Christ. Why didn't you say?' she asked.

The car sped up and she began to drive with a greater sense of urgency.

'By the way, don't think I didn't realise. You're that runner that they're after, aren't you? I heard it on the radio. The other drivers put the word about. So this is the reason you're in such a hurry.'

'Yep, and I feel like shit for what I did. The guy who got hit in the road, that was an accident. I'll put it right, but I have to find my wife first.'

'Why not call the police? They'll sort it out, won't they? It's their job, after all—'

'I know, but they're going to want to talk to me about this taxi fare incident. It's going to take so long to cut through the crap. Meg could be hurt ... she could be dead by the time we find her. I can't risk that.'

Ivy still had the baby. I'd completely forgotten. I turned to Alex.

'Ivy's looking after the baby. I just remembered. She'll probably call the police. God knows what she's thinking.

'You two don't half know how to make an impact!' the taxi driver said, looking at us in the mirror. 'Blackpool is a small town and the locals tend to get to know each other. I know Ivy's, although I don't know Ivy herself. I'm sure I can find out where she lives if you want me to get a message to her. Shall I make a call over the radio?'

'What do you think?' Alex asked, searching my face.

'It can't do any harm. Yes please see what you can do. What's your name, by the way?'

'Jan. Call me Jan. This makes a change from snogging couples and pissheads. We're almost there – this is the road now.'

We were approaching Woodlands Edge. Jan had slowed the car and was looking for a place to pull over.

'Carry on driving,' Alex said suddenly. 'They've got a car watching the home.'

Jan carried on driving, past the home and towards the end of the road where the woodland area began.

'Shit!' I said. 'Though if the cops are still here that might be good news. They can't have hurt Meg.'

'How many were there?' Jan asked. 'I didn't see a cop car.'

'Just one,' Alex said, 'but he was watching. I saw him. Plain clothes.'

'So where is Meg?' I asked. 'If they haven't got her here, where is she?'

'When we were kids there was an old den out there in the woods. I used to go there and smoke with my friend Toni. It was our private place – I don't think any of the adults knew it was there. Some of the kids would go out there with their boyfriends or girlfriends. They might have taken her there.'

'It's pitch black out here now. How far back do the woods go? We could get lost in there.'

'It's not that big,' Jan replied. 'It's years since I went in there. I was a kid then and it would have seemed bigger to me. It can't be much more than an acre or two. It's not huge.'

'What do you think?' I turned to Alex. 'If that guy at the other end of the road is really a cop, shouldn't we tell him? He can get his mates up here. We shouldn't do this on our own. I'm not sure if my leg can take it.'

Alex's phone made a noise. It wasn't a text sound or a phone call.

'Maybe you should check that,' I said. 'The way things are going, that could be anybody.'

Alex's phone lit up in the back seat as she checked her notifications.

'That's unusual. It's a Skype contact request. Probably some porno site trying to send me—'

Alex stopped and hurriedly touched a few more buttons.

'It's from Hannah!' she said, not looking up from her phone. 'She says she needs to speak to me urgently – she can't get in contact with you. It's about Meg. She says it's urgent.'

CHAPTER SIXTEEN

1993 'You'd better get that young girl out of there before she drowns.'

He had to shout to be heard, but he got their attention immediately. He had a pistol pointing in their direction. This is what it took to bring men like Tony Dodds and Russell Black back to the negotiating table.

They'd thought they were alone, that there would be no witnesses. Suddenly everything had changed. Tony Dodds was wondering if a third body might be too much to cover up.

'And who the fuck are you?' Dodds shouted over the crashing of the waves.

'Get the girl. I need to see that she's okay.'

Russell Black signalled to the thuggish man to retrieve Meg from the waves. He would probably be retrieving a body by this time anyway. They'd throw her back in the water once this situation was resolved.

Tom watched as Black's hired help walked into the water, picked up Meg and brought her back onto the sand. Tom rushed towards her, but Simon restrained him.

'Let him go to her. Let's step back towards the cars, away from the noise. We need to speak. The girl had better be alive.'

The man indicated which direction they should walk in with the barrel of the pistol.

'Where did you get that thing?' Dodds asked, clearly scared that he'd got no effective way of dealing with this new situation.

'We didn't go far enough after Hungerford. You of all people should know that. It's still easy enough to get hold of one of these things. And it's my guess this is the only thing you're going to listen to.'

Tom had hung back on the beach with Meg. Her body was limp and seemed lifeless. He'd been taught resuscitation as part of his duties in the children's home. It was one of the few things that Gary Maxwell had introduced which might actually benefit the children.

Tom turned Meg's head to the side. He didn't care what was going on ahead. He was desperate to save his daughter. Her body was ice cold, her hair bedraggled and covered in sand. He began to push down on her chest. There was still a pulse. She was alive at least.

The group of men had gathered by the concrete steps which led back up to the promenade.

'We'll stay down here,' said the man carrying the gun. 'I want you all in front of me where I can see you, with your hands behind your heads.'

Simon looked as if he was about to make a grab for the gun, but Tony Dodds knew how to read a situation. He'd dealt with every form of criminal and thug that you could imagine. This man was the most dangerous kind: an intelligent man, one who would plot and plan carefully to get exactly what he wanted. He was capable of patience and, if necessary, pulling the trigger. They'd have to listen to him first.

'The first thing you need to know is that I caught all of that on video camera. I have you taking the girl out of the boot of the car; I have the car number plates; I have your man here throwing her into the water; I have pictures of her being tossed about in the waves. Oh, and I have some lovely shots of the head of social services and the chief constable presiding over all it. Fairly damning, wouldn't you say?'

'What do you want?' Tony Dodds asked. He could see where this was heading.

'I haven't finished yet!' the man snapped. 'Because I also have pictures of you and Mr Black here speaking to that poor young girl over there in a graveyard, along with her sister, in what has to be a highly inappropriate way, given that both of them may have been giving evidence in an investigation into the Woodlands Edge children's home shortly afterwards. You can get very long lenses for cameras these days. Those pictures have developed beautifully. I'd be delighted to share copies with you if you wish?'

'What do you want?' Tony Dodds repeated, impatient that it was taking so long to get to the point. Further along the beach, illuminated by the thrown light from the street lamps, they could see Tom Yates desperately trying to revive his daughter.

'This latest set of photos might prove to be evidence of murder,' the man continued. 'At the very least they're proof of assault, intimidation, conspiracy … Whatever it turns out to be, it'll be the end of your careers. For your two men here, I suspect it'll be a return to jail. Imagine how much fun the inmates will have with a former chief constable in the shower block.'

'Get to the point. What do you want? We've got that

you've been gathering evidence and that you're going to blackmail us. What's your price?'

Tony Dodds looked weary. He knew how this played out. He was about to be squeezed. Very tightly. And he had no negotiating power. He'd need to see the photos, of course. He wasn't stupid. But they were on the defensive now. The whole thing would blow apart if they didn't comply.

'We need to get her to a hospital. I can't revive her!' Tom shouted from along the beach. He continued to pound on Meg's chest, moving between that and frantically blowing into her mouth to encourage her to breathe once again.

'The murder of a young girl and the attempted murder of her father. That's not going to look good on your CVs gentlemen. So let's get to the point. It's bloody cold out here and I'd rather be watching TV in my hotel room.'

Russell Black was a changed man. Used to being in control and playing the role of bully, this was an unwelcome turnaround for him. He'd been protected and guided by Tony Dodds. He'd felt invincible with the power of the local constabulary behind him, but now he was just a scared man with a semi-automatic pistol pointing right at him.

'Here's what's going to happen,' the man with the gun continued.

'I'm going to get this latest set of pictures developed and, along with the first set of photographs and their negatives, these are going to be placed in a safe-deposit box at a location in London. This safe-deposit box forms a part of my last will and testament. If anything happens to me, the contents will be released to my estate and will therefore become public, along with my handwritten notes with names, dates, times and locations. So don't get any ideas about sending your tough guys after me, okay?'

Tony Dodds and Russell Black nodded. They were caught. Even if they killed him now and destroyed his camera, the first set of images were in circulation.

'Now to the good bit,' the man continued, 'because this is where we get to what I want. I know that both of you gentleman have property and leisure interests dotted throughout Blackpool – and I have no guilt about this, because I know exactly how most of those deals came about. I reckon you all know this stretch of beach pretty well, right?'

'Come on, Meg!' Tom shouted in frustration. He was tiring now, and beginning to despair. He looked helplessly towards the men. Were they just going to let her die?

'Every month, on the twenty-fifth day, you're going to make a transfer to my bank account of two thousand pounds: that's one thousand pounds each. Those payments are going to continue in perpetuity, and the photos are going to remain hidden.'

'A thousand pounds! That's too much money—'

'Shut the fuck up!' the man shouted. 'Don't you think I've done my research? You have several lucrative and bankrolling properties around this resort as well as your large salaries. One thousand pounds each will be fine for both of you. It won't cause too many problems.'

'You piece of shit!' Tony Dodds cursed.

'I'm sorry if you're annoyed, but there's more to come. Should one of you die or be unable to make up your share of those payments, the other will be expected to make up the difference. You're a team, right? I'll expect you both to stay in the black. Ha! Good joke eh, in the black! What do you think of that, Mr Black?'

Russell Black said nothing. He knew that they were beaten. This had come completely left of field. Why hadn't they been aware of this man before? Where had he come from?

'There's one more thing that I want from this, gentlemen, but don't worry, it won't have to come out of your pockets. I'm a journalist and I want a story. My wife is about to screw me for a divorce so I'm going to be in real need of your money and I'm also going to need my job. I have to leave this godforsaken place with a story. I want a fall guy. The only one of you buggers without any money is that toad Gary Maxwell, so let's make sure something sticks with him and you two and your mate Ray Matiz get to walk away. Matiz is lucky. I haven't got anything on him. Not yet, but I'm looking. But that's the deal. I walk away from your lovely seaside town with a great story; you make sure Gary Maxwell takes a hit, and you sign direct debit forms for my easy payment plan. Easy! Alright?'

Tony Dodds and Russell Black looked at each other. They turned towards the man and nodded resentfully.

'I'll want to see copies of the pictures,' Tony Dodds said, 'and if they don't exist, you need to know that I'll throw you from the top of the tower myself.'

'You'll receive a copy of the photos in the mail tomorrow. I took the precaution of posting them earlier in case our meeting didn't quite work out.'

'If you ever break this deal, if those pictures ever surface, you need to know that I will have you killed,' Tony Dodds hissed, 'even from prison. I have the contacts. I'll kill you if you ever break this deal.'

'I won't. I'm not a greedy man. Your secrets are safe with me. I've taken the liberty of writing down my bank details so that you can set up those direct debits. Copies of tonight's photographs will be posted to your home addresses before the first payment is due. If the first payment doesn't arrive, Gary Maxwell won't be the only national news story coming out of Blackpool. Understood?'

Tony Dodds and Russell Black nodded. They had escaped with their careers and their livelihoods, they knew when they were beaten. Russell Black surveyed the piece of paper in his hand.

'Charlie Lucas. You're that bastard from the tabloids.'

Further along the beach, Tom Yates pounded one final time on his adopted daughter's chest. She caught her breath, coughed out the seawater that had filled her lungs and slowly began to take in her surroundings. Kneeling over her was the man she'd once feared would betray her because he simply wasn't strong enough.

Over the howl of the wind and the roaring of the waves Tom Yates heard a word that he doubted he'd ever hear from his daughter's mouth.

'Dad.'

'Can you call her from here?' I asked. 'Is the signal good enough?'

'I think so. Do you want to do it? Alex replied.

I pressed the call button on Skype. Hannah was showing as Away but at least that meant she was connected.

It dialled. We sat in silence as we waited for an answer.

'Alex?'

It was Hannah's voice.

'It's Pete, Hannah. What's this about?'

'Why couldn't I get you on your phone, Pete? You've wasted a lot of time. Meg is in danger. I've received a threat.'

There was silence in the car. Jan's radio control crackled.

'Where are you, Pete?' Hannah asked.

'I'm in a taxi. We're at Woodlands Edge.'

Silence. She'd muted her microphone. I could tell. You don't work in radio for as many years as I have without being to spot every change in sound quality.

'What's happened with Meg, Hannah? Come on. Spit it out. I need to know.'

More silence.

'You know all the deaths surrounding the home?'

Her voice was crystal clear over the speaker in the mobile phone.

'Whoever is killing those people has found Meg and me. They must be looking up whoever was there at the time. They don't want to hurt her, but they want something from me. Well, from you actually.'

'Jesus, Hannah. What's this about? Somebody grabbed Meg in town. I saw it myself. What do they want with her?'

'I don't know who's behind this, Pete. They called me anonymously. But they have to be from our time in the home in the nineties. They want to get to you through me. They must have known that I know you – I have no idea how. They want you to do a job for them. They need you to reach Russell Black.'

'Why me? I don't even know the man.'

'They want you to use your influence to get to him. He's too clever, they haven't been able to get near him.'

'And then what? I get to Russell Black and they kill him? You know we can't do that, Hannah.'

'They have Meg, Pete, and they'll hurt her. They want Russell Black, and you get Meg back in return.'

It was my turn to mute the speaker on Skype.

'We can't do this. We have to get the police involved. We can't do this on our own.'

'You do what you have to, but this taxi is yours as long as you need it. My friend's told me about that Russell Black. He's a slimy git.'

'Thanks, Jan,' I said. 'I appreciate that. What do you think, Alex? Time to call in the police?'

'See what she has to say first,' Alex said. 'Find out what they want you to do.'

I unmuted the speaker.

'Okay, so tell me more,' I said. 'What am I supposed to do? And how do I know that Meg is safe?'

'We don't know,' Hannah replied, 'but they've assured me this is about Russell Black. It's the main men they want: Ray Matiz, Russell Black, Tony Dodds – that's what they said. They got to Meg to get to you.'

'So why did Bob Taylor get hurt?' I asked. 'What did he have to do with anything?'

Hannah's microphone was muted again.

'Has she got someone with her?' I asked.

Alex shrugged.

Jan turned off the car engine.

'Bob Taylor must have been an accident,' Hannah replied after a short wait. 'Wrong place, wrong time. It's a dangerous job being a crossing guard. That's what they said in the papers.'

It seemed an unlikely answer. My gut instinct told me that Bob Taylor was connected with the other deaths, but I didn't push the issue.

'They were quite clear about what they wanted, Pete.

No police. Nobody else but you. You need to bring Russell Black out into the open for an interview and they'll take care of the rest. You won't even know anything is going on. You'll be completely in the clear.'

'And if they kill him? Am I in the clear then?' I was getting angry.

'Look, Pete, don't shoot the messenger,' Hannah snapped back.

'I'm sorry. I know she's your sister and you must be as scared as I am. Who could be doing this, Hannah? Think. Who could it be?'

'Pete, if I knew, I'd tell you. I'm scared about Meg. They want you to contact Russell Black tonight—'

'Hannah, I can't just waltz in there and get an interview with Russell Black. For one, he's not even in post anymore. He's under no obligation to talk to me. And secondly, he doesn't know me.'

'I just want Meg back safe, Pete. Do what you can. I'm on Skype if you need me.'

She ended the call.

'This is really odd,' I said. 'Why would they get in touch with Hannah?'

'She told you. They couldn't reach you so they contacted her,' Alex replied. 'How else would they do it?'

'But how did they even know that Hannah was in the UK? She's hard to reach at the best of times. She prefers it that way—'

'What happened to Gary Maxwell?' Alex interrupted.

'What?' I replied.

'You know, Gary Maxwell, the guy who ran the home. He was in the newspaper articles. What happened to him? Why is nobody looking for him if they're killing all the people who were involved in that inquiry? Where is he in all of this?'

'We never found out, did we? Jan, do you know?'

'I don't know where he is now, but I do know that he went to jail – for quite a stretch, if I remember rightly. He was having a sexual relationship with one of the girls at the home. The big inquiry may have been dropped, but at least they managed to get to him. He was the one that all the kids hated. My friend used to call him the bogeyman.'

'Is he living in Blackpool?' Alex asked.

'I don't know. I doubt he'd dare to return here, not after that. It was a big scandal. It was all over the papers.'

'How did we miss that?' I asked Alex.

'Because we weren't looking for it, Pete. When did it happen, Jan?'

'The nineties, probably 1994 or 1995, something like that. I was still at school, I know that much.'

'What are you going to do?' Alex asked. 'Are you going to speak to Russell Black? What about the police?'

'Yes, I'm going to see if I can get to Black, but I'm also going to ask DCI Summers to tail him to make sure nothing happens to him. That will lead us to Meg. The minute we know Meg is safe, DCI Summers can alert the local police teams. What do you think? Worth a try?'

'You can use this taxi as long as you want,' came Jan's voice from the front of the vehicle. 'I'll do what I can to help. And I'll see if we can get a home address for Ivy. I bet someone has picked her up before. She's had that café for years – one of the guys must know where she lives.'

Jan picked up her radio microphone and started talking to the chap who was on radio duty.

'What shall I do?' Alex asked.

'I'm going to use you to flatter Russell Black and bring him out into the open. It's time we exploited your TV fame a bit. I'm going to tell him you've approached me to feature him in a documentary. He's a vain prick – his sort usually loves that kind of thing. I'll make it about something totally unconnected with what went on at the home. He'll fall for it. But you're going to have to switch on your best TV charm. Okay?'

Alex smiled.

'Of course, Pete. I'll do my best. We need to do this tonight. Meg must be scared out of her mind.'

I thought back to Tony Miller and Meg's terrible experience after he abducted her, fearing for her life, petrified that he would assault her, maybe even rape her. But Meg could look after herself. She'd killed Tony Miller when her chance came – she was tough. This wasn't about sexual intimidation, it was about revenge. If I could deliver Russell Black, I'd be able to get her out of there safely.

'Can I use your phone, Alex? I need to call the guys in the office. They should have Russell Black's phone number on the contacts database.'

I dialled into the news desk and Amy picked up the call. That was good. Amy was experienced and was taking her turn on late-night producer duties.

'Hi Amy. It's Pete Bailey. Can you do me a favour?'

'Hey Pete! Great interview the other day. Loved it! Yeah sure, how can I help?'

'I need a number for Russell Black. He used to be social services head. I don't know when he retired, but it can't be that long ago. He's not very old. Can you find it?'

I heard tapping over the phone line.

'I've got a house number for Ivy!' Jan whispered. I put my thumb up to her.

'Hi, Pete. Yes, it's an old contact. The last time it was

updated was 2007 so it might be out of date. I've got a mobile and a home phone. Have you got a pen and paper?'

Jan fumbled about at the front of the taxi and handed over a couple of business cards and a pen.

'Go ahead, Amy.'

I carefully wrote down the numbers.

'What's up? Anything interesting? I could do with something for the breakfast show. All I've got so far is a runaway Shetland pony and an off-licence theft in Kirkham.'

'It's just a bit of research, Amy. It might turn into something interesting. Thanks for your help. Cheers!'

I hung up.

'Do you want to start driving us to Ivy's place?' I said to Jan, thinking that we might as well be moving while I was making calls. She started up the car again and, after turning around at the end of the road, we began to move slowly along the street.

I dialled Russell Black's mobile number first, thinking that would be a direct route to him wherever he was at that time of night. It didn't even ring. It was a dead number.

'Bollocks, he must have changed his mobile number.'

Then I tapped in the numbers for the home phone. It rang. I hoped Russell Black hadn't moved house since 2007.

I put the call on speakerphone.

'Hello. Russell Black speaking.'

'Fuck, that's no police car. Look who it is!'

Alex's outburst took me by surprise, and I ended the call immediately.

'Damn it, Alex. What's up? You might have timed that a bit better!'

I snapped at her, she might have put my pitch to Russell Black in jeopardy now. He'd think we were pranksters.

'Didn't you see who was sitting in that car? It's nothing to do with the police. It was that blackmailing bastard Charlie Lucas!'

'Pull over, Jan, please,' I said. 'Just along here – don't let him see us.'

'What's he up to?' Alex said, looking out of the rear window.

'Probably hoping he'll witness the next body being dumped there. Imagine the scoop that would be.'

'It seems like a hard way to do your journalism, Pete. Shall we tap on his window and let him know that we're here?'

'I'd rather avoid the sneaky little rat if I can. The less we have to do with him, the better, but I suppose he might know something.'

'You go,' said Alex. 'I might punch the man if I see him again.'

I got out of the car and walked along the road using the stick. My leg was feeling better. It was still uncomfortable, but I was able to move well again.

The fencing that Alex and I had squeezed through to get a look inside Woodlands Edge had been newly secured. There were Keep Out signs attached to each panel, and I could make out the police cordon tape around the tree where the bodies had been left.

Charlie almost jumped out of his skin when I tapped on his window. He was sipping a coffee and it splashed on his trousers. It couldn't have happened to a nicer guy. He wound down the window.

'Did you have to do that?' he snarled. 'You might have given me warning that you were coming.'

'It's very quiet on this road, Charlie. What are you doing here?'

'I've made my name as a journalist getting big scoops, Mr Bailey. They tend not to drop in your lap. You have to control the situation and make sure that you're in the right place at the right time. And what brings you out here?'

'Same thing, I suspect. I wanted to see how the crime scene looked. They've got this place sewn up nice and tight. There won't be any more bodies dumped by that tree, that's for sure.'

'You never can tell, Mr Bailey. I'm surprised that the police haven't left some form of surveillance up here. They removed their man after that lollipop man, Bob Taylor, got killed.'

'How long will you be sitting here? It seems a bit extreme lurking in your car all night when you've got a comfy hotel to go to.'

'I'll be here as long as it takes, Mr Bailey, as long as it takes. This place owes me. It screwed up my marriage. I'd like it to pay up with a big story again.'

'You know what you said about my video and the photos of Alex with the escorts, Charlie? What would it take to make those go away? Alex's first. What would I have to do for you to destroy her part in that story?'

'A good journalist knows how to be patient, Mr Bailey. You never know when you might need a particular piece of information. Sometimes you hang onto it for years before making use of it, and other times it never sees the light of day. There's very little that you could do that would make me destroy that information. Consider it a pension pot. However, if you could get me in a room with Russell Black for ten minutes, that might do for starters.'

'Russell Black? And what would you give me if I could arrange that?'

'It's not enough for you to get your friend off the hook,

but your video isn't worth very much to me. Get me to Russell Black and it's yours. He mustn't know I'm coming. We have what you might call history.'

'I might just be able to deliver that, but I want Alex's information too. You know there's nothing salacious going on there. She's not cheating on anybody. If I give you Russell Black, you let me have any information you have on Alex too. Okay?'

'Not okay, but put it this way. If I get what I want from Mr Black, before some nutter with a revenge mission kills him, I'm prepared to make that deal.'

'You make sure you're as good as your word, Charlie,' I warned.

I walked back to Jan's taxi. The engine was still idling. I kept the conversation to myself – I didn't want to get Alex's hopes up. Neither did I want her to know what a shitty thing I was about to do.

'Let's get to Ivy's house,' I said. 'And I need to call Russell Black. Hopefully he'll pick up again.'

Jan started driving. I dialled Russell Black's home phone number. It rang for some time before he picked up.

'Hello. Russell Black speaking.'

'Hello Mr Black. I'm sorry to disturb you at this time in the evening. My name is Peter Bailey. I'm a radio journalist at North West News FM ...'

'Mr Bailey. I heard you interviewing my friend June Dodds on the radio. I hope you're not going to invite me to endure the same humiliation, as it'll be a polite refusal I'm afraid.'

'I would like to speak to you, but it's on behalf of a good friend of mine. Have you watched Crime Beaters on the TV, Mr Black?'

'Yes,' he replied slowly, waiting to see which way the wind was blowing.

'Alex Kennedy is a good friend of mine. She's staying with me in Blackpool at the moment and is filming a documentary on social care in the nineteen-nineties. She'd love to chat to you with a view to putting you on national television.'

'This is nothing to do with Tony Dodds' death or any of the other unfortunate events at the children's home?'

'It's nothing to do with that, Mr Black. Ms Kennedy happened to tell me that she was looking for a charismatic and capable social services director who was active during the nineties. I told her that I have the very man.'

Alex made a wanker signal with her hand. I smiled. If I was Pinocchio, my nose would have grown one inch longer.

'I could maybe meet with her when all of this has blown over. Perhaps in a week or two?'

'I'm sorry, Mr Black. Alex returns to London next week. You would be the missing piece in the puzzle. If we could speak tonight, that would be really useful.'

There was silence on the end of the line. Alex took the phone from me, sensing that we needed to add a little more seasoning to the lie.

'Mr Black, hello. It's Alex Kennedy from Crime Beaters here.'

She missed out the bit about being newly retired.

'Peter has told me how influential you were in Blackpool in the nineties. It sounds like you're the professional voice that we're looking for.'

'Good evening, Ms Kennedy. It's a pleasure to speak to you—'

'Can I interrupt you? You have a superb broadcasting

voice. It's good enough to be on the radio. Your diction is wonderful.'

This time I made the wanker sign with my hand.

'That's very nice of you to say so, Ms Kennedy. Thank you. So what is this programme that you're making?'

It took Alex less than five minutes to close the deal. I'd suspected he was vain, but he was gullible too. There had been many times in my radio career where I'd talked important people into doing things that they really shouldn't have done. What was it Meg used to say? 'You chat people up for a living.' Well, if that was the case, Alex and I had just had a threesome with Russell Black.

'He'll meet us at the Grande Royale Hotel at nine o'clock. It has to be in the bar, in the open.'

'This is Ivy's street,' Jan said from the front of the car. 'It should be one of these ... number 32 ... number 34 ... Here it is: number 36.'

We pulled up a little way along the road where there was a space.

'What time is it?' I asked. I was missing my phone.

'Twenty past eight,' Jan replied. 'Leave yourself a clear ten minutes to get to the Grande Royale from here.'

I took Alex's phone and called Charlie Lucas. I was brief and curt with him, not really sure if I was doing the right thing. I had to think of Meg. Charlie Lucas could take care of himself. He was a cockroach – a survivor.

'Russell Black will be at the Grande Royale Hotel at 9 o'clock. I'll turn up five minutes late. You've got that long with him. Make it look like a coincidence; tell him you're staying there. And when I arrive, don't show that you know me. Make your excuses and go. Got it? You make sure that you honour your word. Remember our deal.'

'If I get what I want from Russell Black, I'll settle up

with you,' was all he said. Bastard. It was the only chance I had to find Meg, get her out safely and finally get Charlie off our case. It seemed like my best bet.

Alex and I stepped out of the car. We knocked on Ivy's door, number 36. This would have to be a brief visit, but it was one I'd been looking forward to for a long time. I was finally about to meet the child who might have been my son.

CHAPTER SEVENTEEN

1993 Tom and Meg spent that night in a hotel on the seafront, paid for in cash by Charlie Lucas. He was protecting his deal. He hung around long enough to make sure that Meg was fine, but insisted that she didn't go to the hospital. She rallied quickly, the warmth of the radiators in the hotel helped no end. Tom called from a phone box to let his wife know why they'd been delayed. He made up a story about spending some bonding time together and staying out late to enjoy the illuminations. Mavis wasn't at all sure, but she accepted it. She never found out what had happened that night. But in any case, it was over.

Russell Black and Tony Dodds did exactly as they'd been asked by Charlie Lucas. He had both the evidence and the means to get that information out into the open. The men met up in private on the day that they received their brown envelopes from Charlie. They were no idle threats. His photographs would have sunk the careers of both men if they were ever leaked. The direct debit paperwork was completed and payments were made.

Charlie never came looking for more. That wasn't his

game. The payments from the men replaced the income that he lost from his divorce. He honoured his promise. The information stayed locked up in a safe-deposit box.

Things moved fast after Charlie had struck his deal. Tom and Meg gave evidence to support the claims that had been made against Gary Maxwell. Meg was given anonymity and permitted to give her evidence via video. Tom pushed hard for that. The poor girl had been through enough. She'd been traumatised by what had happened on the beach. Both she and Tom recognised that the best deal had been struck. They didn't know about the financial arrangement between the three men, but they were getting their man. Somebody's head was going to roll.

Gary Maxwell was jailed for ten years for the repeated rape of Debbie Simmonds. Throughout the trial, Debbie maintained Gary's innocence, claiming that they were in love, that the sexual contact had been consensual, and that they'd got it wrong. She attempted to avoid all questions that painted Gary Maxwell as the monster that he was and refused to believe he was guilty of a crime. She was distraught when he was sentenced for his repeated raping of a minor. His position of trust and responsibility made things worse. Debbie, like Meg, retained her anonymity throughout Gary's trial.

Meg didn't know what happened to Debbie afterwards, and she didn't particularly care. A part of her felt sorry for the girl and her delusion, but she was an evil bitch who'd sent Meg to her fate that night. Gary Maxwell and Debbie Simmonds deserved each other.

Life returned to relative normality once the outcry in the national newspapers had died down. Charlie Lucas had his name splashed all over the papers; he'd landed exclusive interviews with all of the protagonists who could be identified and his post-trial reporting won him an award for outstanding journalism.

Meg got her first sense of what a stable family life was like. She and Hannah began to see how lucky there were. As Hannah entered her eighteenth year in 1995, things were looking good. The trial was in the past. Hannah was taking driving lessons. They had their whole future in front of them. Meg had made good progress at school for the first time in her life. She was focused and had a sense of direction. She'd taken a great interest in the procedures around the trial and had become determined to find a job within the justice system.

On the bad days, and there were many of them, Meg would burn with indignation about what those men had done. She'd want to kill Tony Dodds, Russell Black and the other men who'd hurt them – she didn't even know their names. She remembered the late-night parties, the drunken men, the cigars and cigarette smoke, the laughter and contempt with which they treated the children. She felt ashamed, dirty, humiliated and wretched whenever she thought back to those times. She wanted to kill those men, every single one of them. One day, when she was older, perhaps her revenge would come. One day.

There had been good times too. David, for instance, was a precious memory. And the adoption: Tom and Mavis were doting parents. She finally had people in her life she trusted enough to call Mum and Dad.

But nothing lasts forever and for Meg Yates the pain had only just begun.

It was almost a year after the incident on the beach. The weather had turned cold again, the heating was on, and the family was gathered in the living room to watch TV.

Like many arguments, it came out of nowhere.

'You still haven't fixed that heater, Tom!' Mavis scolded.

It had been a long day at work. Tom was tired and not in the mood for it.

'It still lights. We can't afford the part for it, alright? If you'd help out by taking a job, that would help to pay for it. Even Hannah and Meg have part-time jobs—'

'Don't start that again!' Mavis retaliated. 'We agreed that I'd be home for the girls. We always said that. The girls come first – we cut our cloth.'

'But couldn't you even take a small job at the corner shop or something? If you want the heater fixed, that's how it gets done. I can barely afford to pay the mortgage at the moment; the heater is the least of my problems!'

'Mum, Dad, we're trying to watch the TV,' Hannah interrupted.

'Enough!' Mavis shouted. 'This is important!'

Hannah stomped off to her room. Meg waited to see if it died down. This was unusual for Tom and Mavis. They had their arguments like everybody else, but the heater had become a bit of a battleground.

The argument escalated. They ended up hurling everything into the pot that they could think of: work clothes that hadn't been ironed on time; Tom's supposedly secret smoking habit that had mysteriously started up again – Mavis could smell it on his clothes. Voices were raised and tempers frayed. Things were said that never should have been.

'And if you think you're sleeping with me tonight then you're very much mistaken!' Mavis shouted as Tom headed upstairs, defeated and worn out by the stupid row.

'Don't worry. I'll take the spare room!' he shouted back. They'd be the last words he would ever say to his wife.

'And you still haven't sorted out that door. I've been

asking you to do that for just as long!'

Tom slammed the spare room door hard. He spent his days fixing stuff that was broken. Why couldn't she appreciate that sometimes he wanted a break from it at home?

Once he'd settled in the spare room, Mavis retired to the sanctuary of their bedroom, leaving Meg alone in the sitting room. There was a gentle tap at the front door. It was their neighbour wondering if everything was alright.

Meg was angry. She felt vulnerable whenever the couple rowed. She feared that they'd be sent back to the home, as if the arrangement was temporary. She had no experience of marital ups and downs. She believed the row was more serious than it was.

'Just my bloody mum and dad,' she raged. 'I hate them!'

She slammed the door on the neighbour and headed up to the room she shared with Hannah. They'd talk quietly in the privacy of their bedroom, and Hannah would reassure her that all couples argued this way sometimes. It would be alright.

Mavis had been right to scold Tom about the faulty gas heater. Meg had forgotten to switch it off. The girls were usually first in bed so she didn't even think about it. They chatted for about an hour and then settled down to sleep. It was school the next day and they'd be up early. The entire family was worn out by the row.

It was the crackling that Meg heard first. She knew it was a threat straightaway, even though she hadn't worked out what it was yet.

'Hannah, are you awake? Hannah. I think I left the heater on downstairs. Can you make sure I've switched it off? I'm not sure what Dad does to turn it off properly.'

Hannah looked at her through tired eyes.

'Oh God, Meg. Can't you go down and do it yourself? Okay then, come on, I'll show you how to do it.'

As they stepped down the stairs into the lounge, they saw the entire room ablaze. The sofa was in flames throwing up thick black smoke. It caught their throats and they began to cough.

'Mum! Dad!' Hannah called. Meg opened the front door to establish their escape route, but the rush of air into the house fanned the deadly flames over to the stairwell. Hannah ran back up to the landing. She tried the door to the spare room. It was jammed.

'Mum! Dad!' she called.

'Hannah, come down!' Meg screamed at her, terrified of the fire, coughing with the smoke.

'I can't get to Dad. Dad! Dad!'

Meg could hear her thumping on the door.

'It's too hot. Dad, jump out the window! Mum, get out the front of the house!'

Hannah emerged from the thick smoke on the stairs, coughing badly, her eyes red raw.

'Mum and Dad!' Meg shouted. 'We've got to help Mum and Dad!'

'We can't, it's too bad up there, it's too hot. They'll have to try and jump from the windows. We have to get out, Meg. Now!'

The girls stepped out onto the street and watched as the flames engulfed the house. They saw their mother pounding at the window and drop to the ground as she was overcome by the smoke. Their father was at the back of the house. They could only pray that he'd get out. The heat was ferocious; they'd never seen or felt anything like it before.

They stood there watching. Defenceless. Helpless. As the street woke up and neighbours piled out into the street to watch, many commented how calm the girls looked, standing there as their house burned down with their parents inside.

Meg and Hannah knew how this played out. They didn't deserve the chance that they'd been given. This was all they'd come to expect in life. Everything they loved was turning to dust.

When I saw the baby it didn't really matter whose it was. It was a baby; it was tiny and gorgeous, and the identity of the father was a matter for another time. Ivy had been great. She'd walked home with the pram, found some formula, baby food and nappies in the bag on the shelf underneath, and was quite at ease with the child. Tom.

Alex had to excuse herself. She was choked up by the sight of me holding the baby and went into the living room to alert DCI Summers to what was going on.

'We can't stay long, Ivy. Thank you so much for doing this.'

I handed Tom back to her. I was awkward and nervous. I hadn't had much experience of handling children.

'I hope Meg is alright,' Ivy said, concerned. 'I almost called the police myself. You looked in a right panic when I saw you.'

'It's complicated, Ivy, but I'm going to get Meg back now.'

Jan was waiting at the front door, which had been left ajar.

'We'll have to go soon, Pete, if you want to get there on time.'

'Okay, Jan. I need to make a quick call. Can I use your phone, Alex? I need to speak to DCI Summers.'

Alex handed it to me and I redialled the last called number.

'Hi DCI Summers, it's Pete Bailey. Where are you?'

'I'm driving back down to Blackpool. I just turned off the motorway.'

'Look, I know this is dodgy, but we need your help, Kate – DCI Summers. Meg is being held as a hostage and will only be released in exchange for Russell Black. I can't wait for the local police. We have to act now.'

'You're playing with fire, you know that, Pete? And I'm going to land myself with a disciplinary.'

'But think how good it'll look for you if you solve a murder case off your own patch. Please, Kate, I really need your help. Can you tail Russell Black? I'm about to meet him at the Grande Royale Hotel. Can you follow us when we leave together? Once you know the location of the exchange, you can call your guys and get them in position. Get them primed and ready, but I only want them going in when Meg is safe.'

'Okay, okay, Pete. I'm twenty-five minutes away. Make sure you don't leave that hotel before 9:15. Text me to let me know where they want to meet you and make the exchange. I'll have our guys there as soon as possible. No heroics, Pete. Alright?'

'No, no heroics. And thank you. Thank you again for helping me with my fucked-up life.'

I ended the call and heard a beep as I passed it back to Alex.

The sound had come from the pram. Tucked in and hidden by the pram cover was Meg's mobile phone. It was new; she'd changed her brand since she was living with me. No wonder I could never raise her.

'That's where it was coming from! I thought I was hearing things,' Ivy said. 'It's been doing that all evening.'

'Lots of texts from someone called Phil,' I said, down-hearted at the sight. 'Must be her new bloke wondering where she is.'

'Pete, we need to go,' Jan reminded me.

'You stay here, Alex. You'd better call this Phil fella and tell him what's going on. Can I take your phone? I don't think Meg will mind you using hers in the circumstances.'

I gave Alex a peck on the cheek and squeezed her arm.

She nodded.

'Be careful, Pete. Bring back Meg safe. Let's get this all sorted for good.'

'It's all I ever wanted,' I replied. 'Meg, the baby, the house. We're almost there, Alex.'

I joined Jan in the car.

'We're going to be later than you wanted,' she said. 'I hope he's still at the hotel when we get there.'

The irony of it, a taxi driver scolding the passenger about getting to the destination too late.

Jan drove fast and assertively through the town. The traffic was almost non-existent, so I was only five minutes late. I looked around for DCI Summers but I couldn't see her. I checked the time on Alex's mobile phone – I'd need to keep Russell Black talking for ten minutes or so to give her plenty of time to get into position.

I could see Charlie Lucas and Russell Black through the window of the bar. It didn't look like a friendly conversation

– Russell Black's face was red with fury. I'd need to call Charlie off. Whatever they were talking about, I didn't want to frighten Russell.

I made sure that they saw me pretending to look for Russell to give Charlie plenty of time to finish off. I waved from the bar, indicating that I was getting myself a drink before I came over. Charlie took his cue. I could see that their body language was changing. I walked over with my Coke. I'd need sharp wits for whatever happened next. My leg gave a twinge and I hoped that the painkillers would help me to see out the evening.

'Russell Black? Pete Bailey.'

I extended my hand while he tried to relax his face from whatever it was that Charlie had said to vex him.

'Sorry if I've interrupted something,' I said, looking at Charlie and giving him his prompt to leave.

'No, no. Russell and I used to know each other many years ago,' Charlie began. 'Imagine bumping into him in this hotel of all places.'

Yes, Charlie, just imagine.

'I think we're finished here, Mr Lucas?' Russell said, barely hiding his contempt for Charlie.

'Yes, I'll look forward to hearing from you on the twenty-fifth of the month, Russell,' Charlie smiled. Whatever had happened here, Charlie was the one who was leaving happy and Russell was the party who'd lost out. My guess was that Charlie had leant on him in some way, much as he'd leant on Alex and me. Well, I'd delivered on my agreement with Charlie. Alex would be in the clear now and hopefully Charlie would release me from his little blackmail trick too.

Charlie pulled on his coat and extended his hand to Russell, who ignored it.

'Nice to meet you, Mr Bailey,' Charlie said. He shook my hand and headed out into the hotel foyer.

'If I was a suspicious man, Mr Bailey, I'd think that little meeting was set up,' Russell said.

'No, no, I've not met him before,' I assured him, wondering if he could tell that I was lying.

'So where is Ms Kennedy if this isn't a set-up? I thought I was going to be talking to your friend Alex this evening?'

'You are, Mr Black. May I call you Russell? Alex has been delayed I'm afraid. You know what these TV celebrities are like. We're going to have to meet her elsewhere in town. Something to do with a new TV series.'

'Sounds interesting,' he said, perking up. 'Do tell me more.'

As I'd thought, Russell Black was a vain man. It didn't take much flattery to make him move on from his conversation with Charlie Lucas and back to the prospect of being on the television.

'If you'll excuse me, I'll contact Alex to see where we're meeting now,' I said, moving off towards the hotel foyer to make my call.

I contacted Hannah via Skype. I could see that she was already online.

It's Pete here, not Alex. I have Russell Black. Can you find out where Meg is and where they want us to meet.

Good. One moment ...

It took a few minutes for Hannah to get back to me. It seemed like an eternity. Russell Black had nipped off to the gents.

Okay, Pete, well done. You need to head to this map loca-

tion. They've told me to warn you – no police. Meg is safe.
Good luck!

I clicked on the map link that Hannah had sent. It was
Google Maps. I opened up the web page so that I could see
it better. Damn, it was the woodland area near the home. It
would be that den that Jan had mentioned. At least she
could get me there quickly; she had the car waiting outside.
I took the map location and texted it to DCI Summers. I
waited for the delivery report on the text, but gave up on it
when I saw Russell returning to his seat and looking for me.
I was going to have to lie to him. He'd know exactly what
was going on when he saw where I was taking him. I
returned to the table.

'Sorry, Russell. She wants to meet us at her hotel. I do
apologise. She's caught up in some big TV deal. It's all very
lucrative, so she had to sit in on the conference call. She
sends her apologies. Are you okay for time?'

Russell looked at his watch.

'I'm fine. For something as important as this, I can make
time. It will be a paid appearance, won't it?'

'Yes, of course. TV pays quite well I hear!'

Another lie. I had to keep him on the hook. We put on
our coats. My leg was growing increasingly sore. I'd left my
stick in the car.

As we stepped out of the hotel, I made a pretence of
getting ready to call a taxi.

'Oh look, there's one over there already. That's lucky!'

Jan had the engine running. She played ball with my
pretence.

'Where to?'

I showed her the map link on Alex's phone and she gave
me a look, asking if I was sure, without alerting Russell
Black. I gave a small nod.

We drove off and I exchanged pleasantries with my passenger. He was filled with a sense of his own importance. He was only speaking to me because I was offering him something that he wanted. I didn't like the man, but I could see how impressive he would look in the right circles.

I surreptitiously tried to glance in Jan's rear-view mirror, assuming that DCI Summers would be tailing us. We'd arrive at our destination, she'd bring in her police colleagues, I'd get Meg, and we'd be sorted. But I couldn't tell if there was anybody behind us. I hoped Jan was staying alert. She knew the plan.

As Russell Black droned on about how influential he'd been in Blackpool's social services, I started thinking about how I was going to get him out of the car and into the woods. As soon as he realised that something was amiss, he'd be on his phone calling a new taxi to take him home. He might even panic and alert the police.

I had two choices. I'd either have to tell him that Meg's safety depended on him helping us and that we were being tailed by a police officer or I'd have to threaten him with my walking stick.

Sure enough, as we drew onto the road on which the children's home was based, the penny dropped and he became aggressive.

'What is this?' he shouted. 'Is this some sort of scam? First it's Charlie bloody Lucas and now you. What are you? His stooge or something?'

'Calm down, Mr Black, please. It's nothing like that—'

'You assured me that we were going to speak to Alex Kennedy and now I see that this is a stitch-up. Is she there with a TV crew? Is this live TV?'

He began hunting around for a camera. Alex's phone

vibrated in my pocket. I ignored it. I had more pressing matters to attend to.

'Mr Black, I need your help. This is not some elaborate con, but I do need you to help me out. My wife is being held as a hostage in those woods. They want to see you. When they see you they'll release her—'

'What am I? Some sacrificial lamb? You saw what happened to Tony Dodds. Are you stupid, man? I'm calling the police—'

'I can't let you do that just yet, Mr Black.'

I snatched his phone from him. He wasn't expecting it. I even surprised myself. I handed it over to Jan.

'*She's* in on it too! I'll see you both go to jail for this. This is abduction. It's kidnap—'

I still can't believe I did this. I smacked him hard on the nose with the end of my walking stick. It started to bleed. It shut him up though.

'The police will be following us at all times. You won't come to any harm, Mr Black, but I do need your help to flush out this killer.'

I could tell that Jan was shocked at what I'd done. She was looking at me in her rear-view mirror. She must have seen violence in the back of her cab before, but maybe she hadn't expected it from me. She drove up to the end of the road and pulled up at a five-bar gate which led to the woods.

'Where is this den, Jan? Can you remember?'

'It's a long time ago, Pete, but if I remember rightly it's down the track, and then you go off the path to the right. Are you sure this is the right thing to do?'

I could see that she was unsure. She'd started the evening helping us out on a bit of an adventure and now she was colluding in an abduction.

'DCI Summers should have followed us up here. Did you see her behind us?'

'Someone followed us into the road, but I didn't get a good look at who it was.'

'Can you walk up the road to meet DCI Summers, Jan? Let her know where we're heading so she can point her guys to the den.'

I could tell that she was scared now. I was scared, but I was getting my wife back. The nightmare had to end. It would end that night.

'You come with me!' I said to Russell Black, sounding as threatening as I could.

'I don't suppose you have a torch in the back, Jan?'

'I do as it happens, for emergencies. Only a small one, but it'll help.'

I took my walking stick with me. My leg was hurting badly once again. The painkillers had only given me a temporary respite.

'Do you know where this place is?' I asked Russell Black, finding the switch to Jan's torch and shining it in front of us.

'I've heard about it but I never came into these woods. I've seen that tree – the place where the bodies were found, where those kids hanged themselves. At least we're not meeting there. I don't want to end up like Tony Dodds or Ray Matiz. There's some nutter on the loose.'

'What's this all about, Mr Black?' I asked. 'What was going on with you and Charlie Lucas? And you must know my wife, Meg? She was at the home in the nineties. You might have known her as Megan. Her surname was Yates. She was also known as Meg Stewart. Ring any bells?'

'Is that what this is about?' he asked, stopping to look back at me. I was glad of an excuse to rest for a moment. The uneven ground of the woods was hard on my leg.

'So you know Meg?'

'Yes, how could I forget Meg Stewart? No wonder you've got mixed up in all of this. You know it was the father of her child who hanged himself from that tree?'

I looked at him, although it was too dark to see his face. Alex's phone vibrated again in my pocket.

'Meg had a child?'

'Yes, of course she did. Didn't she ever tell you? You're her husband, you say? Yes, she caused me a lot of trouble that girl and her family. That's why Charlie Lucas was speaking to me. I won't tell you what it was about, but it all makes sense: Charlie Lucas, Megan Stewart. This is what they call chickens coming home to roost.'

I gave him a push to walk on. I could see where a small path led off to the side as Jan had advised. I could also see some lights ahead. That had to be where we were heading. I turned off the torch so as not to alert whoever was there.

It was hard going when we left the main track. With every step I felt my leg getting sorer and stiffer. We stopped talking as we walked through the trees. We had to take care to avoid twigs and brambles. As we neared the light of the fire, I indicated to Russell to stop.

'I want to check these messages,' I said, 'and make sure DCI Summers is ready to go.'

I could hear a man shouting. There was a woman too. Her voice was stifled, as if she was gagged. It was Meg. The man was angry and pumped up, clearly awaiting my imminent arrival.

I held Alex's phone close to my chest to try to conceal the light that the screen would give off.

There was a Skype message from Hannah.

Hurry up! They're getting impatient. They warned not to bring the police.

Then there were several texts from Alex, sent via Meg's phone.

Pete, don't meet them yet. DCI Summers stuck in traffic. She's going to be late.

Too late. She couldn't be far behind.

Kate Summers has alerted police team. She won't get there in time. Be careful, Pete.

Dare I hang on much longer? It was dark out there. Somebody had been tailing us, Jan said. Was it the police? Had DCI Summers dispatched someone she trusted to follow us?

The man started shouting again. He was waving his hands around, getting angry and increasingly agitated. I'd have to go in and confront him. There was another message. It was the most recent one. I opened it up but never got to read it properly.

Pete, take care. Don't go in before police get there. Please. I know who Phil is. You won't believe it—

'Hello, Pete,' came a woman's voice to my side.

'Hannah?'

I turned around, trying to find her in the darkness.

She laughed.

'What a lovely little reunion. Hello, Mr Black. Remember me?'

Russell Black looked frantically into the darkness, but was unable to get a good look at her face.

She switched on a torch and shone it towards her face.

'Hannah, what's going on?'

'She's not called Hannah,' Russell Black said slowly, a terrible fear in his voice. 'That's Debbie Simmonds. Older, much slimmer now and with a different hair colour as far as I can tell. And you've finally got rid of that terrible complexion.'

I looked towards her, trying to see who it was that Russell was looking at. We were looking at the same person.

'So that must mean I also know that man over there who's making all the noise?' he said, looking at her. 'That'll be Gary Maxwell.'

──────────

CHAPTER EIGHTEEN

'If you want to see that bitch of yours, you'd better head over to Gary.'

He'd been alerted now and was watching us walk over to him.

'But hang on. You're Hannah, aren't you?' I asked. I couldn't get my head around it.

'I'm Debbie Simmonds, as Mr Black said. Actually, I'm Debbie Maxwell. Gary and I got married after they released him from prison.'

'For child sexual abuse if I remember rightly?' Russell Black said.

Debbie raised her arm and struck him over the back of the head with what looked like a wrench. He sank to his knees and fell on the floor of the woodland clearing where the den was located. It was a small brick building with a crumbling chimney and covered in ivy. The fire was lit inside and they'd made a bonfire in the clearing. I couldn't see Meg, although I could hear her trying to shout through the gag.

'Russell Black, you scheming little bastard!' Gary said.

His face was lit by the fire. I struggled to match him with the old photos that I'd seen in the faded newspapers that I'd looked at with Alex.

He'd lost a lot of his hair and his head was fully shaven now. He was leaner than he'd been when younger, and he looked fit and strong. He was angry too.

'Did you know, Mr Bailey, that Mr Black here used me as his fall guy? I took the rap for everything that went on in that home, when it was these bastards that started it all. Me and Debbie, we were always in love. It was always the real thing for us.'

I didn't know what to say. How had I been so stupid as to miss this? I thought back to how Hannah – Debbie – had contacted me via Skype. She'd read the papers, she'd said – seen the terrible things that had happened, claimed to be Meg's sister. I'd thought that Meg's family were dead, but I'd met her mother. I wanted to scream.

'I was raped over one hundred times during my prison sentence, Mr Bailey. They said I was a sex offender and therefore I was fair game. If I ever told, they'd get to Debbie on the outside. I had to take it. And do you know why, Mr Bailey? Because I love that woman. I always have done.'

'My hand was resting on my stick and I realised that Gary was close enough for me to strike him with it. Debbie must have seen my hand tense because she came up from behind and hit my arm with her wrench. I cried out with the pain and she struck me around the head. I fell to the ground, still conscious, very close to the fire.

'You're a nice guy, Pete, and I'm sorry we have to end it this way. You shouldn't have married that bitch. You're the only person who can identify me, so I'm sorry, you have to follow Russell Black and Meg too.'

'No,' I said. 'You told me that Meg and I could walk away from this. You don't need to hurt us. We'll stay quiet.'

What was DCI Summers doing? We should be surrounded by police now.

Gary Maxwell switched on his torch and shone it towards a tree. It took me a moment to realise what I was seeing: three ropes all fastened to a long, strong branch, two rotting chairs and a plastic chair, no doubt recovered from the den. They were going to hang us. Jesus Christ, they were going to hang all three of us.

I tensed and tried to stand up. Debbie struck me again. I stayed down.

Gary came over to me and expertly secured my hands with a nylon tie. He did the same to Russell Black, who was beginning to come round now. I began to shout. The police had to be nearby. Why weren't they coming to help us? Gary struck me with his fist. I fell down to the leafy floor once again. He was strong. He came out of the den with a reel of gaffer tape. He tore off a strip and placed it across my mouth. I tried to cry out again, I could barely breathe, let alone speak.

Gary did the same to Russell Black who'd also seen the nooses and worked out what was about to happen.

'Debbie, let's do this bastard first!' Gary said. They helped Russell Black to his feet and led him towards the tree. It was difficult to see what was going on. The flames flickered in their direction one minute and then away from them the next. I began to inch away from the fire to where I could see Meg. I had to see Meg.

I heard a thud and a guttural sound. The flames lit up a body hanging from the tree. It was Russell Black, his feet thrashing wildly, the plastic chair kicked to the side.

I panicked. I began to kick my own feet furiously, trying to move towards where Meg was, attempting to stand up. I had to do what I could to escape. Where were the police? Where the hell was DCI Summers?

It ended quickly for me. As I managed to get enough balance to stand up, I felt a crashing blow to my head. As I thudded to the floor, struggling to stay conscious, I heard three gunshots. Surely not gunshots? Gary and Debbie hadn't got a gun. I heard Meg's voice. The gag must have been removed. Two names: Phil and then Pete. I heard a helicopter overhead. At last, the bloody police. As I finally faded, urgent shouts.

'Is he dead? Is he dead?'

I'm not proud of what I did. In fact, I'm ashamed of it. I will never forgive myself. If I had never slept with Ellie on that fateful night, none of it would have happened. But I did make that mistake, that single mistake, and it set off the events that would haunt us all for years.

Once again, I woke up in hospital. I was confused. I couldn't remember what it was I'd woken from. Then it came back to me. We'd been in the woods. Who had fired a gun?

I jumped up in bed. A needle tugged painfully out of my arm at my movement.

'Jesus, Pete. I almost shat myself!'

It was Alex. Waiting for me, sitting in high-backed hospital chair, reading some trashy magazine.

'It's over, Pete,' she said, kissing me on the forehead. 'It's finally over.'

I put my hand up to where she'd kissed me. I had a bandage on my head. I'd been on some sort of drip, and my sudden movement had pulled it out of my arm which was now bleeding. I was more interested in finding out what had happened.

'I'll get a nurse,' Alex said. 'Do you want some water?'

My mouth was dry. I nodded.

A nurse came in, replaced the needle, and patched up the minor wound. I was grateful to have a few moments. My mind was clouded and struggling to access what had happened in those final moments.

'Is Meg okay, Alex?' I asked.

'She's fine, Pete. She's unhurt. She had a few bruises, but they let her go home to the baby the same night.'

'How long have I been out?' I asked.

'A couple of days,' she smiled. 'Concussion. You're not cut out to be an action man.'

'Who fired the gunshots? Was it the police?'

'DCI Summers filled me in on the details. No, it wasn't the police. It was Charlie Lucas. Some old gun he had that he'd hung on to since the nineties. Unbelievable!'

'Charlie Lucas? I left him at the hotel. Did the bastard follow us up to the woods?'

'He did. He'd blackmailed Russell Black and Tony Dodds years ago. When Tony Dodds got killed, he'd panicked about his retirement fund. He got jittery about what you were up to with Russell Black, so he followed you.'

'Did anyone get hurt? Is Jan okay?'

'He fired four shots in all. One hit Gary Maxwell in the leg. He was trying to hit the rope that was holding Russell Black but he missed and hit Russell instead. The first shot missed altogether. The final shot was a misfire.'

'Is Russell Black dead?'

'Oh God, Pete. It's such a mess. It's touch and go. He may have sustained brain damage from the loss of oxygen when he was hanging. He's had to have a liver resection from the gunshot wound. But after everything I've learned, it sounds like he deserved it.'

'What about Hannah – or Debbie? Is she alive? What was going on?'

'You were conned, Pete. It was Debbie Simmonds all the time. She read those magazine articles in Spain. That's where she and Gary settled after he was released from prison, out of the public eye. She read your story in the magazine and realised that you didn't know anything about Meg's family. She and Gary had always spoken about getting revenge and when they finally saw a way of getting to Meg again, that's when they hatched their plan. They're a right couple of spiteful shits from what I hear. But you – we – were conned, Pete.'

'Is Hannah still alive then? Does she even exist?'

My head was hurting but I wanted this information. I needed to know.

'She died, Pete. Years ago. Meg can tell you. There are a lots of things that Meg will have to tell you herself.'

On my insistence, I was released from hospital sooner than I should have been. I was on a cocktail of painkillers and I had to promise to report to my doctor every morning for the next week. I said whatever had to be said to get out of there.

Meg wanted to meet me at the graveyard of all places. Alex told me she wanted it to be there to help her to explain things. Jan drove us in her taxi on a sunny winter's afternoon.

Jan had my phone. Alex had taken care of all of the unpaid taxi bills, smoothed things over with the taxi driver who'd got hurt and managed to set things straight with the police. Nobody was pressing charges. Alex had laid on the charm and sorted it all out while I was fast asleep.

I gave Jan a hug when she came to collect me from my flat.

'Thanks for your help that night,' I said. 'And thanks for guiding the police to us. I think Charlie might have caused even more damage if you hadn't been there to help us.'

'It was me and Phil,' she replied. 'We did it together.'

Oh yes, Phil. Alex wouldn't tell me about Phil. It was Phil who'd overcome Charlie Lucas before the police got to us. He'd rushed straight over to Meg to release her. The thing that I'd wanted to do. Save my wife.

Jan stopped outside the cemetery.

'You do this alone,' Alex said. 'Meg needs to explain this to you. Alone.'

I walked into the cemetery. I could see a woman standing in front of a grave ahead of me. She had the pram. Tom's pram. The cemetery was almost empty. I could see a man sitting on a bench, a few elderly people and a guy walking his terrier.

I walked towards Meg. She was crying, but she looked up, happy to see that I'd arrived. She embraced me. It was the embrace of a woman who still cared for me. It was not the embrace of a lover.

'Still having to use the stick then?' she said.

'It's getting better, but yes. I'll be like this for a few weeks yet, I think.'

'I'm sorry, Pete. For everything. For not telling you about all this. I could never ... the time was never right.'

I looked at the graves that were in front of her. Both had fresh flowers: Tom Yates and Hannah Yates (also known as Young). Hannah had died in the late nineties. A car crash.

'It was an accident, Pete. A ridiculous accident. A pheasant ran out into the road. She swerved, hit an ice spot, ran into a tree and died. I honestly thought my life was over. I didn't think it could get any worse.'

'I'm sorry,' I said. 'I understand. You know you could have talked to me. Anytime you could have talked to me.'

'They were abusing us in that home, Pete. How could I have told you? I was so happy when I met you. I didn't want to spoil it. And when I couldn't get pregnant, I thought I was being punished for giving away my baby. It hurt me so much.'

I squeezed her hand.

'It was Russell Black, Tony Dodds, Ray Matiz, they were all in on it. They used to have parties. Gary Maxwell would line us up for that bus. It was horrible, Pete. I can barely even think about it still. With you ... I trusted you. You were the first man I could trust after David. We had a lovely life together Pete. Until ...'

'Until I cheated on you. With Ellie. I'm so sorry, Meg. I hate myself. I don't know why I did it. I'm to blame for all of this. I should have been there for you. I'm so sorry.'

I felt my eyes begin to well up with tears.

'Walk along here with me,' Meg said, turning the pram.

We walked a little way and came to stop at another grave.

The name read David Marshall.

'He was my boyfriend. Before you, he was the only man

I ever loved. He made me feel safe like you did. He made me happy when I was in hell.'

I could see that he'd been young when he died.

'He hanged himself. From the tree outside the home. Along with Hannah's boyfriend, Jacob. David was the father of my child.'

She began to cry. I took her hand.

'I'm not sad those men are dead,' she said. 'I'd like to have killed them myself, but you have to let it go eventually. You have to let it go to move on.'

'I'm sorry, Meg. For everything.'

She took a deep breath.

'I lied to you about my family. I told you the lie once, when we were driving that day, and it was easier to stick with it. I went to see my mum whenever I could. It kills me to see her like that. We couldn't help her. I hate myself for not being to help them. And you know what? It was me who killed them. I had a fall out with my dad. I threw something at the heater when we were arguing. They never knew I did it, but it was a slow gas leak that started the fire from damage to the pipework. Me, Pete. I did it!'

'It's done, Meg. It's all done. We can't bring them back. You couldn't have known. It was an accident.'

'When I killed Tony Miller, Pete, that's when I realised. When he put his hand into my pants, it brought it all back. Those horrible parties. Those drunk men. What they did to us. When he touched me like that, I went mad. I kept on stabbing him until I was sure he was dead. I killed him, Pete. I don't know what came over me. I knew I had to go and sort it out then. I had to deal with it. I'm sorry I went away, Pete. I'm sorry I left you to deal with everything. But I had to ... I had to put my life straight.'

We stood in silence for a moment. I wish to God that

289 THE FORGOTTEN CHILDREN

Meg had told me, but I understood why she didn't. And I understood why she'd done what she did to Tony Miller. She must have been petrified. At least as an adult she could fight back. Each one of those stabs must have felt like retribution for what had happened to her as a child.

'I need to tell you about Tom,' she said, touching the baby's cheek. He was asleep in the pram.

'I was going to get tests done, but I decided not to. I don't care. He might be yours, he might be Jem's. I don't care. I wanted to have my baby. It's not his fault. But I don't want to know, Pete. After giving my baby away all those years ago I couldn't get rid of another child. I hope you understand. I just couldn't do it.'

I understood. When I'd held Tom in Ivy's house, it hadn't mattered to me either. I hated Jem for what he'd done, but he was a child. He deserved to be loved, however he had come into the world.

'There's one more thing I have to tell you, Pete. This is the most difficult thing of all.'

I knew what was coming. This was the bit where she told me about Phil. This is where she told me we were over.

'You see that man sitting on that bench over there? That's Phil.'

'I'm pleased you've found someone new, Meg.'

'He's not my boyfriend, Pete. He's my son. He's the son I had to give away when I was fifteen. I tracked him down. I knew when I was pregnant with Tom that I had to find my first child. It turned out he'd been looking for me. We live together now: me, Tom, Phil and his girlfriend. We're a family. It's the family I always wanted, Pete. I love it.'

'Do I fit into that family?'

'I love you, Pete, but I think we've gone too far. This is

my family now. I don't think we can pick up what we had. I think our moment has gone. You must feel that too?'

'I do. There's so much I need to tell you about Alex too.'

'She told me, Pete. She's lovely. I don't know why I hated her so much. I always thought she'd take you away from me. She explained everything. I don't know why we struggled to make a baby, Pete. Maybe we did make Tom together after all. But I think this is the right thing to do. Don't you?'

'I love you, Meg. I really do. And I will be sorry for what I did to my last breath. But you're right. You deserve this happiness. I won't take it away from you. You have a happy life.'

I held her in my arms, wiping a tear from her cheek.

I leant over to look into the pram and held Tom's tiny, clenched hand.

'I'll see you again, Tom. I'll be in touch, Meg, when things have had time to settle. In a few weeks. Let's get things sorted. It's time to move on. Take care. I'll see you again soon.'

Slowly and painfully, I walked through the cemetery towards Jan's taxi. I stopped off at Hannah and Thomas's graves to pay my respects.

It took me a few minutes to get back to the car. I saw Meg wheeling the pram over towards Phil. They embraced in the distance. I was pleased for Meg. I'd meet Phil later, but I wasn't ready for it just then.

I got into the car, my eyes streaming with tears. They were tears of regret and sadness, but relief too that it was finally over.

'I've got two plane tickets for Spain,' Alex said, taking my hand and placing it on her lap. 'I fly at the weekend. Are you coming?'

I looked through the cemetery gates at Meg, Phil and the baby walking off in the distance.

'Do you know what? I think I will, Alex. Let's go to Spain.'

Find out more about Paul J. Teague's thrillers at http://paulteague.co.uk

ABOUT THE AUTHOR

Hi, I'm Paul Teague, the author of the Don't Tell Meg trilogy as well as several other standalone psychological thrillers such as Burden of Guilt, Dead of Night and One Fatal Error.

I'm a former broadcaster and journalist with the BBC, but I have also worked as a primary school teacher, a disc jockey, a shopkeeper, a waiter and a sales rep.

I've read thrillers all my life, starting with Enid Blyton's Famous Five series, then graduating to James Hadley Chase, Harlan Coben, Linwood Barclay and Mark Edwards.

If you love those authors then you'll like my thrillers too.

Let's get connected!
https://paulteague.co.uk
paul@paulteague.com

Printed in Poland
by Amazon Fulfillment
Poland Sp. z o.o., Wrocław

49078737R00170